Bound Together

"If we don't find those swords in five days an innocent sixteen-year-old girl who never hurt anyone in her life will die." Kameko seized his hand in hers. "Don't turn me away, Sean. You're the only one who can help me save Tara."

He bent to press a gentle kiss on her brow. "Trust me, darlin', you're better off without me."

Snick.

He'd felt the slide of her bracelets against his skin, but had paid no attention to it. Now when he tugged his hand from hers, he couldn't free himself. He glanced down and saw she'd not only slipped one of her bracelets on him, but had cuffed his right arm to her left at the wrists. "What's this?"

"These are my lovers' cuffs," she said. "I should mention that, underneath the enamel and mink, they're standard-issue police handcuffs."

Sean couldn't help but laugh. "And you think cuffing us together will make me change my mind?"

"No." With her free hand, she pointed a gun at his heart. "This will."

**DON'T MISS THE FIRST TWO BOOKS IN
JESSICA HALL'S
WHITE TIGER SWORDS TRILOGY!**

The Deepest Edge

"An amazing thriller that is exotic, passionate,
and exhilarating.
Do not miss this book!"
—*Romantic Times* (4½ Stars, Top Pick)

The Steel Caress

"Do *not* miss reading this riveting, passionate
novel. It's fantastic!"—*The Old Book Barn Gazette*

THE
KISSING
BLADES

Jessica Hall

A SIGNET BOOK

SIGNET
Published by New American Library, a division of
Penguin Group (USA) Inc., 375 Hudson Street,
New York, New York 10014, U.S.A.
Penguin Books Ltd, 80 Strand,
London WC2R 0RL, England
Penguin Books Australia Ltd, 250 Camberwell Road,
Camberwell, Victoria 3124, Australia
Penguin Books Canada Ltd, 10 Alcorn Avenue,
Toronto, Ontario, Canada M4V 3B2
Penguin Books (N.Z.) Ltd, Cnr Rosedale and Airborne Roads,
Albany, Auckland 1310, New Zealand

Penguin Books Ltd, Registered Offices:
80 Strand, London WC2R 0RL, England

First published by Signet, an imprint of New American Library,
a division of Penguin Group (USA) Inc.

First Printing, August 2003
10 9 8 7 6 5 4 3 2 1

For Robin Rue—
an amazing agent, a brilliant woman,
and a wonderful friend

Chapter 1

"What you need, honey, is a stud."

Kameko Sayura stopped arranging the twenty-four-thousand-dollar emerald-and-gold necklace on the black velvet display collar and looked up. "I have matching earrings, but I'm afraid they're hoops."

Brenda Taggart laughed. "No, I mean the other kind of stud—you know, those big primitive male types who eat too much red meat, go crazy for ball games, and dig up the yard every weekend."

"Ah." Meko shook her head. "No, thanks."

The film director's astute gaze flashed over Meko as if she was planning to cast her as the lead for her next feature. "Every girl should have one or two around the house."

Knowing her client—who also happened to be married to one of the state's finest heart surgeons—Meko smiled. "The only problem is, all the good ones are taken."

"Not all of them." Brenda nibbled the edge of one manicured fingernail as she thought for a moment.

"Wait, I know the perfect guy for you—one of our stuntmen, Jack Hammond. Six-three, blond, blue eyes, pretty smile, wall-to-wall muscle—"

The image of a different man from the one Brenda was describing materialized in Meko's mind before she could banish it. A silver-haired man with an easy smile and brooding dark eyes.

Not Sean Delaney. I never want to see him again. Besides, he's probably locked up in some military stockade for the next twenty years by now.

"—shoulders out to here," Brenda continued, emphasizing the width with her hands, "and he doubles for Nick Nolte without makeup."

Meko thought of Nick Nolte, who she'd always thought resembled a thug, and suppressed a shudder. "Sounds nice."

"He is." Brenda pressed her hand over her heart. "The nicest guy in the world. I swear."

Nick Nolte was probably a nice guy. Sean Delaney had been nice, too. He'd been nice from the first moment they'd met, when he'd rescued Meko from two intruders who had broken into her home. He'd been nice when he'd stayed with her after the break-in, to talk to her about her father's death. And he'd kept on being nice, even when he'd pulled out a gun, kidnapped her, and forced her to drive him to San Francisco.

I should have pressed charges. At least then I'd know he was in prison.

Meko was pretty sure he wasn't. A week after the kidnapping, a large bouquet of exotic tiger lilies had been delivered to her home. The card read simply, "Sorry, Sean."

Not as sorry as I am. Being attracted to her own kidnapper had disturbed her so much that she still had trouble sleeping—and the ominous phone calls she'd been getting lately hadn't helped, either. Like Sean, the strange men who called kept asking about her dead father.

Did Takeshi send anything to you from China?

"Meko." The director waved a hand in front of her face. "Earth to Meko."

"Sorry." She forced herself back to reality. "And thanks again, Brenda, but I'm really not interested in dating anyone right now."

"Who says you have to date? Take him home, get him naked, and jump on him. Jackhammer'll do the rest." Brenda winked, then leaned to murmur, "They say his nickname is nothing compared to the size of his—"

Meko swiftly faked a cough, then turned to her young assistant, Tara Jones, who was pretending to polish the top of a nearby display case. "Tara, would you mind checking the teapot in my office? I think I left the warmer on again."

The teenager exchanged an amused glance with Brenda. "Sure thing, boss."

Once Tara was safely out of earshot, Meko smothered a sigh. "Brenda, try to remember my assistant is only sixteen."

"Sixteen going on forty, more like." The director peered at her. "Meko, are you blushing? Can women still do that?"

"No, I'm having a hot flash. Women my age do *that* all the time." She wasn't actually going through menopause, but she had her dignity to uphold. "No stuntmen, okay? The last thing I need in my life is a . . . jackhammer. Now here." She held up the necklace. "See how you like the length with it on."

Momentarily diverted by the rich swirls of gold and glittering green stones, Brenda bent down so Meko could clasp the necklace around her thin throat. "I don't know why I'm so addicted to emeralds—not like I need another necklace, huh?"

"It's not silly to want something beautiful." Meko adjusted the shimmering chain. "People throughout history have considered jewelry important to their lives. Everyone from monarchs with jeweled crowns that conveyed power to shaman who fashioned amulets for protection against evil spirits."

"Power and evil spirits—sounds like Hollywood to me." She caressed the circle of jewels around her neck with reverent fingertips. "So give me the stats on this gorgeous thing."

Meko had worked on perfecting the necklace for several months, so she could recite the facts from memory. "The largest emerald is a natural Colombian, intense blue-green, ten-point-eight-four carats. There are only a few minor inclusions, which are typical of natural emeralds, and the stone hasn't been heat-treated or color-enhanced."

Brenda eyed her reflection. "No artificial colors or flavors, huh?"

"Not a one."

The director lifted the center stone up to examine it closely. "What are these little threads running through it?"

"Those are the natural inclusions—the ones that look like leaves and vines are *jardin*, which is French for 'garden.' The ones that give it a satiny appearance are called silk."

Brenda released a long sigh. "God, Meko, it's so beautiful."

"Thank you. There are another twenty-three carats of pavé emeralds in the setting, which is eighteen-karat gold, and I'll include a two-inch extension piece so you can change the length from sixteen to eighteen inches." She adjusted the counter mirror as the director inspected herself. "I think it looks stunning on you, but I'm a little biased when it comes to redheads and emeralds. What do you think?"

Brenda turned to the right, then the left. "I think Penny Marshall is going to rip my heart out with her teeth when she sees this. But what'll I wear to showcase it?"

"Black. A strapless sheath would be perfect." Meko could just see the lanky director on the cover of *People*, wearing the necklace she had designed exclusively for her. It had already happened three times before with other, famous clients.

"I'd go with Honore Etienne, or Rudolph Aria, or Versace. Matte silk, above the knee," Tara said as she emerged from the back of the store. As the daughter of a high-powered studio executive and a seasoned character actress, she not only knew the best designers but mingled with them during parties at her parents' Beverly Hills estate. "You can't go wrong with classic black, and you've got great legs, Ms. Taggart."

"Hmmmm. Sounds good. Though with Penny up for the same Oscar, maybe I should get Donatella to do me something in Kevlar." Brenda chuckled as she performed one more inspection, then nodded. "Okay, let me see those matching earrings. Hoops, you said?"

Thirty minutes later Brenda Taggart walked out of the shop, on her cell phone with Versace's assistant, and Meko added a thirty-thousand-dollar check to the daily deposit bag.

"Nice chunk of change, boss." Tara whistled as she finished tallying the slip. "Does this mean I get a raise?"

Meko pointed one finger at the ceiling. "It means I get the roof fixed *before* the summer rains get here."

"You're such a Scrooge." Tara pressed the back of her hand against her forehead in mock exhaustion. "After I spent two hours sweating over the hot new display, too."

"Let me see." Meko inspected the case reserved for her costume and trend pieces, where Tara had artfully arranged her newest offering, lovers' cuffs, made from a pair of mink-lined enameled handcuffs. "Very nice work."

"Yes, despite her many abuses, I'm still devoted to my thankless employer." Tara sighed, then glanced at the wall clock. "Better get going if you want to hit the bank before it closes. Do you want me to lock up?"

Meko shouldered her purse and took out her car keys. "No, I have to finish setting that bracelet, so I'll be right back. I'm going to lock you in, though."

"Do you have time to run by the post office?" Tara produced a small sample box. "You wanted to send this back to that German company."

"I'll throw it in the car and run by in the morning." Meko took the deposit bag and folded it in half before slipping it into her purse, then added, "Would you mind pulling twenty-six rubies for me before you go? Use the one-carat brilliant stock that just came in."

The teenager's blue eyes widened. "You want me to match them?"

"You've got a great eye for color." Meko pursed her lips. "And, if J.Lo buys it for her mom tomorrow, you'll get ten percent extra commission." She grinned. "If that's acceptable to you, Ms. Cratchit."

"Acceptable?" Tara's voice cracked on the word. "I think I just became your slave for life."

"I've always wanted to own my own teenager." She went to the door, then recalled another errand and retrieved the duffel bag of clothes she needed to take to the cleaners from behind the counter. "Use the sorting tray on my desk, Tara. The lamp in there has the best light. And remember to wear a pair of gloves."

She made a face. "I hate gloves."

"If you become sensitized to working with metals and stones, your hands will crack and bleed every time, and you'll never be able to work as a jeweler. *Wear* the gloves." She slid on her sunglasses. "Be back in a minute."

Meko rarely left Tara alone in the store, and locking her in was simply an extra security measure. Despite their upscale location on the fringes of Beverly Hills, the store was always a potential target for robbery. With more than two hundred thousand dollars' worth of jewelry on the premises and more in loose stones and precious metals in her work-room, Meko knew the risks. She'd even recently up-graded her state-of-the-art security system to send out a silent alarm. Still, her expensive stock took second place to Tara's personal safety.

Being kidnapped has made me totally paranoid.

There were only two people in the drive-through line at the bank, so she was able to make the deposit quickly, and only stopped on the way back to the store to drop off her dry cleaning and pick up some giant-sized lemon ices from a vendor at the park. Tara loved them, and they needed to celebrate a great sale every now and then.

As she parked in her reserved spot by the curb in front of the store, Meko eyed her reflection in the rearview mirror. "Okay, so I'm spoiling her. Sue me."

Juggling the ices while unlocking the front door took a minute, then Meko walked in. "Got a sur-prise for you, kiddo," she called out as she locked the door behind her. "Three guesses what it is."

There was no answer.

Too busy sorting through the rubies. Meko set the cups down by the register and wandered back to-ward her office. "Tara? Take a break for a minute, these things are melting all over the—"

She stopped in the open doorway and stared.

The room looked like a tornado had raged through it—papers scattered, file drawers hanging open, chairs overturned. But the chaos wasn't what made Meko press a shaking hand over her mouth. Someone had driven a sword into the top of her desk. The ancient blade looked brittle, and strange markings were etched into it. Markings that dripped with wet, fresh blood. And something was hanging, caught on the hilt. A broken bracelet, made of links that looked like dolphins.

Tara's bracelet.

She didn't know how long she stood there, but the sound of something ringing snapped her out of her trance. At first she couldn't identify the muffled noise. Then she recognized the ring.

Her cell phone.

She staggered away from the office and followed the ringing until she found her purse. Her hands shook so badly that she nearly dropped the phone twice before she could switch it on. Yet as she raised it to her ear, she had a terrible feeling she knew who was calling.

"Hello?"

"Your young friend is not dead yet," a man said in heavily accented English. "Do you wish her to live?"

"What?" Meko grabbed the edge of the counter to stop the room from spinning. "Where is Tara? Is she all right? What have you done to her?"

"We want the swords."

Traffic snarls prevented Liam Kinsella from getting into Washington, D.C., and by the time he reached Pennsylvania Avenue he was nearly an hour late for his meeting. He parked illegally on E Street and entered the J. Edgar Hoover Building, scowling at his watch as he passed through security.

He knew the deputy director wouldn't call him

up to D.C. without a good reason, but it sure as hell would have been nice to know what it was.

The director's secretary rose from her desk the moment she saw him. "This way, Agent Kinsella." She led him down a side hall and showed him into a briefing room.

"Ah, Liam, you made it." Howard Stevens came forward to shake his hand before turning to address the other six men present. "Gentlemen, this is Special Agent William Kinsella. Liam, this is CIA domestic operations chief Richard Roan, National Security administrator Adam Liebert, Department of Justice adjunct Ira Rosen, Interpol liaison Peter Spoviki, White House advisor John Taylor, and U.N. security director Russell Lawitz."

Kinsella recognized enough of the names and faces to know he was facing some of the most powerful men in Washington. All the coffee he had chugged in the car churned in his stomach. "Is there a situation, sir?"

"Yes, and that's why you're here." Stevens handed him a file marked CLASSIFIED—NEED TO KNOW ONLY and gestured toward an empty chair at the table. To the other men, he said, "Agent Kinsella heads up an Asian organized-crime task force out of our New York office."

Which is where Kinsella wanted to be, instead of at this meeting. But this many D.C. power players didn't get together unless something major had hit the fan—and that kind of shit usually slid downhill in a hurry.

"Where are you and the team on the Sayura case,

Liam?" Stevens asked as he shut off most of the room lights.

"We're preparing the last of the warrants." Kinsella shifted in his chair as the director's secretary pulled down a slide screen. "The U.S. attorney is ready to indict twenty-six suspects on multiple counts of racketeering, fraud, and conspiracy to commit murder. As soon as we coordinate with the L.A. field office, we plan to—"

"You'll need to put your case on hold," CIA chief Roan said, sounding testy. "Our situation takes immediate priority."

His task force had spent two grueling years patiently accumulating enough evidence for those indictments. He wasn't going to tell his men to sit on their hands without some kind of explanation. "And what would that situation be, sir?"

"We need to bring you in on a related investigation, Liam," Stevens said as he switched on a slide projector. The stern, unsmiling face of an older Asian man filled the screen. "You recognize this man?"

"Yeah, that's T'ang Po, leader of the Shandian tong." He thought of the two agents recently killed while investigating a case involving Chinese organized crime. "Was he responsible for Jennings and Hessler?"

"Indirectly. He was killed four months ago, in New Orleans, while trying to retrieve the White Tiger, a priceless antique Asian sword collection. There's a profile on his past activities in the dossier I gave you." Stevens switched slides to show a street photo of a younger Chinese man with long dark hair. He was smiling, and had his arms around a petite Caucasian woman with fiery hair. Together they held a blond female toddler. "This is T'ang Po's son, Jian-Shan; his wife, antique weapons expert Valence St. Charles; and their adopted daughter, Lily."

The kid didn't look like either of her parents, but Liam found out why a moment later.

"The child is the daughter of Jian-Shan's first wife, Karen Colfax, and her former husband, U.S. senator Phillip Colfax." John Taylor, the White House advisor, leaned forward. "You may remember the Colfax case; Karen was acquitted of murder charges after killing the senator in self-defense."

Kinsella vaguely remembered the scandal. "I do, but I'm sorry, I don't see the connection."

"Senator Colfax was receiving payoffs from Shandian, and through him Karen met Po's son in China. She convinced Jian-Shan to take the White Tiger swords and leave the tong. T'ang Po took his revenge by having Karen Colfax murdered. He tried to do the same to the St. Charles woman and the child when Jian-Shan brought the White Tiger to the U.S. T'ang Po was killed during the attempt, but the swords disappeared." Stevens advanced to the next slide, which showed a two-star army general and a breathtaking tall brunette woman.

Kinsella recognized both—the general from a number of Washington functions he'd attended in the past and the woman's famous face from a dozen magazine covers.

"Army general Kalen Grady and his wife, retired army major Sarah Ravenowitz, also known as the international model Raven," NSA administrator

Liebert said. "General Grady heads the army's Central Intelligence Division and has an ongoing investigation into Shandian operations here in the U.S. General Grady and his wife conducted a covert operation after the swords disappeared in which they successfully infiltrated the Chicago-based Dai tong. They eliminated a high-profile assassin and uncovered a CID double agent working for the Chinese in the process, but were unable to recover the swords. The full report on his investigation is also included in your dossier."

"During Grady's undercover operation, one of his former agents became involved in the case." Stevens brought up another image, this one of a silver-haired man with dark eyes and an easy smile. "Sean Delaney, officially a retired army colonel, unofficially a loose cannon. Grady later cleared him of any misconduct, but our sources indicate Delaney kidnapped a civilian and otherwise interfered during the course of the Dai investigation."

"General Grady did find evidence that indicates T'ang Po intended to use the swords to take over Chinese organized crime here in the U.S.," DOJ adjunct Rosen said. "Which brings us to the main suspect in your ongoing case, agent. Takeshi Sayura."

As an image of the Japanese crime boss appeared on the screen, Kinsella's eyes narrowed. "Sayura couldn't be involved in this; he's dead, and he and T'ang Po were lifelong enemies. Also, I'm not clear on why a bunch of old swords are a threat to national security."

"The swords themselves are priceless—worth millions on the antiquities black market," Stevens told him. "But according to General Grady's information, T'ang Po etched the swords with an encryption. That is what presents the greatest danger to national security."

"An encryption for what?"

"We haven't determined that yet. However, there is a great deal of interest in those swords from other countries." Lawitz, the U.N. security director, paused. "Most of which are located in the Middle East."

"T'ang Po had ties with some of the more ruthless terrorist groups around the globe," Interpol liaison Spoviki added. "They, too, are very keen to take possession of the White Tiger collection."

"General Grady believes Takeshi Sayura orchestrated the theft of the swords and may have hidden them before he left for China. Sean Delaney also believed Sayura had a connection; the civilian he kidnapped was Sayura's daughter, Kameko," Stevens said. "Liam, you had someone operating inside the Sayura organization. We need to use your connections to find those swords."

"Our informant has been incommunicado for several weeks, sir. That was one reason why we were moving forward with the indictments." Kinsella scanned the faces around him. "When we bring the suspects in, we can question them about these swords."

"In the interests of interdepartmental cooperation, you'll have to hold off serving those warrants," Liebert said.

"Sir, the longer we wait, the more likely it is that

one of the suspects in my case will get his hands on these swords," Kinsella pointed out.

Stevens's thin mouth curled. "That's why you're going to California tomorrow, Liam. To prevent that from happening."

"Her back leg looks better, but I'd keep her in another day or so," the vet said as he picked up his case and moved into the next stall.

"Easy now," Sean murmured, and stroked the agitated heifer's shoulder while he added a measure of feed to her bin. "You'll have your chance to gossip with the other girls later this week."

After the cow became more interested in the grain than in kicking Sean, he slipped out, latched the stall, and moved to the next gate. The vet was already on his knees in fresh straw, examining the swollen udder of his next patient.

"This one's got a mild teat infection. She'll need a hosing." The vet stood and prepared a syringe, then glanced at Sean. "Tell your boss to have someone pressure-clean the clusters and lines in the parlor. The hands ought to keep an eye out for porcupines and skunks—they're the carriers. More trouble than the mountain lions, lately."

Sean's boss would probably give the job of sterilizing the equipment in the parlor—the huge shed where the cows were milked by machine—to his newest hired hand. Sean didn't mind. The harder he worked, the less he thought. It was why he'd come to Sonoma Valley and taken the job at the Red Hart Dairy, to do something physical and mindless.

He'd thought there were nothing but vineyards

in the valley. A curious mixture of clay, rock, and gravel made up most of the poor soil in the area, which oddly enough forced local vines to produce superior grapes. But dairy and cheese farms also flourished in the region, and Sean had had more experience with cows. He'd told Jake Hart as much when he'd applied for the job.

"You're older than the men I usually hire." Hart had been equally blunt during the initial interview, which included Sean's demonstrating that he could handle riding a stock horse to herd and pick up feed sacks that weighed a hundred and fifty pounds. "But I don't judge a man by how much snow he's got on his roof. I expect you to put in a full day's work, every day, Delaney. Do that and we'll get along fine."

"That'll do it for today, Irish." The vet left the stall and had Sean sign an invoice form before he eyed him. "Not very talkative, are you?"

Sean Delaney's mother had claimed he could talk his way into heaven while dragging the devil in after him. "Not much to say, Doc."

The vet grunted. "Well, you make sure that equipment gets cleaned, else you'll have more swollen teats swinging around here than at a Las Vegas dinner show." He chuckled at his own joke as he trudged out of the barn.

Sean finished changing the straw in the stalls, then headed up to his cottage to clean up before dinner. Despite the demands of his job and Jake's excellent cook, his appetite had dwindled and he barely ate one meal a day now.

What he craved most he avoided until he knew he'd be alone.

Birds scattered from the old oak beside the cottage as he walked out and started for the main house. There were so many birds in the valley now that neighboring vineyards had to resort to drape nets to protect the grapes.

He stopped to check on the Churro sheep in the south pasture, which their owner, an organic weaver in town, leased from the dairy. Sheep had once dominated the valley's fields, until coyote attacks decimated the herds and forced most ranchers to make the switch to cattle. Local predators remained plentiful, however, and Sean kept a sharp eye on the small herd.

That's all I'm good for now. Guarding sheep, moving cows, and shoveling shit.

He thought of the amount left in the bottle of Bushmills back at the cottage. There was enough to get him through the night, but he'd have to make a run into town tomorrow—

You won't find absolution in a bottle, Mr. Delaney, no matter how many you drink.

He'd gone nearly an entire day without hearing Kameko Sayura's voice, or seeing her solemn little face inside his head. He never went longer than a day, though. Of all the women he'd ever known, her ghost was proving to be the hardest to exorcise.

And he couldn't for the life of him understand why.

"Stay out of my head, darlin'." Sean dragged a hand through his hair and sighed. "Because I don't think there's enough whiskey in the world to get rid of you."

"I can't help you if you don't come back to Los Angeles, Kameko." Max Rubenstein sounded tired and upset—but he usually didn't represent clients who left town the moment they were set free on bail. "If you don't show up at the pretrial, the district attorney will have a bench warrant issued for your arrest. You'll lose everything you own."

"I know." The burning knot inside her stomach flamed higher as she spotted her exit. "I'll be in touch soon, Max." She ended the call and turned off the highway.

Her attorney obviously thought she was crazy, and Meko wasn't so sure she disagreed. Until three days ago, she had been completely sane. A law-abiding citizen, who had never been arrested or received so much as a parking ticket.

Now she was suspected of killing the girl whose life she was desperately trying to save.

After finding Tara gone and receiving the terrifying phone call, Meko had immediately called the police, then Tara's parents. The latter had not been home, but she had impressed on the Joneses' servants the nature of the emergency. By then the authorities had arrived, and they swiftly took over the scene.

Uniformed officers cordoned off the front of the building with yellow warning tape. Others kept pedestrians back and interviewed surrounding business owners about what they had seen. Forensic technicians crawled over every inch of the store, looking for evidence.

Meko stayed out of the way until she was questioned by the detective in charge of the case. She recited her statement three times, detailing her movements and Tara's up until she returned from the bank.

She said nothing about the phone call.

"You claim nothing is missing from stock, and we did find an entire tray of rubies sitting on your desk." The detective, an older man with a remarkably expressionless face, finished reading back over the notes he had taken. "And those rubies are worth how much again?"

"Twenty thousand dollars." Why was he asking her the same questions over and over? "More if they were sold individually."

"You stated that you believe Tara Jones was kidnapped from your store and is being held for ransom." He looked up from his notes. "If they wanted money, Ms. Sayura, why didn't they just take the rubies? Or any of the jewels from your stock?"

Meko blinked. "I—I don't know. Maybe they didn't have enough time."

"Not enough time to even grab a handful of stones on the way out?" The detective's tone changed. "Tell me, do you know if Tara had a boyfriend?"

"No. I mean, not as far as I know." She looked at a technician in a white jumpsuit, who was dusting her front display case for fingerprints. Had they worn gloves? Would the police be able to tell from the fingerprints who the men were?

She couldn't allow that to happen. She had been

given very precise instructions, and if she didn't follow them, Tara would be killed.

"Any problem with drugs?" The detective's voice dragged her back to the present. "She hang out with any gangs?"

"No." Meko felt like shrieking at him and everyone to get out of her shop. "Tara would never get involved with drugs or gangs. She's a sensible girl."

"Could she have stolen something?" He nodded toward the cases. "Something you possibly overlooked?"

She clenched her teeth. "Tara wouldn't steal from me. Look, I told you, I wasn't here. I don't know who came in here while I was gone. But someone *took* her."

"Maybe. Maybe there's another explanation." He gave her a sympathetic smile. "Let's say Tara got tempted. Kids do, you know—they want something, and they don't think about all the hard work we adults have to do to earn a living. Maybe she decided to take something, a little ring or bracelet for herself. And when you came back from the bank, you caught her putting it in her purse."

"Tara didn't steal from me," she repeated, her voice adamant.

The detective went on as if he hadn't heard her. "I know if I caught an employee stealing from me, I'd be pretty upset. My temper might get a little out of control. It happens. No one *means* to hurt someone when they're angry."

"I left the store to make the bank deposit—I've given you the receipt."

"I called the bank, Ms. Sayura. You went through the drive-through. Was Tara in the car?"

"No. As I told you, she stayed here. I stopped to buy some ices, and when I got back, she was gone. I found a bloody sword and her bracelet on my desk, that's all." She met his skeptical gaze and remembered what the man had said over the phone—she hoped his number couldn't be traced, because she was almost positive they would check her phone records. "That's all I can tell you."

"Did you buy the ices as a peace offering? Maybe to get her to go along with you?"

"I just got them as a treat for both of us. Look, they're right over there." She gestured toward the two cups. "Melting all over my counter."

"A treat. Right." He sighed, like a disappointed parent. "And you said this sword is Japanese, right? How did you know that?"

"I'm Japanese." She almost added that her father had collected them, but decided that would only make matters worse. Her father had been the head of a well-known crime syndicate.

The detective pulled out a pack of cigarettes and offered her one before lighting up. "Your people like to do some pretty gruesome stuff with swords, don't they? Like that hara-kiri thing, right?"

Meko recoiled from his exhaled smoke. "It's called *seppuku*, it's a form of ritual suicide, and *my people* stopped doing it about five hundred years ago." Unable to sit another moment, she got up and started pacing. "Look, I've told you everything I know. What are you going to do to find Tara?"

"Everything we can, ma'am. Now, if you'll just go over what happened with me one more time . . ."

And she had, three more times. When she was ready to tear her hair out in frustration, the detective had finally backed off. He scheduled an interview with her in the morning at police headquarters, then let her go home.

As soon as Meko walked out to her car, her cell phone rang. She switched it on. "Hello."

"Did you tell them anything?"

"No." She gripped the steering wheel until her knuckles turned white. "Please, just bring her back. I won't tell anyone, I swear to you."

"Your father stole the swords from us. We want them back first."

Tears of fear and frustration stung her eyes. "I don't have them. My father is dead. Please, don't hurt her. Let her go. She has nothing to do with this."

"She does now. We will trade the girl for the swords."

She turned, looking all around her. *Were they somewhere nearby, watching her?* "I don't know where they are."

"Find them. And remember, don't tell the police anything, or your young friend will die. You have one week."

Sean went up to the main house, where the hands assembled for dinner each night in a communal dining room. Louise, the cook, had already set out huge platters filled with fried chicken, corn on the cob, and whipped potatoes. She brought a basket of biscuits to the table and deliberately dropped two on Sean's plate before handing the basket to the next man. "You pick at my food tonight, Irish, I'm going to knock you on your skinny white backside."

Knowing the black woman's threats were mostly bluff, Sean smiled. "Yes, ma'am."

"Eat." She snorted. "And don't be batting them pretty eyes at me, thinking I won't do it."

There was little talk as the men began to demolish Louise's cooking, which was as tasty as it was plentiful. Sean related the vet's diagnosis to his boss, and agreed to begin cleaning out the milking parlor in the morning. To keep from offending Louise, he rolled her biscuits into his napkin and stuck them in his pocket before he got up to leave.

Louise's plump dark hand caught his arm when he passed by her. "I got pecan pie tonight, Irish." She didn't look angry now. She seemed worried. "Goes down real good with my decaf."

"Thank you, ma'am, but the chicken did me in." He winked and patted her hand before slipping out.

Back at his cottage, Sean resisted the bottle of whiskey for almost an hour before giving in to the craving and pouring out a short measure. He studied the amber liquid for a moment, and wondered why it no longer looked as mellow and lovely as it had before.

A small, serene-looking woman with a quiet, dignified smile appeared in his head. Kuei-fei, surrounded by flowers. He always remembered her that way.

Some of the most dangerous creatures on the earth are small, she had told him once. *And female*.

"That they are," he said, and toasted the woman he had almost loved, then lost.

Her angelic dark eyes narrowed and flashed, and her lips became fuller. Now she was Kameko, frowning at him with that sinful mouth of hers.

You're drunk, Mr. Delaney.

"Not yet, ladies." With a jerk he lifted the glass to his lips and drank half the contents. It burned all the way down to his belly. "But if God is merciful, I will be. Soon."

Chapter 2

Kameko drove slowly through the valley, following the directions the gas station attendant had given her.

"Red Hart's one of the biggest dairy operations around here," the man had told her. "Just up the road, on Petrie Drive. Look for the red-and-white signs. You can't miss 'em."

As she drove, she finished replaying in her mind the events that had compelled her to become a fugitive. The morning after Tara was abducted, Meko had returned to the police station. Tara's parents had been there, too, but they weren't happy to see her. Tara's father had been obliged to hold his wife back to keep her from attacking Meko.

"You bitch, what did you do with my daughter?" Rebecca Jones had screamed as Meko walked by.

The detective who had taken her statement at the store ushered Meko past the distraught couple and into an interview room, where he informed her that Tara's blood had been matched to the blood on the sword. No other evidence of a break-in, however, had been found.

Don't tell the police anything.

"Your doors weren't forced, and you claim nothing was stolen. We do have a statement from a witness who saw you carry a large bag out of the shop that afternoon, just before Tara disappeared." He leaned forward. "Would you care to tell me what was in the bag, Ms. Sayura?"

Meko went blank for a moment. "That was just my dry cleaning." When his expression didn't change, she felt her stomach clench. "I have a receipt, if you want proof."

He didn't respond to that. Instead, in a gentle voice, he asked, "Make it easy on yourself, Ms. Sayura. Tell me what really happened between you and Tara yesterday."

"Nothing." She thought of telling them about her own kidnapping, which she had never reported to the police—but that might endanger Tara's life too.

And he could smell the lie—it was all over his face. "I'm sure you didn't mean to hurt her. Was it an accident? Did she threaten you?"

Bile surged in her throat. She could say nothing of the men who had done this, but she couldn't help trying to defend herself. "Why do you think I'm responsible? I don't have a criminal record; I've never hurt anyone in my life. Tara is a wonderful girl, she's been like family to me. I could never do anything to harm her."

"But you have secrets, don't you? Like the fact that your father was Takeshi Sayura, one of the biggest crime bosses on the West Coast. And your ex-husband, Nick, worked as a bagman for your father's syndicate," the detective said. "Did Tara find out something she wasn't supposed to? Did she threaten to go to the media with it? Were you trying to protect your family—your real family?"

"My father is dead, and I don't hear from Nick anymore." Her voice went toneless. "I have never been involved with their illegal activities."

"But you have to admit this doesn't look good. In light of the fact that a sixteen-year-old girl suddenly disappeared from your shop and you were the last person to see her alive. Before you carried a large bag from the premises and stowed it in your trunk."

"That was my dry cleaning!" Frustrated beyond belief, she flung a hand at the window. "You should be out there, looking for her!"

"Oh, we are, ma'am, and we will find her—wherever you left her." He sat back in his chair. "If you tell me what happened, and where she is, maybe we can work something out with the D.A."

The D.A. couldn't save Tara. Nor could Meko. But there was one man who might be able to help her find the swords, and get Tara back.

Sean Delaney.

"I can't help you, Detective." She rose to her feet, impatient to leave. "May I go now?"

"I'm sorry, ma'am. You just don't get it, do you?" The detective sighed as he stood. "Kameko Sayura, you're under arrest for the murder of Tara Jones. You have the right to remain silent . . ."

It took two days for her attorney to arrange her bail and release from county lockup, and Meko had put them to good use. She used her daily phone call privilege to contact a florist in Los Angeles, who confirmed that her tiger lilies were sent FTD by a Sean Delaney from Sonoma Valley. A second call to the Sonoma Valley florist who had taken the order revealed even more information.

"Yeah, I do remember him—if he had black hair, he'd be a dead ringer for Gabriel Byrne, right?" The clerk laughed. "I tried to talk him into some tea roses we had on special, but he said the lady was a real tiger."

Meko, who had passed herself off as the L.A. florist, laughed along with her. "That's the guy. The recipient called me, wanting to know his address and phone number. I told her I'd check and see, but I couldn't promise anything."

"I have the P.O. box he used on the sales slip, if you want that. Is there some problem?"

She gripped the phone a little tighter. "No. She said she wants to send a thank-you card, so I'll take the P.O. box." After the florist recited the address, Meko asked casually, "Sounds like a good-looking guy. Does he work near the shop?"

"If he did, honey, your customer wouldn't have a chance. I'd be all over him." The other woman sighed. "But he was driving a Red Hart Dairy truck, which means he works on the other side of the valley. That's way too far out in the boondocks for me." She chuckled.

By the time Meko was released, Tara's parents were on all the news stations, pleading for any information that would lead to finding their daughter. Kameko's photo was shown, and she was identified not as Tara's employer but as the prime suspect in her disappearance, and the last person to see their daughter alive. Meko noticed they also regularly mentioned how they were giving up promoting their latest movie in order to search for their missing daughter.

Which was the best kind of promotion in the world, of course.

She didn't have much to do when she left the county lockup. She went home, showered, packed a bag, and then went to the store to pull something from the display case that Tara had been so proud of. She wasn't sure she'd need the last item she picked up, but she felt better taking it with her.

He'll agree to help me, or I'll make him do it.

Then she got in her car and drove north.

Sean polished off the last of the whiskey as he lay in bed, watching the ceiling fan slowly revolving above him. Like most Irishmen, he had a cast-iron liver, and as a result he was only half drunk. To knock himself out, he would need a full bottle, or a club to the head.

Or a woman.

It had been a long time since he'd taken a woman to bed. His boss had already pointed out a few places in town where a man could find uncomplicated companionship—not that finding a willing woman had ever been a problem for Sean. Since his teens, all he'd ever had to do was smile, murmur a couple of sweet words, and he didn't spend the night alone. His mother had called it the Delaney knack.

Your father could convince a nun to forget her vows, boyo. And have her thanking him for it in the morning.

But Kuei-fei had seen through his charm as surely as if Sean were made of glass. A year ago he'd offered to help her find her long-lost son Jian-Shan, and yet somehow she'd known that he wanted to use them to shut down Shandian and capture Jian-Shan's father, T'ang Po. She'd used Sean in return, as the means to escape her own criminal past and get to her son before his father did. And in those short weeks, he had started feeling something for her—something that could have been love, had she lived long enough for them to explore it.

Maybe he was made of glass, Sean thought as he contemplated the empty bottle in his hand. He'd reunited Kuei-fei with her son, just in time for Po to kill her. That had certainly smashed him to pieces. And then the key to destroying Shandian—the White Tiger swords—had been stolen as Kuei-fei lay dying at Sean's feet.

He hadn't been able to face his guilt. He'd blamed his own government—and his own boss, CID's General Kalen Grady—for Kuei-fei's death. Guilt and rage had made him crazy enough to go after the White Tiger swords himself. He'd planned to get them and destroy them, then testify before a military court and do the same to Kalen Grady's career. He'd been wrong, of course. Kalen hadn't killed Kuei-fei.

Sean had killed her, by not following orders. He had been taken off the Shandian case and told to retire. Instead, he had gone after T'ang Po himself, using an unauthorized civilian in a classified international operation.

The only hands covered with Kuei-fei's blood were his own.

Now all was forgiven. He'd helped to save Kalen Grady's life, had been allowed to retire with his rank and citations intact, and had even been invited to the general's wedding. Sean suspected most of it was the bride's doing—Raven's way of paying him back for helping her when she was working undercover for the general during the Dai tong operation.

Sean hadn't gone to the wedding. He'd lost himself here, in Sonoma, hoping it would all go away. Some of it was fading—his memories of the beautiful, tragic Kuei-fei were dim, like an old photograph now. Soon all he'd have left would be the bloody shards of his own heart, and the image of another woman he couldn't have.

"Kameko." He rolled off the bed, staggering over to toss the bottle into the trash. "Shouldn't have let her get away from you, boyo."

He looked at the small table in his kitchenette, and his vision doubled. For a moment, he was back in San Francisco, alone with Takeshi Sayura's daughter, on top of a table, his big hands and heavy body pinning her down as he kissed her, and then—

The little china doll nearly cracked your head open.

As he lumbered into the bathroom, he remembered every detail of his time with Kameko Sayura. He'd been proud of her, little thing that she was, defending herself against the likes of him. He'd been half drunk then, too, on her father's whiskey, his own irrational rage, but that wasn't what made him touch her.

She'd touched him first.

You and I are going to leave this place. I'll take you wherever you want to go. You need help, Sean.

He stared at himself in the mirror, then glanced down at the bathroom sink. Kameko had poured his whiskey down a drain, then had taken his hand to lead him out of her father's house. Her voice had soothed him, but it was the shock of feeling her smooth palm against his, her slim fingers easing through his that had stunned him. It created a strange, vibrant heat that punched through the haze of alcohol and fury and sank into him until he could feel her touch in his bones.

He'd had dozens of women, but not even the most experienced of his lovers had ever bulldozed him the way she had, simply by holding his hand.

Thinking about Kameko was like suffering the old Irish curse: *may you be afflicted with the itch and have no nails to scratch with.*

Sean splashed his face with cold water, trying to clear his head of the memories, then rinsed the taste of whiskey from his mouth. He'd done his best to scare her off. He'd picked her up like the little doll she was, lifting her up to his face, knowing how easy it would be to take her and find out how hot the fire between them would burn. Worse, he had looked into her dark, exotic eyes, and had seen the same heat, waiting there, simmering.

He tried to warn her. *You think you know me? You don't know anything about me. I could do anything to you. I'm a dangerous man.*

She'd only smiled. *You're drunk, Mr. Delaney.*

"That I was. And you got lucky, darlin'." He trudged back to the bed and dropped onto it, stretching out his long limbs and curling an arm over his eyes. "Because if I ever have you in my arms again, you'll be far too busy to bash me over the head."

RED HART DAIRY FARMS.

The heart-shaped red-and-white sign made Meko hit the brakes a little too hard, and the tires squealed as she made a left onto the dirt access road. The gate had been left open, so she drove in toward the largest building with lights on, which appeared to be a ranch house.

She parked toward the end of the drive, where two men were unloading boxes from a pickup truck. Both stopped and turned to watch as she climbed out of the Mercedes.

Neither one was the man she needed. "Hello," she called out. "I'm looking for Sean Delaney. Do you know where he is?"

"Yes, ma'am." The older of the two men pushed back his worn ball cap and eyed her. "And you'd be . . . ?"

A rotten liar, Meko thought as she produced an envelope she'd taken from the junk mail she'd gotten at home. "I work for his insurance agent. I've got a settlement check and a new policy for him to look over and sign."

"Why didn't you just mail it to him?" the younger man wanted to know.

"My boss said Mr. Delaney needed the check

right away." Meko shrugged. "I was called up here to inspect another claim, so I offered to drop this off to him while I was in the area."

"Nice of you to do that. Sean's place is over there, at the end of the lane." The older man pointed to a small cottage about a quarter mile from the main house. "Knock hard. He's probably passed out by now."

"Thank you very much."

Meko's heart was pounding so fast when she climbed back in behind the wheel that she nearly dropped her keys. Aware that the two men were still watching her, she kept a calm smile plastered on her face until she drove out of sight, then exhaled hard and wiped the sweat from her brow. *Don't lose it now, you're almost there.*

She switched off the Mercedes' lights before she turned into the short drive leading to the cottage. The windows were dark and unwelcoming, but Meko forced herself to walk up to the door.

He's probably asleep, the man said.

She lifted her hand, hesitated, and then tried the knob instead. He hadn't locked it, and the door swung inward with a small creak. "Sean?"

As she stepped inside the cool, dark little house, she smelled something, and felt her heart sink down to her heels as she identified it.

Whiskey.

She let her eyes adjust to the lack of light, then spotted a long, still form sprawled on a single bed in one corner. From the deep sounds of his breathing, Sean Delaney was dead to the world.

Tara's life is on the line, I come all this way, and he's passed out cold.

Anger swelled inside her for a moment, then receded under the crushing weight of hopelessness. She started walking toward the bed, her arms crossed over her abdomen. She hadn't felt this weary and frightened and miserable since being booked by the police. What had she been thinking, violating the terms of her bail, coming here to beg this man to help her? He couldn't even help himself.

Tara was as good as dead.

She stood beside the bed and stared down at him. He wasn't snoring, slack-jawed, or drooling, but he was frowning a little in his sleep. His long body looked harder, leaner, and his silver hair needed a trim. The smile lines around his mouth and eyes seemed a little deeper, and there were new nicks and scratches on his hands. Absently she wondered if he'd gotten them from working or brawling in some bar.

Oh, Sean. Who do I go to now?

Meko reached down and trailed her fingers over the backs of his. Tears blurred her vision as she thought of her young friend, alone and terrified, under the power of men who would kill her in less than five days.

Nick can't help me, and my father is dead. Maybe my brothers—

His hand twitched under hers, then jerked and seized her wrist. Before Meko could do more than make a high, startled sound, Sean clamped his other hand on her waist, and hauled her down beside him.

"Sean. Wait." She rolled into him as he reached down and pulled her legs up onto the mattress. That was when she realized Sean was naked, and tried to arch away from him. "I'm sorry, I didn't mean to wake you. I know it's late and I shouldn't be here." She was babbling. "I'll come back tomorrow."

He moved over her, pinning her down with his hard hands and long legs, staring at her as if he didn't believe his own eyes.

She gave his chest a small push. "Let me go, Sean."

"Oh, no." A slow smile appeared on his face. "Not this time, *a chuisle mo chroí*."

Sean's mouth was on hers a heartbeat later, and Meko immediately twisted, trying to wriggle out from under him. He countered, using his body weight to hold her down. His fingers threaded into her hair to keep her head still, then he kissed her again. She went rigid beneath him as his tongue glided in and stroked hers. He tasted of mint and whiskey.

He's drunk. That's why he's doing this.

Outraged all over again, she worked her hands between their bodies and tried to push him away. Then she felt an odd, uneven patch of skin under her fingertips and went still. A long scar, so close to his heart that it made her blood freeze.

"Kameko." He only lifted his head and smiled again. "I've been waiting for you."

She drew in a deep breath. If she couldn't reason with him, she'd scream her head off. "Sean, I need you to —"

"I know." His hand gripped the hem of her skirt, pulling it up until the cool night air washed over her thighs. "I've got everything you need, darlin'."

He caught her lips opening to speak and kissed her again, holding nothing back now. Meko had to tell him he was making a terrible mistake, but she couldn't get away from his mouth, and she couldn't bring herself to claw him. She moved her hands up to his shoulders, then over his back, feeling other scars—thin lines, puckered hollows, and one elongated, twisted knot of tissue right next to his spine.

Who had done this to him? Why wasn't he dead?

She wanted to demand some answers, then she felt the world turn inside out as his palm moved up between her thighs and slipped under the elastic band of her panties.

"So soft," he said into her mouth as he traced a slow, erotic triangle around the trim patch of curls under the silk.

A hard, taut ache throbbed there, reminding her of every sleepless night she'd spent since the last time he'd touched her. That emptiness rolled over her other emotions, driving the anger and despair from her head, until she was caught in the grip of that terrible need. She felt her body take over as her hips lifted to fit herself to his hand, and her legs parted and realigned beneath his to give him better access.

"That's it, yes," he muttered against her mouth as he tugged her panties down out of the way. The head of his full, thick penis nudged her belly—another erotic shock. "I've dreamed of fucking you, darlin', deep and hard and slow, all night long, every night . . . and now you're here, and you're soft and sweet for me . . ."

He meant every word. She could hear the low, rough urgency in his voice, feel it in his touch. Nick had never spoken to her like that—in fact, no one had. Because she was small and delicately built, she had always been treated by her ex-husband and the few lovers she'd taken after him with the utmost respect and consideration. As if she would shatter without that oh-so-cautious handling.

But Meko wasn't a porcelain doll, and she was sick of being treated like one.

Even if he is drunk, he means it. She closed her eyes, gnawing at her lip as Sean's skillful fingers played with her. *He wants me so much that he dreams about it.*

The same way she had.

Kappa mo kawa nagare, her brother Ichiro's voice whispered in her head.

Something collapsed inside Meko, and then she was clutching at him, moaning as he circled her clit with the tip of his thumb.

"That's my girl." He curled two fingers up inside her body and slowly penetrated her that way, moving them in and out, until she was shaking with desire. "Do you like that? Do you want more of me?"

She didn't know what to say. Nick had never encouraged her to talk in bed, and she'd been too shy with the others.

"Kameko." He shifted again, lifting his weight off her, pushing her legs further apart. She shivered as he brought her hand down between them, guiding her palm along the length of his erection, then closing her fingers around him. "Feel how hard you make me?"

His hand moved with hers, making her stroke him. She squeezed, feeling the delicious weight and length of him, and shivered again as he groaned and stiffened in reaction. She wanted to say something, but her throat wouldn't work.

"I'm that way for you. Only for you." He took her hand away and looked into her eyes, making her see what was in his as he gripped himself again and positioned the head of his penis against her. "Will you have me, then?"

Meko knew this was her last chance to say no—and the rational part of her brain was all in favor of that. *Wasn't Nick bad enough? I finally have my life exactly the way I want it, and Sean Delaney can't—won't—be a part of it.*

The rest of her wanted this more.

She met his gaze. For better or worse, she would have this one time with him. For both of them. "Yes, Sean."

He didn't look away as he pushed into her body. He watched her eyes, lifting a little when she shifted under his weight, but he didn't stop. Not even when it seemed she couldn't take anymore, and her thighs went tight at his sides.

His hand traced her contours from breast to hip as he murmured, "Don't tense up on me, darlin', let me inside you. It'll be good for both of us, you'll see." She softened around him, and he brushed her lips with his. "That's the way, that's so good . . ."

Tears spiked on her lashes as the emptiness vanished and the ache changed to a slow, stretching heat that crept up through her abdomen and into her breasts.

At last he filled her, and went still, his head falling back as he dragged in an unsteady breath. "Christ Jesus, you're like a fist. Am I hurting you?"

Meko shook her head.

He gathered her up with one arm and braced himself with the other as he moved against her, testing their fit. "Hold on to me, then."

She lifted her arms and linked her hands behind his waist. Sweat trickled down his back and seeped between their skin as he drew himself out, then pushed in again. After a few more gentle penetrations, Meko felt herself go liquid around him, her body providing the slick heat they needed.

Sean's hand curled around her nape, bringing her face to his so he could nuzzle her cheek. His voice went deep and hoarse as he whispered, "Now it gets better than all the dreams, *a chuisle mo chroí.*"

He thrust hard into her, the stroke fast and deep, and caught her small scream with his mouth, taking it in as she took him. Meko felt her hands slide from his damp back and grab the tangle of sheets on either side of them, her fingers digging in as he moved inside her.

Her first orgasm hit her like a freight train out of nowhere, and Sean held her close and drove her through it, murmuring words she didn't understand against her skin as she shook and cried out and clutched at him.

"Not enough, sweetheart," he said under his breath, rolling with her until he was off the bed and poised over her, his penis still hard inside her. He covered her breasts with his hands, scraping his palms over her nipples as he massaged them in time with his thrusts, now impossibly deep. "Give me more, Kameko."

She fought the rising tide inside her, still dazed and breathless from her last climax, but Sean wouldn't let her rest. He took her like a man possessed by demons, a fierce smile curling his lips when she came a second, then a third time. His hands were all over her, kneading and coaxing as he stroked fast and deep inside her body.

Darkness crowded her vision as she reached up for him and pulled him down so that their mouths were only an inch apart. As she kissed him, she bore down, clamping her internal muscles around him. A deep, helpless sound came rumbling from him, and then he stiffened and groaned into her mouth as he poured himself into her.

They collapsed in a tangle of limbs, Sean shifting to one side as he curled around her. Meko buried her face against his chest, still reeling from the intense pleasure he'd given her. As their bodies cooled, she felt his limbs grow heavier, and realized he'd fallen asleep.

She lifted her head to look at his face, then closed her eyes.

Kappa mo kawa nagare, Ichiro had said to her. Even a water sprite can be carried away by the river.

Chapter 3

Most of the military personnel stationed in Washington, D.C., didn't have to report to work by five a.m. Those who did generally met over matters that wouldn't make the morning report on CNN.

At one of the most restricted areas in the city, the sergeant monitoring the metal detector gate stopped an attractive blond woman after she passed through it without setting off an alarm. "Good morning, ma'am. May I see your identification, please?"

She handed over her wallet and a copy of her orders.

"Thank you." He consulted a typed page of names on his clipboard, then checked off hers. "We haven't seen you here in a few months."

"I was on medical leave." Brooke Oliver nodded to the two armed military police officers who flanked her. "Is this something new?"

"Yes, ma'am, everyone gets an escort now. Please don't leave the designated area without informing security." He returned her credentials. "And welcome back to the Pentagon, Captain Oliver."

Because of the heightened security measures in the aftermath of the September 11 attack, Brooke had already been stopped and searched, so she wasn't surprised when the escort team remained with her until they reached the door of General Kalen Grady's conference room.

"You're looking better," a familiar voice said from behind her.

Brooke turned to see another pair of MPs escorting a lanky, brown-haired man. Instead of proper army attire, Conor Perry wore a battered leather jacket and faded jeans—his version of a uniform. "Lieutenant. Nice to see you again."

"Captain." After their escort teams departed, Conor skimmed a finger over her cheek. "That's either extremely good makeup or those bruises have faded."

Two months ago, Brooke would have taken offense at anyone on the job touching or speaking to her so casually—especially a junior officer. That was before her pride and ambition had nearly sabotaged an important operation.

Now she only shrugged. "I heal fast."

The office receptionist had not yet reported for duty, so the two agents went directly into the conference room. A keen pang of regret twisted inside Brooke as she greeted the two-star general and his ridiculously beautiful wife. "Good morning, General, Mrs. Grady."

"Hey, Brooke." Sarah Ravenowitz Grady leaned over to slap Conor's wrist as he reached for a small plate of biscotti sitting in front of her. "Hands off, Perry, those are mine."

Conor rolled his eyes. "Aren't you a civilian now? Shouldn't you be home knitting booties?"

"I *am* a civilian—a civilian CID consultant, thank you very much—and I buy my booties from Fendi." She pressed a hand against her throat, swallowed, and grimaced. "When I'm not inspecting domestic porcelain, that is."

"Still got the morning sickness, Raven?"

"And afternoon. And evening. We're talking queasy city here." She glowered down at her rounded, protruding belly. "I'm about to starve, too. This baby doesn't like *anything*."

"Except chocolate, pickles, and sardines," her husband reminded her. "Usually mixed together, at three a.m., every night this week."

Raven sighed. "I *said* I'd go get them myself last night."

"Tonight, I might let you. Captain, Lieutenant, there's fresh coffee in that carafe, or ice water, if you want it." He waited until the two agents were settled, then began the briefing. "Bring me up to date first on what you've got on the West Coast situation."

"It's confirmed, the Sayura brothers came in through LAX last night at one a.m.," Brooke said as she handed the file across the table before passing out copies of its contents to Raven and Conor. "The local P.D. followed them to the Hilton, and presently are keeping them under surveillance. No other activity to report as of oh-four-hundred this morning."

Kalen skimmed through the intelligence report. "And the sister?"

"No one has actually seen or heard from Kameko Sayura since her release on a half-million bond. My guess is she's gone to ground." Conor grimaced as he offered the faxes sent to him by the L.A.P.D. "I put in a call last night to her attorney. He claims she's in a private hospital recuperating from the shock, and may not be well enough to attend the pretrial."

"That's what every attorney says whenever their clients jump bail." Kalen studied the airport security camera shots of the two Japanese men, one of whom had a twisted leg and walked with a cane. "She's maintained a regular correspondence with the older brother; she must have known they were coming over. So why does she disappear a couple of hours before they arrive in the U.S.?"

"Either she's running to get away from them," Brooke said as she slipped into her chair at the conference table, "or she knows where the body is."

Raven bit off the end of a biscotti. "Or she's trying to find the kid."

Kalen glanced at his wife, who had kicked off her shoes and was now draped lazily over the chair next to his. Despite the seriousness of the discussion, his mouth curled as he felt her briefly caress the side of his shin with her bare toes. "What makes you say that?"

"I know her. Kameko Sayura's a solid business-woman, well known among the local celebs and reputable as hell." Sarah Ravenowitz Grady finished off the biscotti and reached for another. "She didn't kill Tara. I think somebody snatched the kid to yank her strings." She studied the long, thin biscuit. "You know, these really would be much better with sardines, Kalen."

"Now *I'm* getting queasy." Conor grimaced and took a sip of his coffee. "You think Kameko is out doing whatever it takes to get her back."

"From the tap we put on her phone after the Dai operation, we know both Shandian and the Sayura syndicate have been in contact with her. According to the transcripts, the White Tiger swords were never mentioned, but her father was." Kalen closed the file. "Now her shop assistant disappears and Kameko is arrested for her murder. On the same day her brothers leave Japan to enter the U.S., she jumps bail and vanishes. Brooke?"

"They could be putting the squeeze on her." She glanced at Raven. "Do you how close this woman is to the girl?"

"Kameko worked on a couple of Etienne fashion shows that I headlined in Paris. She always brought the kid with her, and from what I saw, they acted more like mother and daughter than boss and employee." Raven sighed. "It's just not like Meko to panic and run, too—she's a steady, sensible woman. Why didn't she tell the police the truth when they arrested her?"

"She could be trying to protect the girl." Kalen stacked the reports, then addressed his agents. "Brooke, I want you and Conor to head out to L.A. this morning. Set up a command post near her shop, and put surveillance teams on Kameko's house, the Joneses', and any close friends'. The attorney general is giving us carte blanche, so get your taps and bugs in place, right away. The minute Kameko Sayura surfaces, bring her in."

Brooke jotted down notes. "Yes, sir."

"Con, I want you to concentrate on making the rounds. Talk to the local muscle, see if the snatch was contracted. You won't be able to dent the syndicate itself, so work on peripherals—girlfriends, suppliers, anyone who might have a direct line on what the Sayura are doing here."

"Will we have company on this one?" Conor asked.

"Let the local P.D. give you street support, but keep them out of the loop. I don't want one word about the White Tiger hitting the streets." Kalen thought for a minute. "You'll probably have the FBI breathing down your neck. They've lost two men to the tongs, and they want some payback."

"Just what we need." Conor rolled his eyes. "Help from the happily handicapped."

Kalen ignored his wife's chuckle. "That's all. Keep me informed."

Brooke lagged behind, waiting until Conor had left. This was the part she wasn't going to enjoy. She had been jealous of Raven's relationship with the general, so much so that she had attacked the other woman, then turned her over to the Army Inspector General as a deserter. Raven, on the other hand, had led a rescue team to save Brooke and Kalen when they'd been captured by the Dai's thugs. Knowing she owed Raven her life only made it more difficult to face her. Still, it had to be said. "Sir, I just wanted to tell you how much I appreciate this opportunity."

She resisted the urge to examine the surface of the conference table. "After the way I treated you and your wife and screwed up everything on the last op, I didn't expect this. Thank you."

"You're one of my best agents, Brooke. I know I can depend on you." Kalen nodded toward her right side. "How are the ribs?"

"Better now that I don't have to wear that steel brace every day, sir." She went to the door, then hesitated and glanced back at Raven. "Mrs. Grady, my mom says unsalted soda crackers are the only reason she made it full term with me. Might want to give them a try."

Raven grinned, delighted. "I will."

After Brooke departed, Kalen caught his wife's bare foot and propped it on his thigh, massaging the arch with his long fingers. "Will you ever learn to behave yourself during an official briefing?"

"No." Raven picked up the photo of Kameko that Conor had left on the table. "So what's my assignment, General? I mean, other than looking gorgeous and dragging you off to have wild sex in the nearest Pentagon supply closet once or twice a day?"

He patted her foot before easing it back down. "You're going to get on the phone with your contacts over in Europe and pump them for information."

"Lucky for you I'm willing, then. And you?"

Kalen took out his data organizer. "I'm going to talk to our friends in New Orleans."

Meko dreamed of the Dragon Wall.

She saw herself clearing some weeds away from

the beautiful tile wall. Tara stood beside her, watching.

This little blue dragon one is mine, she heard herself say. *Pretty lame, huh?*

Nah, I think it's the cutest one. What's the deal with the big white basketball?

It's not a basketball, it's an enchanted pearl.

You're kidding. Tara's bright laughter. *Imagine wearing a rope of those around your neck.*

The smallest dragon here was given the pearl and told that she had to guard it and keep it safe forever. She was too small to fight the other dragons, and the pearl was too big to fit in her pocket. So she wrapped herself around it and fell into a deep sleep that lasted a thousand years. And when she woke up, she had grown three times her original size, while all the other dragons had grown old and weak. From then on she had no problem fighting them off and protecting the pearl.

Tara didn't laugh at her story this time. She backed away from the Dragon Wall, shaking her head. *Not this time, Meko. You didn't protect me this time.*

"Tara!" Meko jerked awake, but she couldn't move. A heavy arm held her down, and it took a moment for her to register exactly who it belonged to. "Oh, no."

It took a few more minutes to untangle herself from Sean's possessive grip, but with some determined nudging and squirming Meko was able to slip out of bed. The dream had left her so unnerved that she banged her bare hip against the corner of his table. She had to bite her lip to keep from shrieking in pain.

Then she felt a trickle of warm fluid on the inside of her thigh, and realized it was Sean's semen. She hadn't even thought about using protection. Of course, she was on the pill to regulate her period, but that would only protect her against pregnancy.

I'm forty years old. How could I be this thoughtless about sex?

She went to his bathroom and used a washcloth to cleanse the physical traces of their lovemaking from her body. Her thighs felt weak, and her muscles ached in several places, but the sensations weren't unpleasant, only unfamiliar. Had it really been so long since she'd taken a lover that she'd forgotten how it felt?

No. It just never felt like this before.

She used a bit of toothpaste on her fingertip to clean her mouth, but it didn't help. She could still taste him on her lips and tongue. She could still smell him on her skin.

And while you're here making love to a man you barely know, Tara's time is running out.

Meko padded back out and found her clothes crumpled on the floor beside the bed, where Sean had flung them. Picking them up and dressing there while she watched him sleep embarrassed her, but she wanted to make sure he didn't wake. Not yet, not until she decided what to do.

Once she was dressed, she wandered around the room, examining the sparse furnishings as if they would give her some hint of how she could convince Sean to help her. She noticed he had no personal possessions on display—no framed photos, mementos, or other symbols of things that were important to him.

Perhaps he had worked here only a few weeks and hadn't had time to unpack. Or it could be a habit, left over from his army career. Soldiers had to pick up and move often—surely intelligence agents even more so. The fact that she didn't know why he kept the cottage neat but bare only underscored how little she actually knew about him.

He could be involved with someone already. He could even be married.

She spotted a pair of jeans hanging over the back of a chair, and gingerly searched the pockets. She found a handful of loose change, a ring of keys, and a thin wallet. In it was Sean's California driver's license, which he'd acquired only a week ago, fifty-three dollars in small bills, and a photo of two young girls, one redhead, the other brunette. The brunette's eyes were identical to Sean's.

His daughters?

The thought of Sean having a wife and two children made her stomach roll, but she forced herself to carefully replace everything. She picked up the faded denim jacket he'd left on the seat of the chair. It felt oddly heavy, and she found out why when she put her hand into one of the side pockets. The gun she pulled out of the jacket was smooth, balanced and fully loaded, she saw as she ejected and checked the clip.

Her brother Jiro had insisted on teaching her how to shoot. "Our father is an important man, little sister. He has formidable enemies."

Meko had learned to handle weapons, but had

never liked them. After she'd opened K.S. Designs, her security contractor had helped her apply for a concealed-gun permit, and had even arranged for her to take shooting lessons at a local pistol range. Meko was supposed to carry the .22 with her at all times, but she usually left it locked in the store safe.

Why would he need to carry a gun on a farm?

She glanced at the man sleeping so peacefully only a few feet away, then ran her fingers along the dark eye of the gun's barrel. The photo of the two young girls shamed her more than anything she'd done with him.

I ought to shoot myself for being such a blind, trusting idiot.

Something inside her instantly rebelled at that thought—the part of her that had responded so violently to Sean's touch, and had willingly taken him into her body. No matter how easy it would have been to dump the blame wholly on Sean, she had participated—with enthusiasm.

I was overemotional and he was drunk. A dangerous combination under normal circumstances. She put the gun in the pocket of her blazer and sat down on the chair. *I can't change what happened; it's over and done with. I'll wake him up in a few hours and tell him about Tara, and talk him into helping me find her.* She rested her palm on the butt of the gun, taking small comfort in its weight. *One way or another.*

Most of the business in the French Quarter of New Orleans was conducted with the brisk, cheerful indifference of any tourist town, but there were still a few places where service mattered more than making a quick buck.

Valence St. Charles entered one of them, a small antique weapons shop frequented by collectors, many of whom still referred to the Civil War as "The War of Northern Aggression."

The bell over the door tinkled, summoning an elderly shopkeeper from the stockroom to the counter. "How may I help you, madam?" he asked in a distinct, upper-class British accent.

Val kept her head down as she examined the long display case between them, which was filled with antique guns, swords, pieces of armor, and several ordinary-looking black canes. The wide-brimmed straw hat she wore completely concealed her hair and face. "Here I thought it was illegal to sell sword canes in the state of Louisiana."

The old man coughed, then cleared his throat. "It is, madam, but I can assure you these are simply walking sticks."

"And I'm the Queen of Mardi Gras." She lifted her gaze to his. "I sure like the Brit accent, Remy. Can you teach me to talk that way?"

"*Mon Dieu.*" Remy Durreil pressed a hand to his chest as his voice dropped into his natural Cajun drawl. "I'm about to keel over here, *petite*, you trying to kill me?"

"Give me one of those canes and I'll try."

"Still a saucy brat." He came around the counter to give her a resounding kiss, then led her by the hand to his cramped office. "There now, you sit. I'll make you some tea while you tell me what's put that sparkle in your eye. Already heard you got the head curate job over at the museum. That's some nice work, *cher*."

"Thank you kindly. I've been real busy." She lifted her hand to display the etched golden wedding band Jian-Shan had given her. "Got me a husband and a little girl now, too. You come to dinner one night and see how pretty they are."

"Be happy to." Remy fussed with preparing the tea before handing her a delicate Wedgwood cup and wading through stacks of files and packages to get behind his desk. He sat with a grunt and gave her a long, measuring look. "You never looked better, *petite*, but I'm guessing you didn't come here to show off your fine self and ask an old man over for supper."

"You know me too well." Val placed her cup back on the saucer and set it aside. "I'm looking for some hot steel, Remy. Japanese samurai swords, Nagatoki era. They got snatched from outside my museum a few weeks ago. Big truck carrying about three hundred of them up and disappeared."

"Wasn't me or mine." He frowned. "I've been out of them big leagues ten years or better now, you know that, child."

"I know." She picked up a flintlock and admired the highly polished stock. "But if anyone can get a line on who grabbed them and where they went off to"—she sighted down the barrel at him—"it's you, Remy."

He stroked the thin silver mustache under his nose with one fingertip. "I'll take it these were those White Tiger blades you went over to Paris to borrow."

She placed the gun back in its stand. "That's them."

"God's honest truth, *cher*, I haven't heard a peep about them." He pursed his lips as he thought for a moment. "Could have been an out-of-town collector did the job. Wouldn't put them on the market if he wanted them for himself. I know that look, Valence—now who you think took them?"

Val imagined her old friend's reaction if she told him about how she had become involved with the Chinese mafia in Paris. "If I knew, I wouldn't be here. Remy, would you put some feelers out, see what you can pick up for me?"

"You don't even have to ask." He reached over to pat her knee. "Now, tell me about this scoundrel who stole you away from me."

She spent another half hour catching up with the old shopkeeper, then left to walk down the street to a split-level seafood restaurant. On the second floor, she headed for a back table, where a Chinese man sat calmly feeding bits of shrimp to a blond toddler.

She paused for a moment to admire them. *Mine, both of them.* After what they'd endured in Paris, it was still hard for her to believe. Even after they were out of danger, they had been obliged to go through the adoption process, as Lily was not Jian-Shan's biological daughter. Since neither she nor Jian-Shan had a sterling past, Val had been worried that the authorities might try to take Lily away from them. Happily, their friend General Grady had used his influence, and now Lily was legally their daughter forever.

T'ang Jian-Shan saw Val first, and a slow smile warmed his austere face. "Valence."

Lily grinned and bounced in her high chair. "Mama!"

"Hey there." She bent to accept a piece of shrimp from her stepdaughter's chubby hand, then slid into the chair beside her husband. "Sorry I'm late; Remy was heartbroken to hear I'm no longer single."

"He had his chance." Jian-Shan brushed his mouth over hers before he lifted his hand to catch the attention of a waitress. After she took Val's order and left them, he asked, "Did he have any new information?"

Val frowned. "No, and that troubles me. He's not fencing big items anymore, but if anyone had put those blades up for auction, Remy would have heard. How about you?"

"Nothing at all." He blotted Lily's face with the edge of a napkin. "The rumors circulating in the collectors' market are merely speculation. It's as if the swords don't exist."

"We've got Kalen and Raven to help us now," she said, and put her hand over her husband's. "We'll find them, *cher*."

Chapter 4

Had he still been in Tokyo, Ichiro Sayura would have instructed his housekeeper to spend several days of preparation to ensure that the *chaji* would be perfect. The classic tea ceremony represented more than a form of ritual respect for one's family, friends, and business associates.

"A meeting is a remarkable occasion which will never be repeated exactly," his *sensei* at the temple school had taught him. "So it is vital to carefully plan every aspect, and thus, the opportunities that may arise from them."

Ichiro had patiently explained to the hotel staff that he wished a full-presentation *chaji*, with both tea and a meal. Since the Hilton could not provide the Sayura brothers and their guests with a formal *chashitsu*, the staff prepared a makeshift tearoom in one of the smaller meeting areas furthest from the busy lobby and elevator access corridors.

As Ichiro hobbled toward it, his younger brother, Jiro, caught up with him.

"I count four undercover officers in the lobby,"

Jiro told him in a low voice. "There are two un-
marked surveillance units at the front and back en-
trances, and one in the alley covering the delivery
door."

Ichiro suppressed a sigh. "You are late."

"I was busy." His brother made an impatient
sound. "Is this entirely necessary?"

"I do not tell you how to do your work, brother.
Do not interfere with mine." Ichiro halted just outside the tearoom. "Where is Kameko?"

"My men haven't located her yet." The younger
man eyed the dainty hostess waiting at the door.
She wore a full traditional kimono and her hair in
the classic *shimada* style. "I don't think this is a good
idea."

"Traditions are important on both sides of the Pacific." Ichiro inclined his head toward the bowing
hostess, who opened the door for them. "Come, our
guests will soon arrive."

As per his instructions, the meeting room had
been cleared of its original furnishings and decora-
tions. The *kakemono* scroll he had carefully selected
had been hung over the *chabudai* tea table, which
had been placed on tatami floor mats. A heavily
laden cart had been left beside a smaller table sup-
porting a porcelain basin of water. A second hostess
in kimono stood waiting beside a small gong.

"This is nothing but old-fashioned nonsense."
Jiro sounded disgusted. "Better to take them out to
the strip bar and get them drunk."

Ichiro nodded to the second hostess, and studied
the scroll. The Buddhist scripture had been created
by a master of calligraphy, and its ink traces were as

powerful as they were delicate. " 'We will enter and remain in the emptiness that is pure, superior, and unsurpassed,' " he quoted from the scroll. "You cannot find enlightenment in a bar filled with gyrating seminude women, brother."

Jiro studied the tea table and exhaled heavily. "I might."

A small tap on the door made both men turn, and the hostess sounded the gong. The door opened to admit two elderly men, one Japanese, the other Chinese.

Ichiro limped over to the *tsukubai* basin, and washed his hands before proceeding forward to welcome his guests with a bow. No words were spoken as he led the two men to the table. Maintaining silence acknowledged that they were leaving behind the concerns and despairs of the physical world.

As his guests also washed their hands, both hostesses soundlessly glided to assist with the seating arrangements. The elderly Japanese man paused to admire the scroll, then turned his shrewd gaze on Ichiro before bowing again. .

Once they were seated, Ichiro addressed the Chinese man. "Forgive these unfortunate arrangements, Ju-Long-san. Such an occasion calls for the finest meal, and yet I can offer you only this meager fare in less than acceptable surroundings."

"I am honored by your concern," Qi Ju-Long said. "And puzzled by it. Takeshi Sayura paid no deference to me during his lifetime. I find receiving it from his sons most . . . unusual."

Ichiro inclined his head before turning to the

Japanese man. "My sincerest wish is that you bestow your generosity and tolerance as well, Menaka-san. You honor me and my brother with your presence."

Aware that he was being accorded the status of a lesser guest, the dour-faced Eiji Menaka only nodded once.

The hostesses began to serve the three-course *chakaiseki* meal on beautifully lacquered trays. Each man used fresh cedar chopsticks to eat the cooked white rice out of special ceramic bowls, along with sips of miso soup and morsels of pickled raw fish and vegetables. Tiny cups of sake were offered, and Ichiro frowned when Jiro quickly drank three in a row.

"How are you enjoying your visit to the U.S.?" Ju-Long asked. "Have you found time to look into your father's . . . business concerns?"

His father would have been furious at such a bald inquiry, and Ichiro could feel his brother tense. However, he kept his expression impassive. Discussing business thoroughly violated the serenity of the *chaji*, but it served a purpose. A faint trace of disgust appeared in Eiji's eyes, something he could appreciate—and use.

"My brother, regrettably, has not yet had the opportunity to attend to those matters." He made a small self-deprecating gesture. "He tolerates the inconvenience of a crippled brother and constantly puts my personal needs before others."

Used dishes were whisked out of sight as the second and third courses were presented, until the meal was concluded with the *omogashi* dessert of lightly spiced almond cake.

"I regret I cannot offer you the reverie a private garden would afford," Ichiro said as he rose from the mats with some difficulty. "However, if you both will kindly join my brother in the adjoining room"—he gestured toward a side door—"I will see to the final preparations of our tea."

Once his brother and the two men departed, Ichiro ordered the hostess to remove the displayed scroll and replace it with a simple arrangement of ylang-ylang flowers. The other hostess removed all traces of the meal and set out the thirteen utensils Ichiro needed for preparing the *koi cha*.

Ichiro retrieved the *mizusashi*, a stoneware jar that contained the purified water he would use for the ceremony, and transferred it to the table. Canned Sterno replaced the hearth fire he would have used at home, but he'd brought his own supply of *jo matcha*. He removed the elegant ceramic container from his *shifuku* silk pouch, and set the tea in front of the *mizusashi*. Behind him, his hostess set up the *tana* stand he would use to display the chosen utensils. When he was ready, he nodded to the hostess, and she struck the gong five times to summon the men back into the room.

Menaka stopped to wash his hands at the basin, but Ju-Long simply sat down on the mat again.

"The flowers are quite beautiful," Eiji murmured as he bowed to Ichiro.

"I am most gratified that they please you." Ichiro brought the *chawan* tea bowl to the table, and showed his guests the many implements it contained before arranging them next to the water jar. "I hope my brother was also able to do the same."

"Jiro speaks of alliances which have never before been attempted," Ju-Long said, dispensing with the formalities entirely. "I would remind you that you are no longer in Japan, Sayura. Your brother seeks more than he can manage."

The *fukusa* cloth Ichiro used to purify the tea container and scoop was a rich scarlet silk. "My brother is determined, Ju-Long-san. You will find him a formidable ally."

"I find nothing formidable here. Your brother is not your father, Sayura. Takeshi would never have coddled a defective," Ju-Long said. "You may think these traditions bind us, but how you fold a cloth and prepare tea indicates you are only fit for women's work. I will not form an alliance with a weakling and an effeminate cripple."

Eiji hissed in a sharp breath.

"I thank you for your consideration, Ju-Long-san." Ichiro's concentration never wavered as he ladled hot water into the tea bowl, then rinsed the whisk. He placed three scoops of tea in the bowl, and ladled more water until the whisk formed the tea into a thin paste. Carefully he added water until the paste was diluted enough to drink, then offered the bowl to the Chinese man. "May you find enlightenment along the way."

Ju-Long took the bowl and drank some of the tea, grimacing slightly. "This is bitter stuff."

"Like life." Before Ju-Long could pass the bowl to Eiji, Ichiro took it from him and bowed. "The balance of today's conversations must, of course, remain confidential. My brother will be happy to escort you to your car."

Ju-Long's narrow face reddened as he stood. "I can find my own way out."

Ichiro nodded to his brother, who followed the Chinese man out of the room. Tension left Eiji's shoulders as soon as he heard the door close. "Sayura-san, he does not know how gravely he insulted you just now."

"He will, Menaka-san." Instead of preparing a new bowl of tea, Ichiro gestured for one of the hostesses to remove the bowl. She did so, and left the room with the other woman. "I assume by your silence that you are more amenable to our proposal."

"I am not at all certain if it can be accomplished, especially with the Chinese. However, I am more than willing to provide whatever assistance you require."

"Excellent. We will begin today."

Eiji frowned as Ichiro produced a second tea bowl and began the intricate preparations of the drink again. "May I intrude on your meditation to inquire something about the ceremony?"

"Of course." Ichiro politely set aside the whisk.

"I have never seen anyone use two bowls during a *chaji*." Eiji appeared to be searching for the appropriate words. "Is this some particular family custom, perhaps?"

Ichiro appreciated the other man's delicacy in questioning what was considered an elite art form in their native land. "No, only a practical adaptation. I did not wish you to drink after one so unworthy."

"Ju-Long is a powerful member of the Shandian

tong," the other man said. "He can create great difficulties for you and your brother."

"We will overcome them together, my friend." He went back to the preparation, then offered the second bowl. "Let us drink together now, to the future of our new alliance."

Someone drove a rail spike into the back of Sean's head, making him emerge from a dream he didn't want to leave. The pain was so unanticipated and jolting that he sat straight up, ready to defend himself against whoever had bashed him in the skull.

Which was when he discovered he didn't have to wrestle an unknown assailant, and he hadn't been dreaming. The woman of his dream was sitting right there, no more than three feet away, on a chair next to his bed.

Kameko Sayura.

Thin dawn light spilled through the front window, shining on her neatly brushed, matte-black hair. Faint shadows made smudged half-circles under her exotic eyes, but her expression appeared otherwise calm.

And she was watching him like a wary cat.

"Mother of God." Speaking made the invisible spike drive deeper, and he clapped a hand to the back of his head before he squinted at her. "What the devil are you doing here, woman?"

"I've been waiting for you to wake up." Her voice sounded just as sweet and easy on the ear as he'd remembered. "Sean, I need your help. I'm in trouble."

Another beautiful woman in trouble. They'd be the death of him.

He reached down to grab his pants from the end of the bed, and stood to pull them on. From the way she politely averted her gaze, maybe he had been dreaming, at least about part of the evening's festivities. Then he spotted the faint puffiness of her lips, and the unmistakable pinkness of whisker burn on the side of her throat.

No, he'd definitely left his mark on her. But how far had it gone?

"What happened last night?" he said as he tugged his jeans on. "I know you didn't climb in bed with me."

When she heard him pull up his zipper, she turned her head to face him once more. "The door was open. When I came in to wake you, I . . . startled you."

He'd been trained to kill men for less. Another sign of how old and feeble he was getting. "How startled?"

"You pulled me down." She looked down at her clasped hands. "Then you were all over me."

The hammering inside his brain reached a crashing roar, but he went still. "I had you, then."

She nodded.

"Did you fight me?" He knelt down before her and looked for bruises. As her scent filled his head, he started recalling more details—but not whether she had cooperated. The thought that he might have forced her and couldn't remember made him sick. "Did I hurt you?"

"No." Her head dropped another notch, until her chin nearly touched her chest. "It was mutual."

"Mutual." The woman was talking about the blistering, illicit sex they'd shared as if it were some kind of investment strategy.

Maybe it was.

Sean rasped his hand over his beard stubble and rose to his feet. "I need coffee."

He trudged out to the kitchen, and turned on the kettle. He sensed her following, then stopping to hover a few feet away. That pissed him off, much more than her acting as if they'd never been naked with each other, but his mother had raised him to be mannerly.

And mannerly he would be. "I've tea, if you want it."

"No, thank you. I'm fine."

He reached in the cabinet for his bottle of aspirin, only to find it empty. He'd meant to pick up more during his last trip to town, but like so many things lately, he'd let it slide. His headache swelled, and he gripped the edge of the counter until his knuckles whitened.

"Here." A cool hand touched his arm, then opened to reveal two white tablets before she placed them on the counter in front of him. "These will help." She drew back again, leaving behind a faint trace of her scent—lilac, he finally realized. "I often get headaches, so I make it a habit to keep a bottle in my purse."

He took the pills and dry-swallowed them. "And do you make it a habit to jump into a strange man's bed in the middle of the night?"

"I didn't jump and you're not a strange man." She sounded angry, defensive. "But for the record, this was the first time I've ever done anything like this."

"Why?" He swung around and advanced on her. "Why do it with me?"

She moved back another step, then stopped and clenched her fists at her sides. *Acting brave.* "I don't know." *Underneath it, scared. Scared of him.* "It's not why I came here. I need your help."

"You need that, all right. What were you thinking, woman?" He stopped when there wasn't enough space left between them to accommodate two hands. "I kidnapped you." He'd forgotten how petite she was; the top of her head barely cleared the center of his chest. "I held a gun on you, took you from your home. I even made you break into your dead father's house and search it with me. Or have you already forgotten our first date?"

She lifted her chin. "I remember every single second of it."

So did he, damn her. "Do you remember saying how you were going to call the cops on me?" He leaned in, intentionally crowding her. "How you'd testify at my trial and have me thrown in prison for the rest of my natural life? And now you're coming to me for help?"

"Yes, I am. Now, would you please"—she glanced down and bumped the tip of her nose against his chest—"put your shirt on?"

The kettle emitted a sudden, piercing whistle, startling both of them. Sean stalked over to take it off the burner, then grabbed his shirt and pulled it on over his head. Attending to the coffee would keep him from strangling her. He hoped.

What the hell does she want from me?

"This is about those swords you were looking for," she said, right beside him again. She even had the audacity to poke his arm with a finger. "So if you want to blame someone, start with yourself."

"I'm sure I will." She wouldn't be the death of him, but those bloody swords might. He drank down a gulp, scalded his tongue, then swore. "Tell me what's happened."

She recited the facts like a schoolteacher. "Someone kidnapped my assistant, Tara Jones, from my shop. They demanded the White Tiger collection in exchange for her safe return. Tara is only sixteen years old, Sean." She paused, visibly fighting tears. "If I don't find those swords in five days, they're going to kill her."

That explained why she'd slipped into his bed.

"I'm sorry for your troubles." He dumped out the too weak coffee and dropped the empty cup on the counter. "Talk to the police. They can set up a sting at the exchange point."

"You don't understand." She swiped at her eyes with her shaking fingers, making the bracelets around her wrist jingle. "The men who took Tara left an old Japanese blade in my store. On my desk. It was covered with Tara's blood. They even hung a bracelet she'd been wearing on it. The police arrested me. They think I murdered her."

The cops weren't idiots. Which meant—"Sweet Jesus, woman, why didn't you tell them about the call?"

"The man said they would know if I told the police anything. He said they'd kill her."

They would kill the girl anyway—not that Sean was about to tell her that. No, he had to send her back to Los Angeles, and fast. He eyed her. "I can't get involved in this."

"You know about those swords. You were trying to find them."

"Not anymore. I'm retired now—out of the game entirely. I herd dairy cows for a living." He stared out at the mist rolling over the north pasture. Kalen Grady would be looking for those swords, and the general had been very specific about what he'd do if Sean ever crossed him again. Irony made his voice turn bitter as he added, "I have my life exactly the way I want it."

She reacted as if he'd slapped her. "I don't care. You think I *wanted* to come here and beg you for help?"

"Well, you're here, and I can't help you."

"If we don't find these swords in five days an innocent young girl who never hurt anyone in her life will die." She seized his hand in hers. "Don't turn me away, Sean. You're the only one who can help me save Tara."

Something else finally registered in his still-hazy brain. "You were charged in L.A. County, weren't you? You jumped bail to come here. Christ." He lifted his eyes to the ceiling and dragged in a deep breath. "Go back to Los Angeles, Kameko. Tell the police the truth—the whole truth—this time. They're your best chance to get her back alive."

"No, they're not. You know what these men are

like. They could have someone working for the police, or even some cops on their payroll. I won't gamble Tara's life to find out." She clasped his hand between both of hers as her intent gaze searched his face. "Please." Her voice broke on the word. "I can't do this without you. I'm begging, Sean. Help me."

"I'm so sorry." And he was. He bent to press a gentle kiss on her brow. "Trust me, darlin', you're better off without me."

Snick.

He'd felt the slide of her bracelets against his skin, but had paid no attention to it. Now when he tugged his hand from hers, he couldn't free himself. He glanced down and saw she'd not only slipped one of her bracelets on him, but had cuffed his right arm to her left at the wrists. "What's this?"

"These are my lovers' cuffs," she said, and stepped back to raise his hand along with hers. "I designed them for Valentine's Day. The local celebrities are getting into goth in a big way lately."

"Cute." He worked it around his wrist. The cuff was intricately enameled on the outside, and lined with what felt like mink on the inside. "The fur is a nice touch."

"Thank you. I take pride in my work."

He tested the locking mechanism and found he couldn't budge it. "All right, joke's over. Take it off."

"I'm not joking." As he twisted his wrist against hers, she added, "I should mention that, underneath the enamel and the mink, they're standard-issue police handcuffs."

He was a foot taller and at least seventy pounds heavier than her. Sean couldn't help the laugh.

"And you think cuffing us together will make me change my mind?"

"No." With her free hand, she pointed a gun at his heart. "This will."

He might have grabbed it from her, but realized it was his own gun. A gun with a hair trigger. In the hands of a woman who probably had no experience with firearms, there was no deadlier weapon. "All right, then. What now?"

"*You're* going to drive *me* to San Francisco this time, Sean." She picked up his jacket and handed it to him. "Let's go."

Nick Hosyu sat in his car at the back of K.S. Designs and dialed the number to the store. As soon as his ex-wife's polite voice began reciting her business hours from the answering machine, he switched off the phone and climbed out of his BMW. He'd go in through the back, the same way he had the last time. Even if he was spotted, he knew the alarm code, and no one would question a Japanese man letting himself into a Japanese-owned jeweler's shop. Especially when the owner was his ex-wife.

Wherever Meko is, she won't mind me borrowing a little stock. She's in so much trouble now, she probably won't even notice it's missing. The thought of the murder charge his ex-wife faced made his withered conscience give a faint, guilty twinge, until he squashed it. *They won't make it stick—anyone can look at her and tell she couldn't swat a fly, much less kill someone. While if I don't get the money to Little Anthony's boys by noon, I'm dead meat.*

He never would have heard about Meko's problems if he hadn't gotten a certain job offer from the tong. Just the thought of it had turned his stomach, but he had simply stalled for time—not that there was anything he could do for the kid. There was no question of him going to the police. Ju-Long, the new head of Shandian operations on the West Coast, had an even worse reputation than Little Anthony.

Nick used the key he'd copied from Meko's spare to let himself in through the service entrance at the back of the building, and punched in the disarm code on the alarm box just inside. There was a small flicker of red lights, then the indicator turned green.

He hesitated, wondering if he'd accidentally tripped something, but then shrugged. Even if someone showed up, he could explain his presence. He was her ex-husband. He was worried about her. Someone had to look out for her interests—and her valuable inventory.

Especially if she ends up doing time.

Because he genuinely cared about Kameko, Nick resisted the urge to rub his hands together and chuckle. Instead, he went to her workbench, but all the trays of loose stones and boxes of precious metals were gone.

"She cleaned up before she left," he muttered, and headed directly for her office. "Locked everything away. Of course, she'd do that if she was leaving for a while. In case of a break-in or something."

In her office, Nick found the wall safe standing open. Worse, the interior was empty, which made chilly sweat inch down his spine. Little Anthony wasn't known for his patience. He was rather famous for keeping the orthopedic ward at L.A. Medical Center constantly filled with patients, however.

Nick chewed on his thumbnail as he tried to think. "She wouldn't hock everything to make bail." He turned to jerk open her top desk drawer and search through its neatly organized contents. "She's loaded, she couldn't possibly—" He stopped and looked up.

The man standing just inside the door beside a uniformed cop gestured toward the open safe. "Maybe you should run your finger around the edge, see if you can pick up any gold dust."

"I beg your pardon." Nick straightened and assumed a practiced, righteous expression. "The store is closed. You'll have to come back another time."

"I know this dirtbag, Lieutenant. He's the ex," the cop said, and shook his head. "You want me to run him downtown?"

"Tempting, but not yet." The man in the battered leather jacket studied Nick the way he would a small, diseased rodent. "Give us a few minutes."

"Lieutenant?" Nick frowned as he watched the patrolman retreat and shut the door. "What are you, some kind of undercover cop?"

"Lieutenant Perry, Army CID." He flashed his credentials. "You're in a shitload of trouble right now, Nick, so shut your mouth and sit down."

He knows my name. Nick didn't bother to ask how much the cops had told him; the game was up. He'd have to find another way out. "Look, this is my wife's store," he said, trying to stall. "You can't just come barging in here—"

"Kameko is your ex-wife, and under the circumstances, I can do pretty much anything to you I want." Conor pointed to the chair. "Take a seat, or take a ride downtown and get ink all over those sticky fingers of yours."

If Nick didn't get ten thousand dollars to Little Anthony before noon, the loan shark's enforcers would find him and break his legs—whether he was in jail or not. Since he couldn't borrow some of Meko's rocks, he'd better broker a deal with the government, and fast.

He sat down and produced his best cooperative grin. "Sure, Lieutenant. Whatever you say."

Good warriors, Takeshi Sayura once told his younger son, *make their stand on ground where they cannot lose.*

Jiro Sayura thought of his father as he drove the expensive sedan to a remote mountain road overlooking the Pacific Ocean. Takeshi had often quoted philosophy to him, and while Jiro could never stand the stuff, his older brother regularly interpreted it for him.

If you want to win, little brother, fight on your turf.

A pickup truck was waiting on the shoulder of the road, and when he pulled over behind it, two raggedly dressed men stepped out and walked back to meet him. Both looked pale and undernourished, and the thinner one was shivering in the bright, hot sunlight as if it were freezing him.

The heavier of the pair leaned over the driver's side window, giving Jiro a whiff of his pungent body odor. "You the man we're supposed to meet with this stuff?"

"Yes." He despised using junkies off the street, but they were the easiest and most unnoticeable brand of labor for hire. "Get the bag out of the back and put it in the truck."

The men took the bulky black garbage bag from the backseat, while Jiro took a bottle of lighter fluid from his jacket and began squirting it all over the interior. The sharp odor of the flammable liquid helped cancel out the faint smell of urine and feces coming from the bag the men carried to the truck.

"Watch it," he said as the men dropped their burden into the truck bed, beside stacks of square green sod and two shovels. "I don't want anything spilling out."

"I guess not," one of the men muttered. The other gave Jiro a quick, frightened glance.

He lit a match and tossed it into the open window of the BMW, setting the interior on fire, then walked toward the truck. "Let's go."

The two men drove Jiro and their cargo to a landfill south of the city. A large sign hanging on the front gate warned that the site had been closed and trespassers would be prosecuted. One of the men got out of the truck and used a pair of bolt cutters on the padlocked chain holding the gate closed, then pushed it open for the truck to pass through. He closed it behind them before climbing into the bed.

Jiro inspected the site. Takeshi had brought him here for the first time when he was a boy. Now that it was closed, it might serve his purposes even better than it had his father's. "Go to the left, then to the end, there, away from where those seagulls are hovering," he told the driver.

The spot he had picked had been covered over by grass, which disintegrated as the two men took the shovels from the back and began excavating a deep, narrow pit.

Jiro leaned back against the truck and smoked a cigarette as he watched them dig. He didn't like the stench of the rotting garbage they unearthed, but it, too, would serve a purpose. When they stopped digging, he went over to inspect their work.

"It needs to be deeper," he told them.

"I ain't digging no hole to fucking China," the talkative one said.

Draw them in with the prospect of gain, his father would have said. Which Ichiro told him meant, *Gain their confidence with a good bribe.*

"If you want this"—Jiro took out a small plastic bag filled with white powder to show the junkie—"you'll dig until I tell you to stop."

The sight of the heroin made both men pick up their shovels, and they worked steadily for another twenty minutes before Jiro decided the pit was adequate for his purposes. He took off his jacket and draped it over his right arm before joining them at the pit again.

"That's enough." He nodded back at the pickup. "Go get the bag."

The two men carried the bulky bag over to the pit and tossed it in. Jiro heard plastic tear and a liquid thump, and looked over the edge. The bag had ripped, exposing half its contents.

"Holy shit, man." The timid one's eyes bulged. "You didn't say nothing about this."

"What are you, an idiot?" The other one grinned at Jiro. "Looks like we get a little pay raise, huh, Chinaman?"

"Actually, I'm Japanese," Jiro said, then used the gun concealed by his jacket to shoot the smiling junkie in the face. After pushing him over into the pit, he did the same to the second, terror-stricken man.

Filling in the grave and covering it with fresh sod took another thirty minutes, but Jiro was in no hurry. One of the junkies—the frightened one—was still alive, and twitched as the dirt shoveled into the pit fell on him. Jiro found that mildly amusing, but before he completely covered the man, he took out his gun and shot him a second time. Just to be sure.

Vulnerability makes men attack, his father had said. *Preparation makes men invincible.*

Jiro had never needed a translation on that one.

Chapter 5

"Are you sober enough to drive?" Meko couldn't help asking as she accompanied Sean out to her Mercedes.

"I was sober enough to make you a happy woman last night. And I was half drunk then." Sean gave her a sideways look. "What do you think, darlin'?"

She wasn't going to think. Not until they reached San Francisco. "The keys to the car are in the front pocket of my purse." Thank heavens she'd had the presence of mind to make him carry it out; she couldn't hold the gun and search her purse at the same time. "Unlock the driver's side door and open it."

Because they were cuffed together, she had to slide in across the seat first. She did so slowly, keeping the gun trained on Sean, holding her breath until he ducked down and climbed in behind her. She was forced to lean forward when he used his cuffed hand to put the key in the ignition. Their forearms rubbed together, making her skin tingle and tighten.

She hadn't expected the jolt, and it disturbed her. They'd already become lovers, and she was still as jumpy as a teenager waiting for her first kiss. If she couldn't control this ridiculous physical reaction she felt for him, he would definitely notice—and use it against her.

Maybe this isn't such a good idea.

She would have to rely on strict self-discipline to avoid a repeat of last night's reckless behavior. Her father had taught her to suppress her emotions from an early age, and that *was* something she was good at. But keeping Sean chained to her like this was going to be awkward and virtually impossible to hide. It made it all the more imperative that she talk him into willingly helping her before they reached San Francisco.

"Take 37 West to U.S. 101—"

"I know how to get to San Francisco," he said, cutting her off and putting the car into drive. He didn't take his foot off the brake, though. "Kameko, this isn't the way to do this. Stop it now, and we'll call it even."

"You find those swords for me and then we'll be even." She pressed the gun into his side. "Now, drive."

Sean drove. Out from the farm, onto the road that led past town, and onto the freeway. Only when they had merged with the early-morning commuters did Meko relax a degree.

This will work. All I have to do is convince him now, and together we can save Tara. "I received a letter from my father just before he died. A letter, and a photograph of a sword. I didn't tell you about them the last time because I didn't think they mattered. Now I do."

"So?" He didn't sound interested.

Oh, yeah, I'm definitely going to win him over by explaining everything. "I wish I didn't have to resort to this, Sean. You have no idea how desperate I am."

The side of his mouth curled. "Oh, but you're going to tell me, aren't you, darlin'?"

His sour amusement made her feel clumsy and foolish, and what she was doing seem utterly ridiculous. She couldn't allow him to patronize her into giving up, so she would have to do a little posturing of her own. "You should know what we're getting into—it could be very dangerous."

"That much I already know." Daylight streaming in through his window from the east made the lines of his face look like a grim, carved mask. "Do you?"

She was simply going to have to stop looking at him. "I think the men who took Tara called me a few times before the abduction. They asked me if my father had sent anything to me from China. When I wouldn't tell them, they must have decided to kidnap Tara and plant that sword to frame me." She described the blade in more detail for him, as well as how it had been literally driven into the surface of her desk. "When the police tested the blood on it and discovered it was Tara's, they naturally assumed that I'd killed her and dumped the body. That's what whoever took her wanted the police to think, anyway."

His expression remained blank. "Did they find your fingerprints on it?"

"No." She shifted her grip on the gun to make sure the safety was still on. "I use special gloves to protect my hands when I work with heated metals. They found some at my workbench, and assumed I'd used and discarded a pair of those."

He nodded. "How did they explain you leaving the murder weapon out for everyone to see?"

"The detective who questioned me thought I'd arranged everything to make it look like an intruder had abducted Tara." She relived the grinding frustration, how outraged she'd felt, listening to his accusations and being unable to respond to them. At one point, she had bitten the inside of her lip so hard it had bled. "He said I needed to learn how to properly stage a scene next time."

"And you said nothing to them about the calls."

She shook her head. "Tara would suffer the consequences."

"You could have gone to another police department," he suggested. "One outside of L.A."

"They wouldn't have believed a word I said. I'm the main suspect—and how would it look when I told them that I'd left the city? Violated my bail?" She watched as a long tractor-trailer roared by them at an illegal speed. "It doesn't matter. I couldn't risk Tara's life on the off chance that I could find someone who hadn't been corrupted by Shandian."

He swore under his breath and avoided a reckless sports car driver trying in vain to get around the tractor-trailer. "You know about Shandian?"

"I lived in my father's home for eighteen years,

Sean." She rubbed her tired eyes. "I assure you, at no time was I blind, deaf, or dumb. My father and the tong remained rivals for years."

He pulled into the right lane to get away from the sports car. "You're in a hell of mess."

"Yes. I am." That was the spark of interest she needed from him. Now all she had to do was fan it into life. "If this were just about me, I would never have intruded on your life or bothered you. But Tara has nothing to do with those swords or my father. She shouldn't have to die because she works for me." She hesitated, then decided to be honest. "No, that's not true. Tara isn't just my employee. I love her as much as I would a daughter."

He lapsed into silence, as if considering everything she'd said. Meko waited, wondering what she would do if he shut her out.

Finally he slid his cuffed hand around and took her hand in his. "I'll contact General Grady at the CID for you," he said. "He's been trying to shut down Shandian for years, and he has unlimited agents and resources. He'll find the girl."

"General Grady? Isn't that the same man you said killed that woman?" She shook her head. "That kind of help I don't need."

"Yes, I blamed him for Kuei-fei, but I was drunk, and I was wrong." He made an exasperated sound. "Kameko, you don't need a broken-down old warhorse like me. You need the army."

"I don't know this general. I know you." She watched him shake his head, and felt her temper explode. "None of this would have happened if you hadn't come to me looking for those swords!"

"Did your brothers send you after me?" he countered just as harshly. "Or was it someone else? Shandian, maybe? Am I the real trade-off for the girl?"

"No one sent me. I came to you because I couldn't think of anyone else. I don't *have* anyone else." She realized the Mercedes was slowing to a stop on the shoulder of the highway. "What are you—"

It happened so fast that she didn't have time to react. Sean threw the car in park, pinned her cuffed hand to the seat, and snatched the gun away from her. His moves were so decisive and quick they blurred in front of her eyes. Then he was straddling her, using his weight to hold her still.

She turned her head to the side and saw the gun pressed to the edge of the seat, right above her shoulder. Then she stared into his eyes. "Are you going to shoot me now, Sean?"

"Don't tempt me." He flicked the safety off, then on, and tossed his pistol on the backseat. "We're done with waving guns around, sweetheart." Soft words, edged with frost. "Now, I want the keys."

She blinked. The car keys were still in the ignition. "What?"

"Keys, for the cuffs." He tugged up their hands. "Where are they?"

Meko began to laugh. She couldn't help it. The fact that it sounded suspiciously like sobbing didn't matter. She laughed even harder when he grabbed her purse and began searching through the contents.

"Kameko." He gave her a single hard shake. "Where are the goddamn keys?"

She gasped for air, hiccuped, then giggled again at his expression. "In Los Angeles."

Fort Irwin had provided Brooke with a small office building only a few blocks from Kameko Sayura's shop. The former recruiter and processing station had closed only a few weeks earlier, and was still set up with nearly everything she needed for her command post.

"That's the last of it," Brooke said to the soldiers assigned to her as they carried in the boxed equipment from the supply truck. "Get the land lines connected and I'll take care of the computer system." She took a quick look around. "We'll need something to use for interviews."

A staff sergeant pointed toward the west side of the office. "There's an old ASVAB testing room over there, Captain."

"That'll work. Put that box marked VIDEO EQUIPMENT in there, Sergeant." She crawled under a desk to hook up her computer modem line. A dusty spiderweb adhered to her cheek before she flicked it away. "Make sure the windows in there are secure, too."

A phone rang as soon as it was plugged in. "Lieutenant Perry's on his way in, Captain," the corporal who answered it told her. "Says he's got an informant for you."

"Conor always brings me the nicest presents." She crawled out from under the desk and booted her laptop. "Let's go and get that video camera set up. We're going to need it now."

Later Brooke decided that she didn't like Nick

Hosyu, not from the moment he strolled in and showed her all of his caps in a lecherous grin.

"Hi, good-looking." He stepped up to her, but his gaze remained fixed on her chest. "You gonna frisk me? Please?"

"Down, boy." Conor, who was following him, grabbed Nick's collar and yanked him back. "I might let her beat the hell out of you, for the entertainment value."

"Yeah, sure." Nick laughed.

Conor tightened his grip until it cut off the shorter man's air. "How many black belts do you have now, Captain?"

"Seven." She gave the wheezing Nick a cool once-over. "Hardly seems worth my time."

Nick's gaze bounced between her and Conor. "Seven black belts?"

"On the other hand"—she took off her jacket, revealing her sleeveless blouse and her tanned arms—"I did miss my morning workout."

Conor released him. "Well, enjoy."

"Hey." Nick's voice squeaked as he stared at Brooke's well-defined biceps. "I'm cooperating, aren't I?"

"Yeah, yeah." Conor gave him a shove toward the interview room. "Get in there, before I kick your ass myself."

One of the soldiers escorted Nick in, while Brooke and Conor went into a separate office.

"Why'd you bother dragging in a loser like him?" she asked as she turned on the remote monitor. Nick was already checking the windows. "Besides the obvious entertainment value?"

"We caught him lifting some of the ex-wife's stock. He wants to cut a deal." Conor rolled his eyes. "I pulled his sheet; he's run numbers, done some collecting for Sayura and sons. Addicted to poker and ponies, our boy Nick is. Says he's got no problems, but he keeps checking the time."

"No way he snatched the girl and then came *back* to rob the store." She studied the man's nervous movements. He was gnawing at his thumbnail with the intense concentration of a trapped, starved rat. "Think he owes some leg-breakers?"

"I figure. Still, he's got connections. We flash some cash, promise him no jail time, he'll roll over." Conor made a seesaw gesture with his hand. "Could be our in."

She nodded. "Let's scratch behind his ears and find out."

Conor stopped to get a pitcher of water and one cup, then entered the interview room with her.

Nick stopped pacing and threw out his arms. "So? We gonna do this? I got an appointment downtown."

"It will have to wait, Mr. Hosyu." Brooke pointed to the chair at the end of the table. "Have a drink. You look . . . uncomfortable."

"Call me Nick." He dropped down and propped his elbows on the table.

Conor poured the water and handed Nick the cup. "Not every day a man gets caught stealing from his ex-wife, *Nick*."

He drank half the water, then sat back and talked to the cup. "I told you, Meko and I have an understanding. I help her out with marketing and advertising, she gives me a chunk of the profits."

"And I'm Playmate of the Year," Conor said.

Nick began gnawing at his thumbnail again, then grimaced.

Brooke walked around behind him and saw he'd bitten himself so hard he was bleeding. "Sounds more like breaking and entering, and burglary. Not good. Not with your sheet. With all the strikes against you, they'll probably send you up to Folsom for ten to twenty." She propped a hand against the back of his chair. "All you'll be betting on there are cigarettes, or an extra dessert."

"Look, I can help you guys out. You're looking for the kid, right?" He lowered his voice. "I heard Shandian grabbed her."

Brooke exchanged a glance with Conor, who nodded. She bent down to murmur next to his ear, "And you heard this . . . where?"

"I know some guys." He licked his lips. "I hear things."

"Sure you do." She straightened. "You wouldn't be working both sides of the street, would you, Nick?"

"Hey, do I look that crazy to you?" Nick crumpled the now-empty cup. "I don't know where they've stashed her, but maybe I could get you in. Most of Ju-Long's guys don't speak good English. I can talk to them, you know—see if they need some help baby-sitting the kid. You know, someone who can talk to her in her own lingo."

Conor jumped on that. "They ask you to do that?"

"Yeah." He ducked his head, cringing. "I didn't want to get mixed up in it. I don't hurt kids. Or women."

Brooke made a disgusted sound. "No, you only steal from them when they're in trouble."

"We want the girl and the swords." Conor came at him from the other side. "Where are the swords, Nick?"

"That's the thing—nobody knows. The Shandian say the Sayura have them. The Sayura say the Shandian do. Meko knows where they are, that's why the Shandian snatched the girl. They want her to bring them the blades." He checked his watch and wiped a line of sweat from under his nose. "Listen, if I do this, Ju-Long's boys will come after me, and they'll keep coming until I'm dead. I want two hundred grand and that witness protection thing. I need twenty now, up front. A good-faith gesture."

Brooke laughed as she strolled to the door. "More like a health insurance policy." She glanced back at him. "Just how much *do* you owe your loan shark, Nick?"

He gave her an ugly look. "Ten."

Conor followed her. "Excuse us for a minute."

Brooke called Washington from the monitor room. She put Kalen Grady on speakerphone before she relayed the results of the interrogation.

"What's your feeling on this guy, Con?" Kalen asked when she'd finished her report.

"He's strictly nickel-and-dime, but he sincerely wants to save his own ass. It'll cost us ten grand to find out if what he says is true." Conor steepled his fingers. "He's better connected than anyone we have. I say it's worth a shot."

The door opened. "Excuse me, ma'am." The staff sergeant handed Brooke a fax before stepping back out.

"Brooke?"

"One moment, General." Brooke skimmed through the fax. "Our friends at the L.A.P.D. gang activity unit report a BMW belonging to Qi Ju-Long was found burned out on U.S. 101 last night. No sign of human remains inside or around the car. His wife filed a missing persons report this morning."

Conor hissed in a breath. "Nice. Somebody dusts him, burns the car, *then* hides the body?"

"It's the worst kind of insult to the tong." She handed him the fax. "If someone so much as whispers that the Sayura killed Ju-Long, Shandian will strike back. In a big way."

"Our three-way tong war is about to turn into a foursome." Kalen sounded grim. "Options."

"We can try the usual shakedowns. With what crypto has translated off the wiretaps so far, we can get enough court orders to keep everyone's lawyers busy earning their retainers for a week or two." Brooke tapped a finger against her chin. "Not going to make an impact on the street fighting, though."

"The Sayura brothers want to crank up the war," Conor said. "Until we locate Kameko Sayura and the swords, and take out all the leaders, I don't think we have any other option but to use our boy Nick and infiltrate."

"The Sayura may have been keeping tabs on their sister. Even if they haven't, I don't know enough about her to pass as even a casual friend." Brooke eyed her partner. "How good is your Chinese?"

"Lousy, so I guess I'm wearing a wire." He looked at the phone. "General, I'll go in and retrieve the kid. Maybe I can find out who offed Ju-Long and who's replacing him while I'm in. Brooke can work on finding Kameko from here, and back me up."

"All right, put it together. My wife and I are leaving for New Orleans tonight, but I'll be available on my private line. And Brooke," Kalen said, "I want a tail on Hosyu until Conor and the girl are clear."

Brooke watched Nick on the monitor. He was gnawing at the jagged, bloody thumbnail again. "Absolutely, sir."

He could have disarmed her at any time; Sean had just been waiting to hear her mention her brothers or some other outside force. If she'd been co-erced to do this, he had to know. So when she admitted that she'd acted entirely on her own, it allowed him to take control of the situation. And he had.

Only he still couldn't free himself from her bloody lovers' cuffs.

"Damn things." Sean seized Meko's wrist and twisted the metal bracelets against each other, trying to force the single heavy link between them to pop open. "What the devil did you use to make them?"

"I told you, real police handcuffs. You're not going to be able to force the connecting link, either," she said, wincing as the cuff ground into her wrist.

"One of my customers lost her key while I was out of town doing a show, and had to get them cut off at a machine shop."

He stopped and looked down at her. "Why would you cuff yourself to me if you didn't have the key? What if I went crazy and got a hatchet?"

"I was desperate." She dropped her head back against the seat and closed her eyes. "And I knew you wouldn't hurt me."

He slid his hand into her hair, tugging until she looked at him. "You don't know that, Kameko. You don't know what kind of man I am."

"I do." Her dark eyes shimmered with emotion. "I found out last night, *nagare*."

He focused on her mouth, because if he didn't he'd be staring at her breasts, and how they pressed against him with every breath she took. "What does that mean?"

"*Nagare* is the river that sweeps you away. No matter how good a swimmer you are." Her lips moved like poetry. Like her. "That's what it was like. What you were like, last night."

If she kept talking to him like this, he'd be tearing her blouse open and refreshing his memory of just how lovely her breasts were.

Every muscle in his body tightened before he released her and got back behind the wheel. It wasn't what he wanted to do, but the side of a busy freeway was no place for him to play teenager in lust. No matter how much he felt like one.

"I'm not a goddamn river." He rammed the Mercedes into drive and merged back into traffic.

She didn't say anything for a long time. He kept

his attention on the road, and even assumed she'd fallen asleep until she edged a little closer to him.

"Don't even think about trying to grab the wheel," he told her. "I don't like hitting women, but I'll knock you out if I have to."

"You won't." She gestured at the windshield. "Where are you taking me?"

Straight to the police, as soon as he got the cuff problem squared away. Unless he could contact Grady and convince him to take over. "San Francisco has plenty of machine shops."

By the time they reached the city it was noon, and he had to maneuver through lunch-hour traffic to get to his first destination.

"Why are you being so quiet?"

"I don't know." She moved her shoulders. "I guess because I was raised to be quiet around men."

Like Kuei-fei had probably been trained, before her family sold her to T'ang Po. He hadn't understood it when Kuei-fei had described how Asian women were treated, and he hated to think Kameko had been subjected to the same thing. "Hell, why? What's wrong with talking to men?"

"Nothing. It's just the Japanese think American women—all Americans, really—talk too much. You're not comfortable with silence, so you're always chattering about something. Japanese children aren't encouraged to talk or speak up for themselves."

His mouth curled. "So speech is silver, but silence is golden?"

"More like 'hollow drums make the most noise.' " She tapped her temple. "It's a cultural thing. Americans associate silence with tension and resentment, or nervousness. The Japanese consider talking too much a sign of immaturity or stupidity." She looked out the window and saw where they were headed. "Why are we going to Nine Dragon?"

"We're not." He watched both sides of the road, which were clear, and slowed down to get a good look at her father's house.

"Okay." Kameko tensed beside him. "Why are we driving *by* Nine Dragon?"

"I've got fond memories of the place."

Once at the end of the street, he turned left and doubled around, but saw nothing suspicious at the back of the property—except for an exceptionally well-tended garden.

"You said there was an old man who looked after the place for your father. Would he be the one keeping up the grounds in the back of the house?"

"I think so. I came here with Tara, after you and I . . . anyway, the last time I was here, I thought I saw him." She frowned. "Xun must be close to ninety now."

He grunted. "Old men aren't completely helpless."

"It has nothing to do with age, Sean. He had very bad arthritis in his hands ten years ago." She glanced back at the property. "Now . . . I don't know how he could still do the work."

For some reason, it still irked him. "You'd be surprised at what worn-out old men can do."

He drove from Nine Dragon to a less prosperous area, looking for a place that would provide some security and anonymity.

Kameko leaned forward. "The Surf and Sand?"

"It'll do for now." He parked in front of the office and turned off the ignition. "You'll have to come in with me. Behave yourself."

"You've got the gun, and I'm the one wanted by the police," she reminded him as she draped their cuffed hands with his jacket. "Do you want one of my credit cards?"

"No, I've cash enough." He dug a hand in his back pocket, then felt how it was turned. "You went through my wallet."

"Yes, but I didn't take anything." She adjusted the jacket. "Your daughters are very pretty, by the way."

"Laney and Neala aren't my daughters. They're my nieces."

The balding, heavyset clerk working the desk stopped eating an enormous burrito long enough to take Sean's money, and after studying Meko, handed him a single key on a cracked plastic tab. "Checkout is eleven a.m. sharp. Extra towels are five bucks." He belched and used a fingernail to pry something green from between his front teeth. "No working your girl in front of the motel, and if I get a noise complaint, I call the cops."

Meko drew herself up like a small cobra, ready to strike. "I am *not* a prostitute."

The clerk took another bite of the burrito, then spoke through the mouthful as he chewed. "Whatever you say, mama-san."

Sean imagined hauling the man over the counter and stuffing his lunch into another opening of his body, then led Meko out of the office. She was still stiff with outrage. "It's a roundabout compliment, you know," he told her. "He couldn't believe a beautiful young thing like you would be with me, unless I owned you."

"Cretin." She stepped over the remains of a smashed beer bottle. "Do you usually stay in such nice places?"

"Beats wading through a pile of manure every day." Their room was on the first floor at the farthest end of the parking lot, and smelled strongly of recently applied pine cleaner. Beneath that lingered years of cigarette smoke. He shut the door and bolted it before surveying the premises. "Or not."

An avocado and burnt-orange paisley spread covered the queen-size bed. Black caterpillar-shaped cigarette burns were scattered over the spread, the carpet, and the tops of all the furnishings. The single light in the room came from a kitschy gold ceramic lamp with a smoke-stained pink plastic shade. An ancient television set had been bolted to the wall between two battered black Formica dressers.

"Five full-length adult movies for ten dollars a night," Meko read from a small cardboard sign taped to the wall beside the TV. "That's quite a bargain. I take it they don't offer any Merchant and Ivory films."

"Not unless Merchant is doing Ivory." He tugged her along with him to inspect the closet-size bathroom, where the pine smell was the strongest. "Next time you abduct someone, make your own hotel reservations."

Sean didn't like the place any better than she did.

The thin razor slash marks on the dresser tops meant they had been regularly used to dice and portion up various drugs. Besides the burn marks, the industrial-grade pink carpet had a number of large, suspicious-looking dark stains. And the parking lot had been filled with late-model cars that were rusting out or had piles of clothes and cardboard boxes stuffed in their backseats.

She surprised him by not making more of a fuss. "What now?"

"We get some food delivered, and I get these cuffs off." He went toward the phone, only to be brought up short when she stood her ground. "You can pick whatever you want, as long as it's not sushi. My fish has to be cooked."

"Let me go, Sean."

"I intend to."

"No, I mean really, let me go. We can ask that clerk if he has a toolbox. Once we're out of the cuffs, I'll go." She glanced at her watch, then at the window. "I can make it back to L.A. by tonight. I'll leave you enough money to get back to Sonoma, and I won't bother you again."

"You're thinking of going after this kid yourself."

She lifted her shoulders. "I'm all she has."

And she'd end up dead in the street, trying to get her back. Sean's temper, which had been teetering on the edge of exploding all morning, finally broke through the shreds of his restraint.

"Not for long. You go after Shandian, and they'll catch you. When they find out you don't have the swords, they'll shoot you in the back of the head and dump you in an alley." He grabbed her chin.

"I'll turn you in to the cops myself before I let that happen."

"You won't help me. The police think I killed her. Even her parents are using the whole thing as tragic publicity to advertise their next movie." Her voice rose. "Tara has *no one*, and *no chance* but me, Sean. What else am I supposed to do?"

"She's probably dead already!" he shouted back.

Her eyes widened, and he wanted to drag her back onto the ugly bedspread, and hold her down, and keep shouting at her until she listened to him.

Someone thumped on the other side of wall behind the bed. "Keep it down in there, will ya?" A muffled masculine voice yelled.

"She's not dead." The tears he'd watched her hold back stayed put, but she tried to hug herself with her arms. "Not yet."

She spoke with the blind hope of a mother who refuses to believe a child could be taken from her.

She really loves this girl.

Sean pulled her stiff, resisting form to him and held her close. "I'm sorry, Meko," he murmured against her hair. "But even if she is still alive, they'll kill her before you make the exchange. They have to—she's a witness."

"You're wrong." She jerked out of his embrace and grabbed her purse. "I'll prove it to you."

He watched her yank out her cell phone and dial a number. "Who are you calling?"

"The man who told me to get the swords." She lifted up a hand when he would have spoken, and identified herself. Then she gestured to him, and held the cell phone out enough for him to listen in on the conversation. "I want proof that Tara is still alive," she said into the phone.

"Do you have the swords?" a male voice snapped out.

"I'm not going to get them unless I talk to Tara."

There was silence, then the crackle of static as the reception faded in and out. Finally, the man snarled something vile, and another voice cried out.

"What?" a girl's voice said. "I don't understand you!"

"Tara?" Meko called into the phone. "Tara, honey, it's me, can you hear me?"

"Mom? Mommy?"

She began shaking, and yet kept her voice calm. "It's Kameko, honey, are you okay?"

"Oh, God, Kameko," the girl sobbed out the words. "They got into the store and then they drugged me and took me with them. I don't know where I am now—Kameko, I'm so scared!"

"It's okay, I'm coming to get you, real soon, I promise—" She halted as Tara's voice abruptly cut off, then the man came back on the line.

"Five days left, Miss Sayura. You'd better hurry."

The line disconnected.

Sean took the phone from her limp hand and switched it off, then dropped it onto one of the dressers.

"You see?" She tried to smile. "I told you. She's still alive. There's still time. I can save her—I can—" She covered her face with her hand and wept.

Sean pulled her against him again and held her, and this time she didn't fight him. When he had abducted Kameko before, Sean had noticed the photos of the redheaded girl on her mantel. Now he had her terrified voice inside his head, to go with the image of the young, smiling face. She didn't resemble Kameko in the least, of course. But if Sean had had a daughter, she might have looked a little like Tara Jones.

It seemed his retirement was over, after all.

"There, now." He slipped his free hand over her shoulder and stroked her back. "You were right and I was wrong. I should be the one crying my eyes out."

"She sounds so afraid." Kameko choked out each word, then lifted her face. "I can't bear knowing they have her. She's alone and frightened and with those awful men and it's all my fault, Sean. All my fault."

"Come over here."

She was shaking so much now that her legs gave out, and he moved his free arm down to her waist to pull her back toward the bed. He sat and she ended up on his lap, her face pressed against his chest.

"Look at me." When she did, he wiped away her tears with the tips of his fingers. "She's alive, that's what matters." One tear had trailed down to the corner of her mouth, and seeped across her trembling bottom lip. He bent his head to kiss it away. "Don't cry, *a chuisle mo chroí*, you're breaking my heart."

"I can't stop." She sobbed out a small laugh. "Ever since they took her, I haven't cried once. But hearing her like that—calling for her mother—"

"I know, I know." He could feel her pain and fear

as surely as he felt the delicate pulse of her heart with his thumb, and it struck him just as deeply as the sound of Tara's voice. Hearing her frightened pleading had cut into his heart.

Kameko was already a part of it.

At that moment he decided there was nothing more to be done. However she needed him, for however long she needed him, he would be there.

"Shhhh." Sean brushed his mouth over hers, giving her what comfort he could. "We'll sort it out."

"Thank you." She sagged against him, leaning into his tender, feathery kisses. Her lips tasted of tears. And then her hand touched his face. "*Hontou-ni moushiwake-gozaimasen.*" *I'm so sorry.*

The words whispered against his skin, and he didn't even think as he dragged up the rusty dregs of what he knew in her native language. "*Ii-desu-yo. Goshinpai-naku.*" *It's all right, it doesn't matter.*

Sean eased her down, their bound hands between them, and stroked his free hand over her hair. It was the softest stuff, he thought, so fine it clung to his skin like a dark web. Then her breathing changed, and Sean lifted his head.

There were a thousand things he needed to do. Yet not one of them seemed more important than this. Sean curled an arm around her, closed his own tired eyes, and slept with her.

Chapter 6

Tara Jones watched through her lashes as Stickman and Weasel climbed the stairs, leaving her alone again. This time they left the single lightbulb hanging overhead on, and she got a better look at her surroundings.

Wherever she was.

As soon as she heard the door at the top of the staircase close, she lifted her head. She still felt dazed and headachy. The last thing she could remember before waking up here was being in Meko's office, and the tall, corpse-faced one she'd nicknamed Stickman clapping a funny-smelling towel over her mouth and nose.

She still couldn't figure out how they got into the shop. One minute she was carefully picking out rubies for J.Lo's mom's bracelet, the next she looked up into the beady eyes of the man she'd dubbed Weasel. She would have run, but he pulled a knife on her.

No, a three-foot-long sword.

Something began clanging overhead, making her

jump. She held her breath and listened until the sound died with a rush of water.

The cloth they'd used to knock her out must have been soaked with chloroform—just like in the old movies—but why had they kidnapped her? To get money out of her parents? What would they do when they found out her mother was in London getting drunk with royalty while her father was out shooting some cheesy remake of *The Mummy's Curse* on the edge of the Sahara?

"They'll probably go on *Good Morning America*, soon as they find out," she muttered, rubbing her forehead against the dirty pipe she was chained to. "Dad would never pass up the chance at all that free publicity."

The clanging sound started again, this time vibrating through the pipe and jolting into her face. She recoiled and tugged at her arms, then tried to stand.

The concrete floor was cold against her legs, and she tucked her feet under, pushing herself up to her knees. The chains wrapped around her were old but tight, and bit as they dragged over her skin. She couldn't feel her hands at all, but remembered that Weasel had bound her wrists together with rope.

"I can do this." She gritted her teeth and stretched her aching muscles, hauling herself and the heavy chains up the pipe until she was able to stand. She rested against the cold steel for a moment, panting. "See? Not so hard."

She was in some kind of basement, judging by the clutter of boxes and old furniture, and the musty, damp smell. Too big to be under a single-family home, unless it was a mansion. There were signs that the space had once been used by a building maintenance crew, too—a broken floor buffer, boxes of air-conditioning filters, and an empty tool rack hanging above an immense workbench.

Besides the staircase, the only other way out seemed to be a row of dust-blocked outside air vents lining the top of one wall. Even if she could work herself free and stand on something, she would never be able to squeeze through one of the small openings.

The strangeness and grunginess of the place only made her feel worse. She didn't know where she was, or how far away from home they'd taken her. She could be in another state, for all she knew.

What are they going to do to me?

The whole situation reminded her of another of her father's movies—a high school prom night slasher flick that had earned him his first twenty-million-dollar box office weekend.

In the movie, the killer had disemboweled his victims, then hung them from beams in the basement, because no one bothered looking down there. Except the shrill-voiced heroine, naturally, who didn't find the bodies until ten minutes before the movie ended. Tara could still recall the blood and gore dripping off the victims and running down into the drain in the concrete floor.

She focused on the same kind of drain, not three feet from where she was chained. If they killed her, Stickman and Weasel could hose down the floor, washing away all the traces of her blood. Just like in the movie.

Not if. When.

"No." Chains grated into her flesh as Tara twisted her numb arms, desperately trying to work them free. Something buzzed in her ears, and the entire room suddenly rocked from side to side. "Shit!"

The weight of the chains dragged her down as she lost her balance, and she landed hard on her knees, tearing her jeans. The door at the top of the staircase opened two seconds after her shriek of pain.

"You quiet! No talk!" Stickman shouted as his footsteps pounded down the staircase.

Tara cringed as her kidnappers approached, and cried out when Stickman seized her by the hair and shouted in her face. It didn't sound like the Japanese Meko sometimes used when she hammered her thumb or broke something.

A phone rang, making both men look at each other. Stickman rapped her head against the pipe, while Weasel pulled a cell phone from his jacket. He uttered a few terse sentences, then thrust the phone at Tara's face and ordered her to do something.

"What?" She shook her head, her ears still ringing. "I don't understand you!"

"Tara?" A woman's voice came from the phone. "Tara, honey, it's me, can you hear me?"

"Mom?" She couldn't believe it. As the man shoved the phone against her cheek, she sobbed like a little girl. "Mommy?"

"It's Kameko, honey, are you okay?"

"Oh, God, Kameko." She put her mouth next to the receiver and talked fast. "They got into the store and then they drugged me and took me with them. I don't know where I am now—Kameko, I'm so scared!"

"It's okay, I'm coming to get you, real soon, I promise—"

Weasel whipped the phone away and talked into it, then shut it off. Stickman exchanged a few words with him before turning back to Tara.

"You." He shook his bony finger in front of her nose. "No talk."

That they would do this to her was terrifying. That they would use her to do something to Kameko made a dark and furious rage build up inside her. Meko had never hurt another person in her life. She looked into Stickman's slightly bulging eyes, and deliberately spit in his face.

That earned her a vicious slap across the face, then a brutal kick in her side. She huddled over, instinctively making herself a smaller target, and tried not to vomit. At the same time, Stickman screamed at her in his gibberish language, only stopping when Weasel pulled him away.

"What's going on here?" a male voice demanded—in English—from the doorway above them.

Tara could have wept again, but she was too busy straining to see around Stickman and Weasel. A third man climbed down into the basement. He was tall, lean, and had curly dark hair, but his features were Caucasian. He wore a battered leather jacket and faded jeans, and carried a large open cardboard box.

"Please, help me," she said. "These men have kidnapped me."

Stickman whipped around to hit her again, but the American caught his arm.

"You don't want to do that," he told Stickman. "Take off, I've got her."

Tara's eyes widened as the two Asian men stalked away, then she locked her gaze on the American. "Will you untie me?"

He took a knife from his pocket and flicked the blade open. "Hold still and I'll cut your arms loose."

Trembling with relief, she obeyed him, and watched while he cut the ropes binding her wrists together. "What's your name?"

He met her gaze for a moment. He had light brown eyes the color of milk chocolate. "Vincent."

She hadn't realized her arm was bleeding until he tugged it out of the loops of chains. Needling, burning pain from returned circulation made her bite her lower lip. Some of the blood on her arm was fresh, but dark, dried rivulets ran up into her sleeve. She craned her neck, and saw the whole front of her T-shirt was bloodstained. "Vincent, I need help. Get me out of here."

"It's okay." He pocketed the knife, knelt down and reached for her arm. "Let me have a look at that." His hands were gentle as he took a damp cloth from the box and wiped away the blood. "They cut you?"

If they had, she couldn't remember. Then she saw her bare wrist. "Those creeps—they took my bracelet!" She looked over his shoulder, saw Stickman hovering on the staircase, watching both of them. "We have to get out of here," she added in a whisper. "As soon as they go."

Vincent didn't say anything, but reached into the box again and produced a first aid kit. There was food in the box, too, she could smell it. Something warm and wonderful that made her empty stomach clench and her mouth water.

I can't think about food. She watched him swab down and bandage her arm with a frown. "Vincent, didn't you hear me?" she asked, a little louder.

"I heard you." He tucked in the edges of the gauze and reached back, this time producing a round pint container. "Do you like vegetable soup?"

She grabbed the front of his jacket as best she could. "These men abducted me from my job. They're holding me for some kind of ransom."

"I know," Vincent told her as he eased her hands away. He glanced back at Stickman. "I work for them."

Brooke adjusted the receiver to better pick up Tara's low murmurs, then tugged off her headset before rubbing her tired eyes. It was a relief to know Conor was in place. "Hang tough, kid," she muttered under her breath.

The door at the back of the office opened and closed with a snap. "Who's in charge here?"

She got up from the console, covering a wince as her still-healing ribs twinged, and headed toward the voice. A big man in a rain-spattered, rumpled dark gray suit met her halfway. "Who's asking?"

"Agent Kinsella, New York office." He took out his ID and opened it for her to read. The hard-edged face and military-short light brown hair matched the official identification.

"Brooke Oliver." She held out her hand, noted his brief, careful grip and the scars across his knuckles. Most FBI agents reminded her of polite college boys, but this one had the face and the touch of an experienced brawler. "What can I do for you, Agent Kinsella?"

"You can get your boss on the line and tell him I'm here to see him." He walked past her and performed a brief inspection of the main room. Despite his large, blocky build, he moved like a feline. "I'll also need all reports, case files, and whatever new intelligence has come in on Shandian and the Sayura syndicate. Get started making the copies." He glanced back at her, his dark blue eyes narrowed. They resembled a cat's, too. "Any coffee around here?"

Brooke almost laughed. Almost. "There's a bagel shop across the street."

"Good. Get me a large with cream, no sugar." He stalked into her office and shut the door. Through the window, she saw him pick up the phone.

Son of a bitch.

Brooke remembered to count to ten, then used the extension at her console to call her local FBI contact. After verifying that Special Agent William Kinsella was indeed on temporary assignment to L.A. from the New York field office, she hung up and considered how to handle the situation.

Without feeling the slightest bit of guilt, she picked up her spare headphones and jacked into the line Kinsella was using.

"—now that I'm here," he was saying, contempt making his voice harsh. "Your usual military fuckup. The knuckle draggers left the airhead to answer phones."

Bad enough that he thought of army personnel as knuckle draggers, but now she wasn't just a secretary, she was an *airhead*. Brooke curled her short, neat fingernails into her palm, and imagined it was Kinsella's face.

"Stomping through the ranks won't get you anywhere, Liam," an amused older female voice replied. "Be polite, be firm, but don't mix it up with the brass. Last thing I need is the army on my back. And be nice to the pretty little blonde. Who knows, you might even get lucky."

That did it. When she got back to Washington, Brooke was dyeing her hair black, or shaving her head. And who was he calling a pretty *little* blonde, anyway? She was only an inch or two shorter than him.

Brooke missed Kinsella's response, and only dimly heard him promise to contact the woman tomorrow before he ended the call.

I can kick his ass and end up in the stockade, or I can get back to work.

She disconnected her lead and plugged back into Conor's frequency, which was impeded by a wash of static. She concentrated on returning the receiver until she eliminated most of the crackling interference, then switched the recorder over to the backup system so she could slide a new CD into the burner. Something tapped her shoulder as she finished queuing up the audio files on the computer.

She slid her headset down to her neck and idly considered the merits of ramming an elbow into Kinsella's abdomen and splintering a couple of his ribs. Instead, she focused on the monitor. "Yes?"

"My coffee?"

Now she did turn around and nearly collided with him. This close, she could smell a trace of aftershave—something clean and crisp—and the rain on his jacket. "I'm sorry, can't you cross the street unaccompanied by an adult?"

"Oh." A line formed between his brows as he studied her again, as if seeing her clearly for the first time. "I didn't know you'd take offense."

"Not at all." She swung back to the console. "The airhead remark was pretty unforgivable, though."

That made him shut up for a full thirty seconds. She could almost feel his gaze on her hair and neck, and it was making her face hot. *No, it's just my temper, and not being able to clock him.*

Finally he said, "Let me guess. You're in charge."

"Aren't you intuitive?" Brooke rose and brushed past him, eager to escape the building tension. "I'll have to revise my opinion of Quantico's training standards."

She went into her office to check the fax and sort through the reports that had been sent from Washington by courier the day before. Kinsella didn't take the hint, but followed her and sat down in front of her desk. "Are we going to dance around all day, or can we get past this?"

Brooke took her time reading the report in her hands before she regarded him. "I don't dance, Agent Kinsella. I don't make copies, or fetch coffee.

This is an official CID operation, and *the pretty little blonde knuckle dragger* is the ranking officer in charge." Pleased with the amount of ice in her delivery, she inclined her head toward the back of the building. "You already know where the exit is. Have a nice day."

"Ms. Oliver—"

Now she just might clock him anyway. "*Captain* Oliver."

"Captain." He sighed. "I didn't mean to insult you, but I'm running low on time and patience. I need whatever you've got, now."

"Why?"

"The FBI has already lost two agents to this tong war. We're going after the generals and shutting it down." He shrugged. "That's all I can tell you at present."

"How fascinating." Did he really think she wouldn't know how to play the game? "What I've got here, Kinsella, is an active, classified military operation. And, until you get security clearance through the CID, I'm not obliged to give you so much as a Post-it note."

"Then get me clearance."

She tilted her head to one side and pretended to think about it. "Tempted as I am to assist someone as congenial, perceptive, and unbiased toward gender in the workplace as you are, it's like the coffee." She gave him her loveliest smile. "Get it yourself."

"Fine." He stood. "You'd better put the word out to whoever you're running with the tongs. My task force will be ready to move in by the end of the week."

Conor. "I have an agent and a civilian on the inside."

"That's your problem, Captain. Not mine." He went to the door, then stopped. "Do I get clearance *now*?"

She had no choice, and he knew it, the jerk. "Get back here and sit down, Kinsella." He did. "I want full disclosure on both sides."

He didn't bother to rub it in. "I can do that."

"Shandian snatched a kid a few days ago, and they're using her to put pressure on Takeshi Sayura's daughter. They want the White Tiger swords, and they think she's got them." She pulled file photos and handed them across the desk. "I've got an agent in—Conor Perry—to retrieve the kid."

He picked out Tara's photo and turned it around. "What's the holdup?"

"We're not storming in just to get her killed in the crossfire. Perry is going to smuggle her out at the first opportunity." She filled him in on the rest of the operation, then added, "Your turn to play nice."

"We know the Dai were responsible for taking out two of our agents," he said. "And we're going to shut down the triad. The director has teams working in every major city now, taking gang members in under witness protection to get testimony against their leaders." He took a folded paper from his jacket pocket and offered it to her. "That's the list. So far, we've nailed everyone with the grand jury except Shandian and the Sayura. Qi Ju-Long disappeared yesterday, presumed dead. The Sayura brothers entered the country last week, but they're holed up in a hotel. No one seems to know who's really running things on either side."

The names on the list were impressive. So was his intelligence. She might actually revise her opinion of the FBI, after all. "We need to work together."

"That was the idea when I came in here."

She ignored that. "You don't have anyone in place yet, do you?"

Kinsella didn't want to say it, but he finally produced a "no."

Checkmate. "Then, since my op is already rolling, it's only logical for you to work with us."

"Under your command, you mean." He made it sound like laboring in the tenth circle of hell.

Which for Kinsella it might be. "Yes." Now she could relax and enjoy herself a little. "I know you're going to astound me, Agent Kinsella, and tell me you don't have a problem working with female agents."

He grinned, and it transformed his broad dockworker's face into something much more attractive. "You heard my boss. She's a female."

"Yes, and I'll have to pray for her later." After glancing at the clock, she grabbed her jacket and shrugged into it. "I've got a ten o'clock with the Sayura brothers. You're welcome to tag along."

"Long as I drive."

Brooke nodded. She wouldn't mind having a Quantico-trained chauffeur at all.

The rhythmic pounding against the wall woke him up first. From the sound of it, and the high-pitched feminine cries coming through the drywall, their neighbors were putting their bed to good use.

Kameko lifted her head. "I think they put us next to the honeymoon suite."

"Sounds that way." The room was dark, but he could see the glitter of her dark eyes watching him. "Feel better?"

"Much, thank you." She stretched like a lazy feline. "What time is it?"

He tilted his watch until the faint light from the crack in the curtains spilled over the face. "Half past midnight." When she tried to sit up, he pulled her closer. "You're exhausted, and we can't do anything until morning. Go back to sleep."

The pounding became so forceful that it sent vibrations through their bed. "I don't think I can, at least not until Romeo and Juliet do." Her breath warmed his cheek. "Are you hungry?"

"Starving." And not for food. "Though we're probably limited to pizza or Chinese." He reached over to turn on the lamp. "What'll it be?"

She winced as the recipient of the pounding next door uttered a single extended shriek of pleasure. "Um, do you mind anchovies and green peppers?"

If only she knew some of the things he'd been forced to eat in his life. "No, that's fine." He picked up the phone and dialed the front desk to get the number. "What pizza places are still delivering now?" He memorized the number the clerk recited, hung up, and redialed to place the order. "I'd like a large with extra anchovies and green peppers, delivered to room one-fourteen at the Surf and Sand

Motel on Baker. Throw in a six-pack of soda. Whatever's cold. Thanks."

"Sean."

He looked back at her. The lamp's rosy light cast
an artificial blush over her features, giving them a
pretty glow. "Hmmmm?"

She jiggled their cuffs. "I'm sorry, but I have to go
to the bathroom."

That meant he had to go with her. Maybe it
wasn't the lamplight. Luckily, the bathroom was
small enough to preserve her modesty. "We'll take
turns standing outside while the other goes."

"Thanks." She edged over the bed until she could
stand, and made a face as she inspected her crumpled garments. "I wish I could take a shower."

Not if he wanted to preserve his own sanity. "Tomorrow, after we officially break up."

They took care of their needs as quickly as possible, but the enforced proximity made it an awkward
business. By the time they had both taken a turn in
the tiny bathroom, their meal arrived.

"Twenty-two fifty, please." As he handed over
the flat box and the soda cans, the skinny Latino delivery boy gave Sean a wink. "Woke you folks up,
huh?" He jerked his head in the direction of the next
room, where the amorous couple was now busy en-
gaging in a noisy round two.

"As it happens"—Meko raised their hands and
rattled the cuffs—"*we* woke *them* up."

Sean closed the door on the wide-eyed boy and
tsked. "A woman your age, corrupting a young
mind that way," he said, trying to sound stern. "For
shame."

"He was being rude." She sniffed. "And we're not *that* old."

"Time for pizza, I think," he said, guiding her over to the bed, then changed his mind and decided the floor was safer. "Damn, I forgot to ask for napkins."

"Here." Meko opened the zippered section of her purse and produced a neat stack of folded tissues. "Use these."

He peered into the open flap. "What else have you got hidden away in there?"

"A woman's purse is like a *himitsu-bako*—its secrets must never be revealed." She offered him the first slice of pizza, then selected a triangle for herself. "Or the magic is lost forever."

In the next room, Juliet began shrieking, "Harder! Harder!"

"The magic. Right." Sean almost choked on his soda. "What exactly is a *himitsu-bako*?"

Meko wiped her free hand before she reached into her purse to produce a small rectangular wooden box. "This is." She placed it in front of him. "Go ahead, try to open it."

He picked up the box, but it was nothing more than a solid block. "With or without the tire iron?"

She grinned. "Without, of course."

The outside was decorated with beautiful geometrically inlaid bits of wood in a star design. Yet when he shook it, he could hear something rattling inside.

"Wait, I think I've seen these before, overseas." He checked the seams. "It's a trick box, isn't it?"

Something fell over in the next room and shattered, but the pounding didn't stop.

"A puzzle box," she corrected, her face red as she took it from him. "*Himitsu-bako* are made in the Hakone-Odawara mountain region of Japan."

Juliet told Romeo how well endowed he was. At the top of her lungs.

"Are they?" Sean kept his expression blank. "How interesting."

"Yes. The process is quite involved. The mosaic woodwork is called *yosegi-zaiku*, a marquetry technique that originated in the late Edo Period." Meko took a sip of her soda. "Actually, there are only about thirty people in the world who know how to make these boxes."

Romeo began praising Juliet's endowments, his voice deeper but equally as loud.

"Thirty." Sean used a tissue to wipe the sweat from his brow. "Imagine that."

Meko nodded and cleared her throat. "The youngest of them is about sixty years old."

The pounding picked up speed.

He stared at her hands, remembering how they felt on him. If the serenading next door didn't soon stop, he'd be all over her. "So how do you open it?"

"There are twenty-seven steps that have to be followed in order. Watch." She pressed her thumb against one of the stars, and a seamless thin sliver of wood slid up. Then she did the same to a side panel, then another sliver, and kept sliding out otherwise invisible pieces until the box looked as if it might fall apart. Finally she pushed back the top, revealing the contents—a small hollowed cache, with two keys, a photograph, and a folded piece of note-paper.

"I think I'd have to take the tire iron to it," he muttered, shaking his head, then reached for the box.

"The keys aren't for the cuffs," she said as he examined them. "They're my spare house and car keys."

"They're safe enough in that thing." He took out the photo and the notepaper. "What's this?"

"My father mailed them to me before he was killed in China. A woman in New Orleans thought the sword in the photo might be one of the missing Nagatoki blades." She took the paper and unfolded it. "This is what he wrote: *'Use this historic evidence to identify. Good example rank sword, the real evidence as specified under research. Everyone is skeptical, guarded. Until a representative delivers everything, don't betray your dear relatives.'*" She paused, then read the last line. "*'All goodness only needs someone to find it.'*"

"What does that mean to you?"

"Nothing, I'm afraid." She turned to look at the wall as their neighbors at last reached a noisy mutual climax and the pounding came to an abrupt halt. "Thank goodness."

"Do you think they've killed each other by now?"

She cocked her head. "No, but the bed is probably in critical condition."

The way she said it, with her prim-and-proper voice coming from that sinful mouth, finally did him in. "And the wall." He chuckled. "The wall's definitely taken a beating."

"Twice." A giggle escaped her before she quickly

regained her composure. However, a mischievous light entered her dark eyes. "But considering that he's the greatest *lover* that she's ever *had* . . ."

Her diplomatic paraphrasing did him in, and he began to laugh, harder than he had in years. He watched her eyes light up as she joined him, until they were holding each other up and gasping for breath.

"Oh . . . I needed that," she said, and reached for her soda. "This is wonderful, by the way. Thank you."

"My pleasure." And it was, to see the worry lines smoothed away from her brow, and the wash of color in her cheeks. He leaned over and kissed her, just to taste the smile on her lips, then he pulled back. She was staring at him with the oddest expression—as if he had all the answers in the world. The delight of the moment faded. She had no idea who he was, or what he'd done.

Or what he could do.

Laughing with her like this reminded him of how much he'd enjoyed making love to her—and how much he'd despised himself the morning after. He'd been half drunk then, or it wouldn't have happened. She was a woman he could never have. A woman who, if he wasn't careful, he might end up getting killed.

He would have committed homicide for a bottle of whiskey and a dark corner at that moment, but contented himself with a promise to do just that once they were done. As soon as he found the girl for her, he'd get them both to safety, and go back to the dairy. Then he could drink himself into oblivion.

"Sean? What's wrong?"

"Nothing." He glanced at the photo and the note between them. "The pizza's getting cold." He handed her a slice and ignored her puzzled frown. "Go on, darlin'. Eat."

Chapter 7

"Try some of this," Conor said, holding a spoonful of the vegetable soup up to Tara's mouth.

She swallowed hard, then her eyes moved to the two Chinese guards standing at the foot of the stairs, watching them. Her pale, dirt-smudged face turned back toward the pipe. "No. I don't want any."

The kid simply would not give in.

Conor had grown up in a houseful of women, and had learned early on that when his mother or one of his sisters made up her mind, it was best not even to argue. At the same time, he couldn't let Tara starve herself.

Conscious of their audience, he lowered his voice. "Honey, you have to eat. You'll just get weaker if you don't."

Her thin shoulders hunched in. "Go away."

"Can't. Taking care of you is my job now." He set aside the container of soup and held up a bottle of mineral water. "You're already dehydrated. Take a sip." A thought occurred to him, and he drank from the bottle himself. "See? It's not drugged, I promise. Come on, now."

This time she reluctantly took a few sips.

"Good girl."

"You said you were taking care of me." She glanced over his shoulder, then back at him. "Does that mean when they get the money from Meko, you're going to kill me?"

He couldn't tell her who he really was, not as long as the other two guards were within earshot. He could try to reassure her in other ways. "No, you'll be going home soon. I won't let anyone hurt you."

She jutted her chin toward the Chinese guards. "They already have."

The realm of possibilities contained in those three words sank into him like long, sharp claws. Blowing off the whole op, and the two thugs' heads, would get him court-martialed.

Looking at her thin, defiant face, Conor decided it would be worth it. "What did they do to you?" he asked, very gently.

"Slapped me, pulled my hair. Kicked me in the ribs." She tried to shrug, but she didn't cringe or avoid his gaze—the way she might if she'd been raped. "I've had worse fights at school."

He brushed a piece of hair back from her mouth. "There won't be any more of that, now that I'm here."

"My parents have a lot of money, you know." She leaned closer to him. "They'd give someone who helped me a big reward."

"I bet." Sixteen years old, kidnapped, weak, utterly helpless and scared out of her wits, and still she was trying to bargain her way out of this mess. Conor could already feel the cracks forming in his heart. "Now, how about you make me look good and eat some of this soup?"

She eyed the container before shaking her head again. "I'm really tired, and my stomach hurts where that jerk kicked me." She tugged at the chains. "Can I lie down and go to sleep now?"

"Okay." He needed to check her abdomen for signs of internal bleeding anyway, and this would give him the excuse to touch her. "Let me get this chain off you."

He took the ends of the chain off the open hook they'd been looped over, and began unwrapping her.

One of the guards stepped forward. "No. She stay there."

"She's all worn out, she isn't going anywhere." He dropped the chain, tossed his jacket on the floor, and bent over to help Tara lie down.

Then the weak, utterly helpless teenager rammed the top of her head into his chin and threw him back so hard and fast that he landed flat on his back.

"Tara, no!" Conor managed to catch her by the leg as she stumbled past him, and yanked her down to the ground, rolling with her until his back was to the guards. Her sharp little nails raked down his cheek before he could pin her hands. "Knock it off!"

"Asshole!" She struggled wildly. "*Let—me—go!*"

He had to put on a good show, so he raised his hand up high, and brought it down at her face. She cringed, but before he actually struck her, he shifted the angle and hit the inside of his own arm, making a convincingly loud smack.

Tara's eyes rounded as she stared at his arm, then his face.

He shifted, using his back to further block the guard's view. "Little brat, I'll teach you some manners!" he bellowed, then leaned forward and added in a whisper, "Yell."

Her eyes widened as he repeated the fake slap, then she opened her mouth and cried out sharply, as if he'd really slapped her. He hit his arm faster and harder, all the while keeping his gaze locked on hers.

"It's okay," he barely breathed the words. "I'm a friend."

Tara caught on quickly, timing her shrieks with the impact of his slaps, and started sobbing very convincingly.

He knew he didn't have much longer before one of the men came over, so he bent closer. "I'll get you out when they sleep. Hide your face now."

Tara was sobbing loudly now, and nodded before shrieking after his last, hardest slap.

Conor pulled her hair forward so that it covered her face, then stood and made a production out of dragging her back to the pipe. "Now you'll behave, won't you, girl?"

She nodded and curled up, keeping her face averted.

"You show her, eh?" The taller of the guards came over and slapped him on the shoulder. "Good job."

As he scowled down at Tara, Conor imagined

breaking the man's fingers, one by one. "Thanks. I do my best."

"Incoming." Raven sat on the sofa next to her husband and accepted a glass of ginger ale from Valence, but shook her head at the mini patisseries on the tray. "Thanks, but Shikoro's excellent dinner is still settling on my hips."

"What hips?" Val teased as she handed Kalen his scotch and returned to the bar. "You do look wonderful, Raven. Pregnancy agrees with you."

Raven smiled to herself as she thought of their flight from Washington to New Orleans. She enjoyed the private jet—one of the perks of being married to a general—and Brooke's suggestion of soda crackers had kept her stomach from rebelling. Which had allowed her and Kalen to relive a number of fond memories in the friendly skies.

"I'll reserve my opinion until *after* the labor and delivery portion of our program." She turned to her husband. "And what were you and Jian-Shan doing in the city for so long? Val and I were about to send the marines after you."

The most powerful general in army intelligence exchanged a glance with the son of the former most powerful tong leader in America.

"We went shopping," Kalen said.

Jian-Shan didn't blink, but Raven thought she saw his mouth twitch. "So? What did you buy?" she demanded. "Nothing for your devoted wives, obviously. A few more rumors about the Star King?"

"Nothing worth the purchase price," Jian-Shan said.

"Remy turned up some odd gossip about that."
Val brought a cup of tea to her husband, then curled
up comfortably beside him. "From what he told me,
it sounds like one of your father's swords, *cher*."

"There was a star blade in the collection," her
husband replied. "But I believe the term refers to
something more complicated—and dangerous. So
does the general."

"I'm no expert on these blades," Kalen admitted.
"If anyone can piece this together, Valence, it's you
and your husband."

Jian-Shan absently stroked his wife's hair. "I am
flattered by your confidence in us, but I think this
must be a cooperative effort."

After finishing their drinks, the four relocated to
the large study at the back of the house, where Jian-
Shan had a wall map of the U.S. marked with pins.

He started with the map, explaining how he had
traced reports of the truck carrying the collection,
from the New Orleans museum where it had been
stolen to the point of entry into California, where it
abruptly vanished into thin air.

"We suspect the theft of the swords was contracted by Takeshi Sayura before his death. He had
been in competition with my father all his life; he
knew it would be a terrible blow to his pride. And
the Sayura syndicate operates here." Jian-Shan
moved a pin to San Francisco. "Unfortunately, none
of my contacts on the West Coast will confirm that.
Takeshi is dead, his sons have claimed to know
nothing about the collection, and his daughter,
Kameko, as you know, has not yet surfaced."

Val took over from there. "Talk on the black market is thin, but that's because some scary men are involved. Shandian's Ju-Long wants those swords, and he's willing to pay a million dollars to whoever delivers them. So does someone else, an Asian collector only known as the Monk. Remy says he's offered two million."

"Ju-Long has disappeared, and we've assumed he's been assassinated," Kalen said. "Who do you think this Monk is, Jian-Shan?"

"One of Kameko's brothers, probably Jiro. He has been charged with a number of crimes, but never convicted."

Raven studied the map. "What about the older brother?"

Jian-Shan shook his head. "Ichiro is something of a recluse, with no prior history of criminal activity. I believe he's also disabled."

"So the swords are probably in California, no one knows where, and when two major players offer big money, one disappears. That's eliminating the competition." Raven tapped the pin at San Francisco with her nail. "Takeshi takes delivery here, hides them, and leaves for China, where he's murdered before he can tell anyone where they are."

"When I called her a few months ago, Kameko said that before her father died, he wrote a letter to her about a sword he was sending to her," Val added. "The last time we spoke, she claimed that she never received that sword."

"If Shandian is out of the game, then the Monk is after Kameko." Raven focused on the subtle change in Jian-Shan's expression. "But the Star King isn't about the swords. You and Kalen both think it's something else."

"I believe I do, but I need to . . . access some computer files. Sarah?"

"No problem." The former model flexed her fingers as she sat down in front of Jian-Shan's computer. "Nice system, Jay. Kalen, go be a general somewhere else for a few minutes."

The general turned his back on his wife so he didn't have to watch her break several federal laws. "Valence, this is the blade the police found at Kameko Sayura's jewelry shop." He handed her the crime scene photos. "Would you compare the sword driven into the desk to the other photos you have of the key swords, please?" He went to the computer while she retrieved an envelope from the filing cabinet and spread the photos out on the desk.

Kalen sat beside her. "Does anything look familiar, Val?"

"It's hard to tell with the blood on the blade." She reached into a drawer and pulled out a magnifying glass. "The blade appears to be a Nagatoki, but the tang is wrapped, so I can't be sure."

While their spouses discussed the photographs, Raven quickly hacked into the Chinese Meteorological Administration's database and converted the display to a split screen so she and Jian-Shan could read it in Chinese and English. "Okay, what are we looking for?"

"A file from 1994. It will contain the words 'Feng Yun' and 'Xing Huangdi,' and will be under CMA's satellite program files."

She paged down through the file directories.

"Weather forecasting, news releases, yada yada yada. Here we go, satellite program." She brought up the encrypted file and made a tsking sound. "Where did they get this pitiful little cipher? At the dollar store?"

Jian-Shan smiled. "They are not as sophisticated as you are, Sarah."

"No one is." She tapped a few keys. "ElgamaL algorithm, SHA-1, and Triple-DES. Oh, Jay, this is *so* not secure."

"Can you access it?"

She rolled her head from side to side. "In a coma." It took her less than thirty seconds to find the side door through the encryption sequencer, and then the screen went blank.

Jian-Shan leaned in. "Did it crash?"

"It's a zap back from my dial-in back door." She shook her head. "Watch."

The screen reappeared and began scrolling, first displaying the encrypted files, then automatically translating each line of code into readable text.

"Okay, we're in business. Looks like the files go back fifteen years, so we should go string search by year." She entered the date, which brought up a number of files. One with a header of "0494" took up three times the memory of the others. "This thing happen in April?"

"That's probably the one."

She double-clicked on the header and brought up the enormous file, then began to page through.

"Okay, we've got your basic satellite launch schedule, duty assignment list, telemetry, rocket boosters, weather conditions, final checkout list, ho, big mess." She stopped and examined the report. "They lost the whole shebang, right before it launched. Explosion and fire, one dead, twenty injured. Traces of RDX found at the accident site. All evidence turned over to the Chinese military."

"RDX?" He leaned in. "How much?"

"Enough to leave a blast crater the size of a city block." She lifted her gaze from the screen. "Jay, somebody packed this sucker with so much C-4 that they blew it and everything within a quarter-mile radius to kingdom come."

"Hold on to the edge of the dresser," Sean said as he positioned his tool.

Meko eyed the arrangement of their limbs. "This looks like it's going to hurt."

"Trust me."

As he applied the tire iron they'd retrieved from her Mercedes, the tip gouged through the link between the mink-lined cuffs. Meko closed her eyes as metal scraped against metal. Then the bar and the link slipped against the slick surface of the Formica and Sean swore.

She thought for a moment. "I have an idea, but I need to get something out of the car."

He accompanied her to the Mercedes, where she took the sample box out of the glove compartment. "What's that?"

"It's a new type of pitch," she said as they reentered the room. "A company in Germany sent it for me to test." She opened the box and removed the wad of resin from its envelope. "Jewelers and goldsmiths use pitch to hold pieces in place while they work on them. This one can be shaped by hand."

Sean examined the black puttylike material. "It's too soft to do us any good."

"Not for long." She took out the accompanying bottle of setting solution. "Come on, I'll show you."

Meko placed the wad of pitch on top of the dresser, and pressed the link between their cuffs lightly into the surface. "Hold still now." She gave the resin a spray of solution, and counted to thirty under her breath before giving it a tug. The link was stuck fast to the pitch. "There, try it now."

He wedged the bar between them again, and worked it against the link. As he pried, Meko tugged her wrist. The resin held the link so well that the metal beneath the mink lining bit into her wrist. Watching Sean's grimace made her feel guilty, and as beads of sweat appeared on his brow she almost begged him to stop.

"Come on, darlin'," he said through gritted teeth. The muscles in his arm bulged as he pulled from the other side and bore down on the tool. "I know you're stronger than you look."

If he wouldn't give in, neither would she. The thin bones in her arm felt ready to splinter, but she kept pulling until something suddenly gave way and sent her staggering backward to land against the bed.

"There." Dragging in a deep breath, Sean dropped the tire iron and backed away from the dresser. "We're not going steady anymore." He sat down on the edge of the bed beside her and eyed the pitch on the dresser, with the link still stuck to it. "You won't use any of that on me, will you?"

"That was all I had." She almost laughed her relief, until she saw the blood on his wrist. "You're hurt."

"It's nothing."

"You're bleeding." She seized his hand and held it toward the lamp. He'd pulled so hard that the cuff had cut through the lining and left a deep laceration on the top of his wrist. "This is my fault. I should never have done this."

"It's only a little nick, love." He cradled her cheek for a moment, then used some of her tissues to wipe away the blood. "Next time, just bring the keys with you."

She was going to throw out her entire inventory of cuffs, at the first opportunity. "You're going to leave me now." It wasn't a question.

"I'm going to walk down the block to get us some supplies and a bit of breakfast, and then we'll see to getting your girl back." He nodded toward the bathroom. "You were wanting a shower, weren't you? Take one while I'm gone."

"All right." Her voice wobbled, but she wasn't a child. She wouldn't make him promise to come back. "Don't be long."

Meko waited until he left before she undressed, then spent a good thirty minutes showering in the tiny bathroom. Any other time the sluggish water pressure, claustrophobia-inducing stall, and minuscule bar of courtesy soap would have annoyed her, but she felt too relieved to complain.

Sean would stay with her. He would help her

save Tara. He wouldn't abandon her, he wouldn't dismiss her problems.

For the first time in her life, she could depend on a man to share her troubles and help fight her battles. Unlike her father and Nick, Sean would be there when she needed him the most. And once they found the swords and rescued Tara, they might even have a future together.

I don't have to be alone anymore.

It was a wonderful feeling. As if a crushing weight had been lifted off her shoulders—a burden that she'd been carrying all her life but hadn't realized it until that very moment.

Humming under her breath, Meko dried off and stepped out of the bathroom to take her clothes from where she'd left them, neatly folded on the bed. She didn't want to put the same thing on, but her overnight case was in the Mercedes and she hadn't thought to ask Sean to get it for her. It took a minute for it to register.

The clothes she'd left on the bed were gone.

"He took them." She looked around the room to be sure, then stared at the door in utter shock. "He came back and *took my clothes*?"

She gripped the edge of the towel and stalked over to the dresser to get her purse. Which was also gone.

"Oh, no. He didn't." She hurried to the window. The parking space in front of the room was empty.

Like her clothes and her purse, the Mercedes had also vanished.

*   *   *

The man in the hooded jacket climbed into the back of the limousine and slammed the door. "Go," he ordered the driver before he eyed the folded wheelchair across from the other passenger. "I see your usual ruse worked."

"The handicapped are more invisible than you think." Ichiro removed his hat and sunglasses. "Did you have any problems with Ju-Long?"

"None at all."

"Excellent. And our sister?"

"There are indications Meko may have gone north, to Sonoma Valley. I sent two men to investigate." Jiro removed the jacket and tossed it aside. "When they find her—"

Ichiro held up a thin hand. "We will bring our sister back to safety, and protect her. It is our duty."

His brother made a disgusted sound. "You obviously do not remember how stubborn she can be."

"No one knows Kameko better than I, brother."

"Then tell me something—why would he entrust her with this?" Jiro sliced the air with his hand. "He also knew her very well—knew how she felt about family business. Why did he not come to you, or me?"

"The most effective ally is an antagonist who aids you unaware," Ichiro reminded him. "Perhaps he believed the secret was safer with Kameko than anyone else, for precisely that reason."

Jiro produced an ugly smile. "Not for long."

The limousine pulled up a private drive to a modest home set back from the street. The discreet Oriental styling of the architecture reminded Ichiro of their home in Japan.

As Ichiro bypassed the front entrance and hobbled back into the garden, Eiji Menaka met him and bowed deeply. "I am honored by your presence, Ichiro-san."

"It is I and my brother who are flattered by your kind invitation, Menaka-san." Ichiro bowed in return, and inclined his head toward the other three guests. "Thank you for meeting us here, gentlemen."

Ichiro's bodyguards formed a short wall behind him. The trio of Chinese men had also brought a small army of guards.

Jiro arrived a few seconds later, and bowed before murmuring to his brother, "No sign of official surveillance, but there are more Shandian waiting in a van at the side of the house." He eyed the unsmiling Chinese men. "I suggest you make this quick."

Eiji introduced the three men, all of whom were related to the now-missing Ju-Long. Before Ichiro could speak, the youngest of the trio stepped up in his face.

"My uncle is dead because of you."

"Gan." Eiji took hold of the young man's arm. "You forget to whom you speak. All we know is that your uncle Ju-Long is still missing."

The scowling boy looked Ichiro over, then spat on the ground in front of his feet. *"Hum kah chan."*

Death to your family. Ichiro smiled a little. "I understand your feelings, young man. We recently lost our father." He glanced at the older men. "It is good that we can share our pain."

Gan ignored the subtle hint and turned on Jiro.

"They say *you* were the last to see him. Did you kill him yourself, or do you use the cripple to keep your hands clean?"

Jiro seized the boy by the front of his jacket. "Would you like to find out what I can do with my hands, *kisama*?"

"Enough." One of the older Chinese men hauled Gan away from Jiro, and gestured to one of the bodyguards, who marched him out of the garden. "I apologize for my son."

"Do not trouble yourself; I understand completely." Ichiro nodded to his brother, who stepped forward with a briefcase. "Let us set aside our animosity and discuss the business at hand."

Eiji led them into the teahouse, where a map of the region had been hung on the wall. Large sections of the state of California had been shaded with see-through colored overlays. Bodyguards from both sides lined the walls as the men sat on the tatami mats around a low table.

Jiro went to the map. "These are the territories as they stand now. Shandian in blue, Sayura in red."

"Shandian has far more territory in other states," one of the Chinese men pointed out.

Jiro nodded. "Yes. But you lack the leadership to control them, particularly in the major cities, where two other tongs continue to attack your positions daily. With the proposed alliance, we can unify our forces and act as one army."

"Your syndicate has yet to recover from Takeshi's tragic death." Gan's father smirked a little. "We expect to prevail over the tongs very shortly."

Eiji brought Ichiro a cup of tea, which he refused with a small shake of his head.

"By using our sister to gain possession of the White Tiger?" Jiro gazed at each of the three men. "That we will not allow."

"I know nothing of your sister." The older man's face turned to stone. "And the Sayura do not make our decisions for us."

"Reconsider, old man," Jiro said. "While you are still able to make a decision."

"We are through here." Gan's father rose. "I will accept the loss of my brother for your father, but no more. Go back to Japan, where you belong."

The Shandian contingent left en masse.

Ichiro sent their bodyguards out of the teahouse, then limped over to the map. "They despise tradition, and yet they cling to the old prejudices so tightly. They are deserving of our pity."

Eiji exchanged a glance with Jiro. "Will we move ahead with the plan?"

"I will meditate on the matter," Ichiro said, then made his way back to the garden.

"Let my brother pray, Menaka-san." Jiro pulled down the map and crumpled it between his hands. "We must attend to more earthly matters."

Chapter 8

Sean shifted the bags he was carrying to one hand so he could let himself into the hotel room with the other. Finding an open Oriental market had taken longer than he'd expected, but it was worth it, just thinking about the look that would be on her face when he spread out all the goodies.

"It's just me, darlin', are you"—something flew at his head, and he caught it out of reflex—"decent?"

She was huddled on the bed, with a towel wrapped around her, sarong-fashion. "Don't you *darlin'* me, you thief!"

He looked at the Gideon Bible he'd caught. "What's this about?"

Kameko stood and raised her arm. "It's about my *clothes*."

"Your clothes—" He whipped his face to the side, and the damp bar of soap she threw at him clipped his chin.

"Are gone." The towel she wore was very small,

and gaped on one side as she advanced on him. "Like my *purse*."

Her bare legs distracted him, which was why he didn't see the roll of toilet paper until it smacked his eye. "Woman, will you—"

"And my *car*." She picked up something from the dresser. "You left me here. Naked."

"Kameko, you're not naked, and will you for the love of God stop—" A wet towel slapped him in the face, so hard that the back of his head slammed into the door. He swatted it away. "All right. *All right*. Would you like the gun now, to finish things off properly?"

"Don't tempt me." She stalked back to the bed and sat down, and the towel's gap widened. "And don't ogle me, either."

"Darlin', I didn't want you to go after Tara by yourself, that's all." He put down the bags and cautiously approached her. "It was for your own good."

She closed her eyes for ten seconds. "I've changed my mind." She pointed at the door without looking at him. "Go get the gun."

He started to chuckle, then saw the way her hand shook and knelt down before her instead. "I'm sorry. I didn't mean to scare you." He kept his attention on her face, because if he looked any further south he'd start to drool on her. "Don't you want to see the presents I've brought for you?"

The line of her mouth tightened. "I want to see my *clothes*, and my *purse*, and my *car*."

"Clothes we've got." He retrieved the bags and brought them to the bed. "There's a little women's boutique across the way. I've jeans and blouses and all the unmentionables." And a fine time he'd had picking them out for her, too.

She folded her arms, making the edge of the towel droop dangerously low over her breasts. "My purse?"

He took it out of one of the bags. "Right here." He had to distract her now or there'd be hell to pay. "Why don't you try on these things while I lay out our breakfast?"

"Don't move." She snatched up the bag of clothes and marched into the bathroom.

He used the time to take his other surprises out of the bags, so that when she came out the first thing she would see was his little feast.

"Everything fits," she said as she walked out of the bathroom. Then she eyed the takeout containers he'd arranged on the bed. "What's this?"

"Grilled salmon, miso soup with spring onion and tofu, steamed rice, seaweed, stirred egg, and some honeydew." He handed her a Styrofoam cup filled with green tea.

"I see." Kameko leaned over and picked up a sheet of dried seaweed. "You like Japanese food?"

"I've never tried it, but the man at the market said this was a traditional breakfast. He even had his wife warm up what needed it." He checked the containers. "Did I miss something?"

"I really wouldn't know."

He glanced from her to the food. "But you're Japanese."

She sighed. "Sean, I've lived in the United States

since I was nine. My idea of a traditional breakfast is an Egg McMuffin."

"You're kidding."

Her lips curled. "Do you have Irish coffee with your corned beef and cabbage in the morning?"

"Only on Mondays." He felt like an idiot. "I'm sorry."

She poked around the containers. "At least he didn't sell you any *natto*."

He opened the orange juice he'd gotten for himself. "*Natto*'s no good, I take it?"

"*Natto* is fermented soybeans. It smells to high heaven, and looks like acorns laced with snot." She shuddered. "Hurry and wash up, and let's eat."

Pleased that he'd brought her around, Sean slipped into the bathroom. He didn't know he'd been hustled until he turned on the water in the sink, and heard the door slam. "Damn it."

He didn't have to go far to find her—she was standing just outside the door, staring at the Jeep parked in front of their room.

She swiveled toward him, her eyes narrowed. "You didn't. You *wouldn't*."

"Now, sweetheart, I had to do a little horse trading, is all." He took her arm. "Come inside now."

"I don't have a horse. I have a silver *Mercedes-Benz CL 600*." She yanked free and gestured at the Jeep. "And *that* is not *it*."

"I know. Like I said, I had to do some trading." He opened the door to the room. "You've got insurance, don't you?"

"Oh, no you don't." She planted her hands on

her hips. "You drive this *thing* out of here and go get my Mercedes back. Right this minute."

"Can't. It's in about ten thousand pieces by now. The guy who owns the chop shop gave me the Jeep free and clear, though."

Her sweet, gentle voice rose three octaves. "You left my Mercedes at a chop shop?"

"Quiet." He spotted the patrol car approaching from the south. "Cops." Without another word, he picked her up like a rigid doll and carried her inside.

"Put me down, you lunatic!" She kicked him so hard he nearly dropped her. "How could you trade my Mercedes for that piece of junk out there? Do you have any idea how much I paid for that car?"

"There's an APB out on you, Kameko, and that includes your license plates and an excellent description of your vehicle. I had to do it." He put her down on the bed beside the food. "That seaweed doesn't look too bad. What's it taste like?"

"I'm turning myself in." She got up and headed for the door.

"No, you're not, darlin'." He caught her around the waist and brought her back to the bed. "And if you try to run on me again, I'll take all the clothes and keep you naked permanently."

She looked at him the way she would *natto*. "You are a pig."

"All the way down to my hooves. Now, come and get in touch with your roots while I make a few calls." He locked and bolted the door, then got on the phone.

*　　*　　*

Hacking into the Chinese military's database, which was much better safe-guarded than the CMA's files, took Raven until midnight, but she finally broke through with one of her fastest Trojan horses. "I'm in—let's do this fast. They've got continuous scanning."

Kalen had gone with Val to her office to get some file photos, but Jian-Shan remained at Raven's side. "Find the April '94 satellite file, and see if you can locate a list of components."

Her fingers flew as she skimmed through the database. "Yeah, right here. Feng Yun One, some meteorological stuff, transmitters, various and sundry solar power cells . . . here's a diagram. And another." She opened the first, then accessed the secondary design schematic. The second image superimposed itself on the satellite image. "This looks like a SYBIL."

"Who is Sybil?" Jian-Shan studied the screen.

"Not who, what." She sat back and studied the screen, then looked up as her husband and Jian-Shan's wife entered the study carrying files. "Babe, my Trojan horse just found itself a role model. I think China was trying to send a SYBIL up in '94."

Val repeated her husband's question.

"SYBIL stands for 'Space Yielded/Based Integrated Laser system.'" Kalen joined them and examined the schematic, then quickly pulled up a chair beside his wife. "They'd need a huge fuel cell. Isolate the orbiter module diagram."

Raven cleared the screen of the first image, then slowly sat back in her chair.

Jian-Shan studied the image. "Does it accommodate enough fuel to power the laser?"

"Oh, yeah." Kalen tapped the keyboard, rotating the diagram. "They installed *three* fuel cells."

"It's too big." Raven tapped the screen with a fingernail. "What is that, like a hundred-and-fifty, two-hundred-pound storage capacity?"

"From the cells' dimensions, more like three hundred." Kalen typed in an inquiry. A small pop-up appeared with a short list of symbols. He hissed in a breath. "Christ, they used Pu-238."

Raven closed her eyes briefly. "It must have been shielded. Otherwise they'd have had a mini Chernobyl and Beijing would still be glowing in the dark."

Jian-Shan frowned. "I'm not following."

"The Chinese tried to launch a laser system that could fire on a target from orbit. Normally, a ground-based laser cannon is aimed at a reflector satellite, which sends the beam to a combat satellite mirror, then the space-based laser, which delivers the beam to the target."

"Has to be done that way," Raven added, "because the laser eats up a huge amount of fuel, and there are no gas stations in space."

"But not this one," Jian-Shan said, eyeing the screen.

"No. With this autonomous design, they don't need the ground-based cannon, or a reflector. One signal is sent directly to the combat satellite, which generates the beam itself." He pointed to the same fuel cell Raven had. "They enabled this by storing the fuel for the laser aboard the satellite. It's plutonium dioxide, Pu-238."

"And since that type of plutonium is two hundred and eighty times more radioactive than the kind released during the Chernobyl disaster," Raven added, "when the launch site blew, it should have been sprayed all over the place. Since several thousand Chinese didn't die after the explosions, we'll assume someone removed the contents of the laser fuel cells before they blew up the launch vehicle. Which would *not* be the people launching it, I think."

Everyone fell silent.

"A treasure of power and death," Val said softly. "This plutonium certainly qualifies." She looked at Kalen. "General, I must examine that third sword. If it is the final part of the key, then it will unlock T'ang's code encryption."

Raven's husband nodded. "We'll leave for L.A. first thing in the morning."

I should have waved down those cops myself.

Meko ate a little rice and some of the melon before the thought of her beautiful Mercedes being reduced to a pile of expensive parts made her appetite disappear. Of course her insurance company would replace it—she kept comprehensive policies on all her assets—but it was more than a car.

The Mercedes was a symbol of her independence—the first car she'd ever bought herself, with her own money. Every other car she'd driven had been chosen and paid for by her father, then Nick.

Like Sean, they hadn't ever asked for her permission or her opinion.

And now? She had a Jeep. Picked out by a man who didn't trust her enough to leave her clothes behind.

She eyed the back of Sean's head. He had been on the phone for close to an hour, speaking in low murmurs and completely ignoring her. Why would he do such a thing? Had he been drinking? Or was he in some kind of withdrawal?

As he ended the call, she decided it was time to find out. "Sean. We need to talk."

"I've a few more calls to make."

She went to him, took the phone out of his hand, and put it down on the receiver. "You can speak with your friends later."

He glanced at the phone, then sighed and rolled his hand.

Might as well go for the worst first. "Sean, have you been drinking again?"

"At"—he made a show of checking her watch—"nine o'clock in the morning?"

"That's not an answer."

"No, Kameko." He gave her a thin smile. "I haven't had a drink since we got naked together. Would you like to kiss me? That's how my mother used to check my father's breath."

"I know it's hard to stop suddenly." She tried for a reasonable tone, but she sounded cold. "Maybe we should end this relationship now."

He folded his arms. "Why? Aren't you interested in chasing bad guys with a worthless drunk anymore, darlin'?"

"I don't think you're worthless. It's just I might be better off handling this on my own." She sighed. "Please don't make this any more difficult than it is already."

"You dragged me into this mess, Kameko." He rose to his feet. "I'll just run along back to the dairy, then."

The phone rang. When he didn't answer it, Kameko snatched it up with an impatient hand.

"Irish, got a line on that missing girl," the voice on the line said before she could speak. "Word on the street is, they're holding her in a crib, waiting for some big delivery before they dust her. She's somewhere in East L.A., but no one's talking shit about it. Gimme five large, I can maybe get a street for you."

Shaken, she handed the phone to Sean, and drifted over to the window while he asked the caller to repeat the information. She stared at the battered Jeep, feeling smaller and more petty than she ever had in her life.

He finished the call and came up behind her.

"That man said *before they dust her.* That means kill her, doesn't it." It wasn't a question.

His hands rested on her shoulders. "As long as they think you're looking for the swords, she's worth more alive than dead to them. We still have time."

"I would have never found that out on my own—what that man said." She turned around and absently straightened the collar of his shirt. "I really can't do this without you. If I try, Tara will be killed."

He cradled her face between his palms. "I'm right here. I won't leave you."

"I've never been able to rely on anyone before, Sean." She traced a fingertip around one of his buttons. "All my life I've been surrounded by men who were too obsessed with their own needs to notice mine. And every woman in my family was a doormat."

"You must be adopted."

"I should never have forced you to get involved in this. And I have no right to question you about your drinking." She lifted her head. "All I can say is, I'm worried—no, I'm terrified."

"You've reason to be." He bent his head until their brows touched. "But I'm here, and I'm doing all I can. We'll get her back, darlin'."

"All right, *nagare*." It hurt to smile. "You're the boss from here on out."

"Good." He gave her a brief, hard kiss. "Now get your purse, woman. We're going for a ride to Chinatown."

"I believe Mr. Sayura is out on the Waikiki deck," the front-desk clerk told Brooke. He gave Kinsella a cautious look. "I can notify hotel security, if you need assistance, Captain."

The FBI agent answered before Brooke could. "Thanks, pal, but we'll take it from here."

As they walked out of the lobby to the central courtyard leading to the pool decks, Brooke scanned the perimeter. Her companion's sour expression convinced several guests to move quickly out of their path. "Try to lighten up, Kinsella. You're scaring the straights."

He grunted. "You be the good cop today; I'm not in the mood."

The Hilton had several oversized pools, each styled after some famous resort area around the world. The Waikiki deck sported three bars in open-sided grass huts and a water slide that resembled an erupting volcano.

"I should have brought my bikini," Kinsella muttered.

Brooke tried to imagine the big man in a very small Speedo, but failed. Kinsella was definitely the trunks type.

The Sayura brothers proved easy to spot, as they were the only two Asian men on the deck. The younger brother was swimming laps around the edge of the pool, but the older sat in the shade, reading a book. Both looked up as Brooke and Kinsella approached.

Before they got within twenty feet of Ichiro Sayura, a large Japanese man stepped up to them. "What do you want?" he demanded.

"Not you." Kinsella gave the man a shove, sending him down the volcano water slide into the pool.

Brooke sidestepped the splash with a sigh. "Very nice."

"He looked overheated." Kinsella pulled out his creds as he closed the gap and showed them to the reclining Ichiro. "Special Agent Kinsella, Federal Bureau of Investigation. This is Captain Oliver with Army Central Intelligence Division. You are Ichiro Sayura?"

"I am he." The man reached for a cane and rose with some difficulty. He smiled at Brooke when she caught his elbow and steadied him. "Thank you. How may I help the army and the FBI?"

"We'd like to ask you and your brother some questions, sir," Brooke said before Kinsella could respond. "About your sister, and some missing antique swords."

"Of course." He gestured toward a nearby table.

Brooke sat opposite Ichiro, while Kinsella stood behind her. The way he hovered got on her nerves, but she imagined he liked using his physique to intimidate people. *Next time, I make him wait in the car.* "Mr. Sayura, have you been in contact with Kameko since you arrived in the U.S.?"

Pain flickered in the man's eyes. "Regrettably, no. My sister's disappearance has me deeply concerned."

"Not concerned enough to keep you from working on your tan," Kinsella said. He picked up Ichiro's book from the table. "Enhancing your personal power base, Sayura?"

"Sun Tzu was my late father's favorite philosopher." Ichiro's gaze moved past Kinsella, where a group of young Asian men stood waiting, along with the sodden, glaring bodyguard who had climbed out of the pool. "Excuse my brother's men. In this country, during these troubled times, they are an unfortunate necessity."

Kinsella unbuttoned his jacket, letting it fall open enough to show his shoulder holster. "So are a lot of things."

Brooke muffled a sigh. *Why don't men just get a*

ruler and whip out their penises the minute they meet?
"When was the last time you saw your sister?"

"During my last visit to the States." Ichiro looked up. "That was two years ago, was it not, Jiro?"

His younger brother mopped his face with a towel before slinging it around his neck. "Yeah, I think so." He regarded Brooke and Kinsella with a frown. "What do you want?"

"We have some questions for you and your brother." Brooke took out a crime scene photo. "Do you recognize this weapon?"

Both men reacted subtly to the sight of the photo. Ichiro reached for it, then let his hand drop. Jiro raised his hand, gesturing for one of the guards.

"We're not answering any more questions." When Ichiro glanced up at him, his brother added, "Not without our attorney present."

"We can all wait together for him," Kinsella offered, "down at the L.A. field office."

"Or we can come back tomorrow, which is probably best for all of us." Brooke got up and offered Ichiro a card. She could feel a tidal wave of animosity coming from Kinsella, and silently vowed to brief him thoroughly as soon as they got back to command. "Call me this afternoon and let me know a convenient time, if you would, Mr. Sayura."

He inclined his head. "I will. Thank you, Captain."

Kinsella waited until they were in the lobby before he caught her arm and stopped her. "What the hell was that?"

"That was called not antagonizing a potential suspect, Agent Kinsella." She nodded to the smiling doorman before handing over their parking stub to the valet outside. "Don't they teach you guys how to interview at Quantico anymore?"

"Interview? I've seen mall Santas get tougher with kids at Christmas."

"Our presence was enough, this time." She paid the valet and climbed in the back of the van. As Kinsella got in behind the wheel, she flipped on her console. "Find a place to park."

"We've got four surveillance teams out here already," he reminded her in a testy voice.

Now she did sigh. "Just do it."

He screeched into a parking space and shut off the van. When he joined her at the console, she turned up the audio receiver so he could hear the two men speaking in rapid Japanese.

"Who the hell is that?"

"They're talking about the sister." She lifted a hand for quiet and concentrated. "Ichiro is saying their priority is to get Meko back safely . . . they can't risk losing her. Jiro wants to move on with the next phase. He has an appointment to see someone in the hotel restaurant, he's leaving now." She glanced up at him. "While you were busy flexing and posturing, I planted a bug on the older brother."

"You sneaky little bitch." He made it sound like his highest compliment. "Pressure-sensitive, short-range?"

She nodded. "As long as Ichiro wears that jacket, we'll hear whatever he and anyone within a five-foot radius say." She set the console to record, then grabbed her bag. "Come on."

"Where to now?"

She handed him a small duffel bag. "While the boys are relaxing in Waikiki, we're going to tag their suite, too."

Nick took off his courier's cap and jacket as soon as he was in the hotel lobby rest room, and stowed them under the sink. Dodging the surveillance teams wasn't making him sweat as much as what he was about to do, but Little Anthony had called in his paper, which ten grand only dented.

You're into me for another twenty, Nick. Get the rest by tonight, or pick out your cast colors.

If the government hadn't been so cheap, none of this would have happened. He could have fenced a handful of Meko's loose rocks and paid off the sharks with cash to spare.

"So it's sink or swim." He used a paper towel to dry his face and tucked in his shirt before heading for the restaurant.

The maître d' led him to a remote corner of the room, where his former brother-in-law sat waiting with a bodyguard.

"Jiro." Knowing the routine, Nick bowed. "Thanks for seeing me."

"Hello, Nick." Jiro waved a hand at his guard, who withdrew a few feet to lean against a wall. "Where is my sister?"

"I don't know." This wasn't the way he wanted to start the conversation. "She took off after the cops busted her for that business with the girl she had working for her. I haven't heard from her in months anyway."

Jiro took a sip from his ice water. "Yet you were told—and paid by my brother, I believe—to watch over her."

"Hey, I did my best, but you know Meko. She gets stubborn, thinks she can do it all on her own." A new angle occurred to him, one that would bail him out and help his ex-wife as well. "This time, though, she's in real trouble, Jiro. It's good you and Ichiro came over to take charge." Nick leaned forward and lowered his voice. "The government is going after her now."

"How?"

"You know how they've been trying to shut down Shandian for years, right? Well, I hear they got an agent on the inside, with that kid. Soon as Meko tries to trade the swords for that girl, they're going to bust everybody." He met Jiro's flat gaze. "She'll probably end up being charged as an accessory."

"She can't turn those swords over to Shandian." Jiro ignored the No Smoking signs and lit a cigarette, then offered one to Nick. "They belong to us."

"Sure, but how are you going to stop her?" He lit his cigarette off one of the candles in the table's centerpiece. "She won't come to you or your brother. Or me. But she'll do anything for that kid." He paused. "With your help, I can get the girl."

Jiro exhaled a stream of smoke. "How much?"

"Thirty to get in the door." Feeling more confident, he decided to press a little. "Forty and I can guarantee—"

"Baka kuso atama."

The bodyguard snatched Nick out of his chair and dragged him out the side door. Being flung up against the wall knocked the breath out of him, and then the bodyguard pinned him with one hand clamped on his neck.

Jiro moved in, lifting the tip of his lit cigarette until it hovered in front of Nick's right eye. "Where is the girl?"

"Jiro—no—" Nick cringed back as he felt the heat from the glowing red tip. At the same time, the bodyguard's hand tightened, cutting off most of his air. "You won't . . . get in . . . without me."

The cigarette singed the edge of his eyelashes, then retreated.

"Tell me," Jiro said, "or lose the eye."

Urine spread down the front of his trousers as his bladder released, but Nick didn't dare blink. "I need . . . the money . . . or I'm dead!"

"Let him go, brother."

Jiro muttered something filthy, but let go. Nick clapped a hand over his watering eye and doubled over, coughing uncontrollably.

"Are you crazy?" Nick demanded when he could speak, only to find himself alone with Ichiro. "He tried to burn my eye out!"

"Our brother can be impatient at times." Ichiro looked down. "Oh, dear. You should perhaps go home and change."

"Yeah, look what he did to me." Nick stepped out of the puddle around his shoes. "He's crazy, just like your father was!"

"We are very worried about Kameko. I know

you will forgive him. Here." He slipped a thick envelope into Nick's hand. "Go and settle your debts,
little brother."

Nick nodded, and headed for the parking lot.

"Nick."

The way Ichiro's voice changed made him turn
around.

Ichiro nodded toward the envelope. "Don't use it
for more gambling. Pay the Italians what you owe
them, then come back and see me."

Chapter 9

Traffic and pedestrian tourists made it necessary for Sean to park several blocks from the entrance to Chinatown, but Meko didn't complain. The Jeep badly needed new shocks, and riding in it only reminded her of the Mercedes.

"Have you ever been here?" she asked as they passed through the infamous green tile-capped triple gate on Grant Avenue and Bush Street.

"A few times." He eyed the small sign hanging down from the center. " 'All under heaven is for the good of the people.' "

Meko raised her brows. "You can read Chinese?"

"Same thing I got in a fortune cookie once." He winked at her.

Walking into Chinatown was, as always, a shock to the senses. Long vertical columns of Mandarin characters appeared on every storefront, street sign, and billboard—even the graffiti in the alleys were written in Chinese. Vividly painted building facades competed with the crimson banners hanging from windows and fluttering from lines crisscrossing the streets.

The sidewalks resembled any found in major Asian cities—crowded with narrow-eyed, dark-haired people with a wide range of exotic features and skin tones. Voices around them chatted in Chinese, Japanese, Vietnamese, Thai, and a dozen other Asian languages and dialects.

"My father brought me here a few times when I was a little girl," Meko said as she passed the shops and stalls selling everything from fat golden Buddhas and fine ceramics to brightly colored rayon *qipao* and cheongsam dresses. The smell of food cooking and garbage rotting blended and radiated from the crowded shadows of the alleys. "He would never let me come here when I got older, so I'd sneak out every chance I got."

"So you were a bad girl."

"Not really." She glanced down one alley. "I met my ex-husband here, in the park near Washington Street. At the time I didn't know it was where all the boys went to gamble."

"How long were you married?"

"A couple of years. Long enough for him to lose our house and almost everything we owned." She avoided a group of men installing a new sign on a gift shop's facade. "I realized Nick loved gambling more than me when I came home from work one day and found he'd pawned my wedding rings to pay off his bookie. I should have never taken them off, but it's hard to work with metal and gems wearing rings." She shook off the bad memory. "Enough whining about my one and only lousy marriage. Are you hungry? I noticed you didn't eat much breakfast."

"It was the seaweed, I think. Next time, we get Egg McMuffins." Sean paused to study the racks of roast duck displayed in a food market window. Beneath them, customers sorted through open bins of imported specialty vegetables and mushrooms, and selected huge sacks of *gohan* and natural rice. Further back were the livestock cages. "I can't imagine the appeal of watching your food swim, skitter, or cluck before you eat it."

"Me either." Meko had thought the unfamiliar environment would intimidate Sean—here, he was definitely the alien—but he seemed to be enjoying himself. "Do you know where we're going?"

"I do." He steered her around a pair of protesters carrying signs against animal cruelty, who were arguing with a shopkeeper in English while he shouted at them in Burmese. "Have a little faith, darlin'."

He guided her along the tourist havens, stopping a few times to speak with shopkeepers and street kids. He spoke so low that Meko couldn't hear what he said, but she got the impression it was a name. They all shook their heads and replied with a curt "no."

A scrawny old woman in a beautifully embroidered cheongsam pushed an odd-looking cart directly in their path, and planted herself in front of it.

"You find pearl for girlfriend?" she demanded, gesturing at the tank of clouded water strapped to the top of the cart. A thick layer of oysters covered the bottom of the tank.

Sean peered into the tank. "How much?"

"Five dollar." The old peddler held out her hand.

"It's a tourist rip-off," Meko told him. "Most of them probably don't have pearls in them."

"Have pearl. Have *plenty* pearl," the old woman insisted.

"Maybe we'll get lucky. All right, ma'am, one oyster for my lady." He took out a five-dollar bill, then held it just out of the old woman's reach. "I get to pick, okay, sweetheart?"

She glared up at him. "Your hand clean?"

"I wash them three times a day." He rolled up his sleeve, plunged his arm into the tank, and came up with a rather moldy-looking specimen. "Do I get to eat the oyster, too?"

"That five dollar more." The old woman produced a shucking knife, and with the ease of an old pro, she popped open the oyster. Her scowl deepened as she removed a tiny white ball. "You lucky man."

"That I am." He took the pearl and presented it to Meko as if it were the Hope Diamond. "What do you think, darlin'?"

"I think this qualifies as the world's *smallest* pearl," Meko said, then laughed and pressed her cheek to the side of his shoulder. "But you're still my hero."

As they walked along, she rolled the milky sphere between her fingers. No man except her ex-husband had ever given her jewels—and in the end Nick had pawned all of them. That such a tiny gem could make her feel so happy made her understand her clients' pleasure a little better.

No, it makes you want to kiss Sean a few more times, a sly voice inside her said.

"Hard to believe that was once a grain of sand," he said, dragging her attention back to the present.

"More likely it was a glass bead, or a barren oyster egg." She lifted it up to have a better look, and the sun brought out a dazzling rainbow of colors. "Wait, this one might be a paragon."

"Of course it is." He sounded smug. "I picked it out, didn't I?"

She nudged him with her elbow. "I mean a paragon pearl, a *virgin* pearl. They form exclusively in the oyster's tissues, and they're often opaque. Sometimes, like this one, they resemble opals." She held it against her skin. "I think I'll set this in a ring. Gold, maybe with rubies on each side to coax the color out . . ." She thought of Tara, and quickly tucked the pearl into a pocket in her purse.

He gave her a sharp look. "Are you all right?"

"Fine." She squared her shoulders. "Where to next?"

They continued down Grant, with Sean stopping every so often to talk to the locals, until one grimy-faced teenager said something and held out his hand. Sean placed a folded fifty in it, and only then did the boy point out a street leading into the residential blocks.

Meko immediately became uneasy. "Sean, this is not the best part of Chinatown for a Caucasian to be wandering around. Even during the day."

He only folded his hand over hers. "Good thing I have you to protect me, then."

In this section of the community, the cramped living conditions and shabby tenements held little appeal for tourists, but Meko spotted another cluster of animal activists protesting the open-air markets on Stockton Street. Finally Sean led her across the street and headed into a building with a red and green facade.

Meko read the sign above the entrance and tugged him to a stop. "Sean, I definitely can't go in here."

"Why not?"

"This is a Chinese bathhouse." When his expression didn't change, she added, "For Chinese *men*."

"We're not here to take a bath." He squeezed her hand. "And we're not Chinese."

Meko felt like tiptoeing down the dark corridor leading into the bathhouse, and felt invisible eyes watching her. This was the sort of place where her father had conducted his business while in Chinatown, after he sent her off shopping with one of her brothers.

There were several older men in the wide, shallow main pool, most leaning up against the tiled walls as they talked, drank tea, and even played checkers. Others, swathed in towels and robes, gathered around small china bowls watching cricket fights.

And as soon as Meko stepped out of the hall, every single one of them turned to stare at her.

The proprietor, an elderly man with a towel draped over each shoulder, appeared an instant later. "This is not a bathhouse for women," he said in perfect English. "She has to leave."

"*Ni hao*," Sean said, in equally flawless Chinese. "*Wode mingzi shi Sean Delaney. Zai na li Fa Yun-Liang?*"

The old man pointed at one of the private rooms, then burst into a spate of protests in the same language.

"*Xie xie*," Sean thanked him, and led Meko around the central pool.

She eyed him. "You didn't get all *that* from a fortune cookie."

"I've been to Hong Kong once or twice." He knocked on a door, then stepped inside.

The room was so steamy Meko wondered if they'd entered a sauna, then she smelled mugwort, and realized from the stone walls and floor that they were in a medicinal bath. An obese man lay naked on a marble slab, and a masseuse was scrubbing his back with a dark green mixture.

"Fa, you've lost some weight," Sean said.

The Chinese man turned his moon-shaped face to look at them. "Irish, it's been too long." He smiled at Meko. "And you've brought me a present. How decent of you."

"Sorry, boyo." Sean put a casual arm around her shoulders. "This one's mine."

"Pity." The obese man snapped out an order for the masseuse to leave, then sat up, completely unabashed about his nudity. "She has quite lovely breasts."

Meko looked down and saw that the humid air

had caused her thin T-shirt to cling. Red-faced, she tried to discreetly tug it out.

Fa Yun-Liang climbed off the slab and waddled over to the bubbling herbal bath, knocking aside some of the decorative stones around the edge. "Will you join me? Mugwort cleanses the body of its toxins and helps ease old, tired bones." He gave Meko a small leer. "I would enjoy seeing more of your lovely little *nu wang*."

Meko knew the Chinese were never very sensitive about modesty or personal space, not when they were used to living together with large families under one roof. Even in the bathhouse it was not unusual for men to scrub each other's backs or douse one another with water.

That didn't mean she was going to strip down in front of Fa.

"I still haven't gotten over the Mercedes," she muttered to Sean under her breath. "Remember that."

"We've had our bath today," Sean said as he brought her over to a bench beside the pool and sat down with her. "But thank you for the kind offer."

"Always so private, you Americans," Fa said, and scooped up some water to rub it across his bloated chest. "We Chinese like to do things together." Again he ogled Meko. "Many, pleasurable things."

The way he looked at her made Meko want to take a bath. And stay there. For a month.

"We'll be out of here soon, darlin'," Sean murmured. In a louder voice, he said, "I'm looking for some information, Fa."

"You can pick up tourist books at any shop on Grant," the fat man said. "Some of them are even accurate."

"I'm more interested in the kind of information the man who imports half of everything that comes into Chinatown has."

"Ah, that would be me." The fat man preened a little as he slicked back his short hair. "However, I cost a bit more than the tourist books."

"I'm looking for some missing property. The White Tiger blades."

Fa pursed his cherubic mouth and thought for a moment. "I've not heard of any stolen knives coming into Chinatown. From where were they taken?"

"A museum in New Orleans. And they're swords, not knives."

"It's time for my facial." He rose from the pool and trudged over to a second, smaller pool. Before he gingerly lowered his bulk into the colder water, he pressed an intercom button near it and asked for someone, then switched it off and stroked his triple chins. "My skin is so sensitive these days, even shaving is a chore. I might know someone who can help you find them, Irish, for the right price."

Sean came back to Meko. "Give me your watch."

"Why?" Like her Mercedes, the Rolex symbolized a landmark of her independence—she'd bought it to celebrate being in business for five years.

"Mine's a Timex, we're not carrying enough cash to bribe him, and Fa doesn't take credit cards." He watched a young man carry in a large bowl of what appeared to be mud. "When the girl is safe, I'll get it back for you."

"It doesn't matter." Being reminded of Tara made Meko slip off the watch and place it in Sean's hand. "Is it enough?"

"Let's hope."

As the masseuse knelt by the cold-water pool, Fa examined the watch. He tried to slip it over his own plump hand, then pouted. "Your *nu yang* has slim wrists."

"That she does. I need a name, Fa."

"Go to the alley off Pacific and Powell." One fat hand waved in the direction of the street. "Go to the third door down on the right, ask for Jimmy Yi. He brings in what cannot be listed on a purchase order; he will know where your White Tiger is."

"Thanks." Sean took a towel from the stack near the massage table to dry his face and handed another to Meko. "See you around, Fa."

The importer gave Meko one more smirk. "I look forward to it."

"Damn it." Brooke pulled off her headset and blotted her temples. The van's air conditioner wasn't the greatest, and three hours of sitting and sweating inside it had her feeling damp and sticky.

Kinsella lifted one side of his earphones. Like her, his face was damp, but his hair was soaked. "What's wrong?"

She gestured toward her side of the console. "Big brother changed jackets, and I'm not getting anything from the suite. I'm switching over to auto." She checked his receiver. "Anything from Conor?"

"Not much. Some metallic clanging, and a couple of whimpers from the kid. Sounds like she's sleeping." He pulled the headset down around his neck. He'd discarded his jacket and rolled up his sleeves, and now used a handkerchief from his pocket to wipe his face. "What's your take on that last conversation Ichiro had with this ex-husband?"

She didn't know what to make of it. Hearing what Ichiro had said to Nick had her a little worried. "We know Kameko's ex isn't all that popular with her brothers."

"You don't threaten to burn a man's eye out unless you want something from him," Kinsella said. "Something he's very reluctant to give up."

"In Nick's case, that would be money, and it sounded like Ichiro gave him some at the end." She thought about it for a moment. "Unless older brother is playing the good cop."

He nodded. "You can nail a gambling junkie with money and sympathy a lot faster than popping one of his eyes."

"Switch places with me."

As she sat down, she felt the warm imprint of Kinsella's body on the chair. Being bear-sized, he generated a lot of heat, and was probably suffering a lot more than she was. Still, the sensation made her vaguely uncomfortable. So did the lingering scent of his cologne. She didn't want to know how warm he was or what he smelled like.

After she switched the console over to speaker, she sent a short, brief tone over Conor's earpiece. If it was safe for him to transmit, he would respond.

And he did. "Hello, gorgeous."

"Hey, handsome." Brooke tuned the receiver. "Talk to me."

"I think I've got some vacation coming, real soon." Conor sounded as tired as Brooke felt. "I'll need you to give me a ride to work, gorgeous. All kinds of shit going down here."

She began taking notes. "How's the baby?"

"Baby's taking a nap. Her uncles have been fussing over her." His voice dropped. "Don't drop in, though. You might wake the dogs."

Her pencil stilled. "When?"

"Tuesday, but call me first."

"Handsome, think twice about Vegas. It's getting hot out there now. Talk to you soon." She switched off the transmitter and turned to bump knees with Kinsella. "What?"

"What the hell was that?"

"That was a coded transmission, Agent Kinsella." The heat was making them both cranky, she guessed. "If we don't know whether anyone is listening, then we use code."

"Christ, I need a damn decoder ring to keep up with you on regular transmissions." He gestured at the console. "So what does all that spy talk mean?"

Brooke consulted her notes. " 'Vacation time' means the extraction point, when we get the girl out. 'Ride to work' means Conor can't transport her away from the site by himself."

"And the 'all kinds of shit'?"

"The dogs—the other guards—are armed with AK-47s. The 'fussing over baby' means they've beaten Tara. We can't move in until Conor signals. Tuesday means he thinks it will be at least forty-eight hours." She put down her notepad. "That means security is very tight, and he's having trouble finding a way out."

"And Vegas is Nick, and the weather changing is him possibly flipping on us. I think I'm finally getting the hang of this stuff." Kinsella shook his head. "Why doesn't Perry take down the guards and just get the kid out of there?"

"Conor had to go in unarmed, and he's got two men with automatic weapons keeping watch. If he tries to take down the guards, he or Tara could be killed. The same thing could happen if we make a move on their location." Her ribs ached, and she pressed a hand against them under her jacket. She was dying to take it off, but her blouse was also soaked, and she didn't want Kinsella seeing her support brace—or anything else—through it. "His one and only priority is to get her out alive."

"Why does he call you gorgeous?"

She arched a brow. "Because *Captain* would be rather telling, don't you think?"

"Well, at least he's not blind." He tapped the headset around his neck. "How long do you plan on us sitting in this van and monitoring the lint on Sayura's jacket and the air in his suite?"

"As long as it takes, Agent Kinsella." His offhand compliment made her put her headset on and switch the console back to manual. "But if the glamour and excitement of real intelligence work gets to be too much for you, just say the word."

Jiro found his brother annoying at times, particularly when he interfered with simple pleasures

like burning out a man's eye, but he decided Eiji
Menaka was much worse.

The man crouched down inside the compound
wall, shivering like a terrified female. The bright
sunlight made the sweat on his face look glassy.
"Why are we doing this now? They will see us."

"Most of the guards do not report until twilight,
and the ones who are here now are inside eating."
Jiro took out a pistol. "If anyone does see us, we
will shoot them. Come on. I don't want this to take
all day."

Eiji reluctantly followed him, keeping to the
shadows as they approached the back of the large
house. In the yard was a brightly colored children's
jungle gym, a plastic fort, and an enormous swing
set. Through the large window Jiro could see Gan's
extensive family gathered around low tables for
their afternoon meal. There were wives of various
ages, a few teenagers, and several young children,
all busy eating with chopsticks. The men sat at a
separate table, drinking and smoking.

Jiro had already been to the Shandian's compound once, to make the preparations. All he
needed was visual confirmation before he finished
the job.

"There are children in the house," he heard Eiji
say. "We cannot do this."

He heaved a mental sigh. "You agreed to do
what was necessary, Menaka-san. Besides, we cannot stop it now."

"There is no honor in killing infants." He started
backing away, and spun around, ready to run for
the wall.

More inconvenience. Jiro took out his gun and shot Eiji in the back, then removed the remote signaling device from his pocket and flicked the only switch.

A series of five explosions went off beneath the house, each successively louder and more destructive, until the final blast practically leveled the structure. A huge ball of flame and black smoke billowed up into the sky.

Jiro stripped Eiji's body of its identification before he dragged it down to the burning ruins. The man was no lightweight, and it took considerable effort to toss the body into the flames. His last task was to confirm that there were no survivors, which was relatively easier. He simply sat down on one of the swings and watched what was left of the house burn.

He knew Ichiro had liked Eiji, so he would have to come up with a plausible excuse for killing the man. Eiji was too loyal to brand as a traitor. Perhaps he could blame the explosives for being too powerful.

As the sound of sirens approached, Jiro took out a cigarette, and picked up a piece of burning timber to light it. Then he walked away.

As Sean followed Fa's directions, he noticed how quiet Meko had become. "What's on your mind, darlin'?"

"Nothing." When he looked at her, she made a little face. "Do you really trust that man?"

"Not as far as I could throw him, which might be a half inch at most." He checked the alleyway, then led her to the third door.

" 'South Sea Creations,' " she translated the small Chinese sign. "Probably a garment factory."

A Eurasian man with yellow streaks dyed into his black hair opened the door shortly after Sean knocked. A strong chemical odor wafted out around him. "What do you want?"

"Fa Yun-Liang sent me to speak with Jimmy Yi."

The name worked like magic, and the man immediately bowed. "Come in, come in. This way."

Stacks of boxes and cartons formed the walls of a narrow passage that led through the back of the warehouse. Sean noted that most contained electronics, clearly labeled in English.

Meko covered her nose and mouth with her hand as the chemical odor intensified. "Sean, they're using a lot of lye and other things in here. We shouldn't stay long."

The fumes were making his eyes itch. "We won't."

The Eurasian man led them past a long wooden table where a dozen middle-aged Chinese women were working over small trays of what looked like irregular-shaped white rocks. Each woman used a stained cloth to apply black shoe polish to a handful of stones. Along the wall behind them, an old man dumped more rocks into large sinks filled with cloudy blue water.

Meko caught his arm and gestured for him to bend down. "Sean, those sinks were filled with toilet bowl cleaner," she said, her voice low.

"I know." He urged her along.

"You don't understand. They're soaking chunks of howlite in that cleaner to stain them blue, then rubbing them with shoe polish after to highlight the cracks. And I saw one of those women using a hammer to break up some old Bakelite." At his blank look, she added in a whisper, "They're manufacturing fake turquoise and amber. This is a counterfeit gem operation."

Sean cursed inwardly—no wonder Fa had sent him here—and turned her around. "We'll go."

"You must be Irish," a smooth voice said, startling both of them. "I'm Jimmy Yi."

He had no choice but to turn and hold his hand out to the well-dressed Chinese man. The stylized snake tattoo on Jimmy's forearm clinched it—Sean recognized the mark of a tong assassin when he saw one. "Fa Yun-Liang said you might help me find some missing property."

"You're the one asking about the old swords, right? I'm sorry, but they haven't come into Chinatown." Jimmy gestured toward a large pyramid of boxed DVD players. "Can I interest you in some Sonys instead?"

Sean heard a rustle behind him and shifted his weight from one foot to the other. "We don't watch movies that often."

"Too bad." Jimmy's bright eyes moved to Meko. "Miss Sayura, it's a pleasure to meet a fellow professional."

"Hello." She drew close to Sean.

"Fa didn't recognize you, but my grandmother did—she's the old woman with the oyster cart." Jimmy smiled, showing both rows of small white teeth. "She's interested in increasing her stock; maybe you could give her some advice."

Sean couldn't pinpoint Jimmy's men, but felt them hovering somewhere behind them. After he studied the arrangement of boxes around them, he rested his palm against the small of Meko's back.

"People have been making fake pearls for centuries." Her muscles tensed under his hand. "All she needs are some fish scales and plastic beads."

"Ah, you noticed our ladies' work. We've always done a brisk business in Chinese turquoise, but since those *Jurassic Park* movies came out, the demand for amber has quadrupled." He gestured toward another workroom. "We haven't been able to perfect our emerald process yet. Perhaps you would act as a consultant."

Sean bent down. "Go along with him," he murmured against her hair.

"Sure, I'll take a look," Meko said, her voice tight.

Jimmy led them into the workroom, where industrial shelves held a bewildering array of chemicals and what appeared to be a king's ransom in emeralds filled several plastic basins on a table. Meko went over, picked up one beautifully faceted gem, and held it up to the light.

"Well? The color is excellent, you'll agree."

Sean moved until his back was against one shelf, and turned to one side so he could watch Jimmy and the outside warehouse.

"The color is flawless," she said, lowering the gem to sort through the others. "As are all of these. You haven't worked with emeralds very long, have you?"

"No." Jimmy rounded the table. "Why?"

The Eurasian man and the teenager in the leather jacket from Grant Avenue appeared just outside the door. When Sean saw that both were armed, he casually reached back and took two containers from the shelf behind him.

"Natural emeralds are almost never flawless. Most dealers regard flaws and inclusions from the matrix as an indication that the stone is natural." She lifted her hand from the box and rubbed her fingertips together. "Using oil for coloring leaves a telltale residue, as well."

"I see."

"Most emeralds are so unstable they can't be used for jewelry. They disintegrate too easily." She picked up a huge stone and smashed it against the table, then held the intact gem for Jimmy to see. "Your emeralds are too hard, Mr. Yi. What did you use to make these? Epoxy?"

Sean coughed, using the sound to cover the popping sound the containers made as he opened them.

Jimmy's mouth thinned. "What would you suggest as a replacement?"

"You use beryl and a little chromium to form the stones." She tossed the fake jewel back in with the others. "Suspend it in a mixture of lithium oxide, molybdenum oxide, and vanadium oxide solvent, and you'll grow your own emeralds."

"We could *grow* them?" Jimmy's avid gaze dropped to the basin. "Like flowers?"

She nodded. "Only takes a year or two."

The furious look on the counterfeiter's face made Sean chuckle. "I think that's enough of a consultation, darlin'. Say good-bye to Mr. Yi. It's time we were on our way."

Jimmy glared, and gestured toward the door. "You may go, but Miss Sayura stays."

Chapter 10

Sean moved back as the two men came in. "No, boyo, I don't think so." He circled around the table, coming up behind Jimmy and catching him by the arms from behind. "Meko, come here."

Jimmy laughed. "My men are armed, Irish."

"Are they?" After he passed the second container to Meko, Sean jammed the open end of one bottle against the counterfeiter's mouth. "Now, you and I know swallowing this drain cleaner might not kill you, but it'll do some damage. Just how attached are you to talking and swallowing solid food, Jimmy?"

Jimmy clamped his lips shut and waved frantically for his men to back away.

"Drop your guns first, boys." Sean watched as the two men placed their weapons on the floor, then retreated. He glanced at Meko. "Get those for me, will you, darlin'?"

"Sure." Meko went over and swiftly retrieved the guns, then placed them in her purse and rejoined him. She lifted the spray bottle of mildew remover. "What should I do with this?"

"Keep it handy." Sean began edging Jimmy toward the door. "It's like mace, only permanent."

He kept the drain cleaner in Jimmy's face as they backed out of the workroom. He paused to give the pyramid of DVD players a solid shove, sending them toppling over between them and Jimmy's men and effectively blocking them off. None of the wide-eyed women in the workroom interfered as Sean dragged Jimmy out to the alley.

Once outside, Sean tossed the bottle into a nearby Dumpster and thrust the counterfeiter up against the wall. "You're done with us. Do we understand each other?"

The man's lips peeled back in a snarl. "If I don't kill you, Fa will."

"Take a nap first." Sean rammed his head back against the wall, then let him drop.

Meko discarded the spray bottle as they ran from the alley. "We'd better get out of here."

"Not yet." Sean scanned the street, then flagged down a cab. "I'm sending you back to the motel."

"You are *not*." She planted her hands on her hips. "I want my Rolex back."

"They know who you are." Sean scowled down at her. "It's too dangerous."

"Tough." She pushed him toward the cab. "Come on, I don't feel like walking all that way again."

When they entered the bathhouse this time, the central pool room was completely deserted.

"Stay here." He strode back to the door leading to Fa's private pool room.

Meko had no intention of letting Sean out of her sight. After checking to make sure no one was left in the bathhouse, she went to Fa's room and opened the door.

Sean was standing hip-deep in the churning cold-water pool, his arms locked as he held Fa's head under the surface.

"Sean!"

"Give me a minute, darlin'." As he jerked the sputtering importer up by the hair, he bent over. "One more time, you can of piss. Where are the swords now?"

"I don't know. I *don't!*" Fa screamed the last word, then choked out more water. "Takeshi hired two of my men to take them from New Orleans. As soon as they got here, I sent them to Nine Dragon. That's the last I saw of them."

"I know your kind, Fa. You didn't deliver those blades right away; you kept a couple for yourself. Didn't you?" When he didn't respond, Sean dunked him again, then yanked his head up. "Where are the blades now? How many did you steal from Takeshi?"

When he could speak, Fa shouted, "One, only one! And I sold it! The rest went to Sayura—and he left the next day for China!"

"There's where the blade in your desk came from, darlin'," Sean told her. "Our friend Fa here stole it from the White Tiger and sold it to Shandian. I'll bet they paid him a little extra, too, to watch out for you. Isn't that right, boyo? Or was it someone else?"

"Jimmy will pay top dollar for her, Irish. So will

the tong." The importer blinked the water from his eyes. "We can split the highest bid, fifty-fifty."

Sean took the pistol from the back of his belt and shoved the end of it into Fa's mouth. "Not if you've got a great big hole in the back of your head, you fat bastard."

"No, Sean." Meko rushed to the edge of the pool. "Don't do this."

"Have you told me everything, Fa?" He cocked the pistol. "Not left out any of the little details?"

The importer nodded frantically.

Sean raised the gun and struck him across the temple, then shoved the unconscious man back against the bench seat in the pool

Meko released a long breath. "You can't leave him there like that, he might fall over into the water and drown."

"I'm not hauling him out." Sean bent down and grabbed something under the surface, then climbed out of the pool. The water level began to descend as the pool drained. "Are you okay?"

"I'm fine." No, she wasn't. "Sean, we didn't find the White Tiger blades the last time we searched my father's house. What if he took them with him?" She thought of Tara's thin, smiling face. "What if they're in China?"

Sean took her hand in his and slipped her Rolex back onto her wrist. Then he pulled her into his arms and held her close. Against her hair, he murmured, "If we have to, we'll go to China. But first we're going back to Nine Dragon and have another look."

*   *   *

Tara woke up in complete darkness, and nearly screamed before she remembered where she was. "Vincent?"

A hand touched her shoulder. "I'm right here."

Tara lifted her head and tested her arms. During the night he'd untied her from the pipe, taken her to a tiny, cramped bathroom, then made a bed for her out of something. As her eyes adjusted to the dark, she saw she was curled up on an old, dusty mattress, with his jacket draped over her. Vincent was sitting up against the wall beside her.

He nodded toward the staircase. "They've been playing cards up there for a couple hours, but keep your voice low."

She crept off the mattress and sat beside him. "Are you a cop? Can you get me out of here?"

"Sort of, and yeah, I will. Soon." He took out a small flashlight and switched it on. "How's the arm?"

She flexed it and grimaced. "It hurts. What does 'sort of a cop' mean?"

"I work for the army." He held the light on her arm and peeled back the makeshift bandage. "When did you have your last tetanus booster?"

"Before school last year." A soldier—but he didn't have one of those awful jarhead haircuts. "Why would the army send someone after me? Are we like bombing Asia or something?"

He grinned. "Not lately. We've been trying to shut down the Chinese tongs operating here in the U.S. You just got caught in the middle, honey." He replaced the bandage and pressed his hand to her forehead. "Are you thirsty?"

She nodded, and he handed her a half-filled plastic bottle of water. "What, no canteen?"

"I'll bring one next time."

Tara crawled off the mattress to sit next to him, and drank half the water before handing it back. "Do you have any chocolate?" When he shook his head, she sighed. "Rats. I would kill for some. Or a hot fudge sundae. A jumbo hot fudge sundae."

"Me too. With pecans and caramel."

"And extra whipped cream." She gazed up at him. "So what's the plan? When do I get out of here?"

"As soon as I figure out a way that won't get us killed. Don't worry, we've got friends listening in." He lifted the edge of his T-shirt, exposing a wire taped to his abdomen. "Now, do you know where Kameko is?"

Tara shook her head. "She called once, but I only got to talk to her for a few seconds. They're blackmailing her? *That's* why they kidnapped me?"

"I'm afraid so. They knew how close you two are."

"That's sick." She hugged her knees with her good arm. "I can't believe this is happening. Kameko is such a sweet person. She doesn't deserve this."

"Neither do you." Vincent slipped his arm around her. "Just hang in here with me for a little longer, and we'll get you both out of this mess."

He had nice brown eyes, Tara thought. The kind that seemed ordinary, until he smiled, and then they lit up from the inside. A small piece of her heart melted before she reminded herself that he was an adult, a secret agent, and way too old for her. "You promise?"

"Yeah." He rubbed his knuckles down her cheek. "I promise."

Nine Dragon would have been more at home in Chinatown than at its prestigious address in the up-scale San Francisco neighborhood where Takeshi Sayura had commissioned it to be built. Designed to resemble one of Emperor Qianlong's palaces, the striking home lay safely guarded behind a ten-foot-high wrought-iron security gate.

Sean parked the Jeep a block away from the house, then helped Meko out and walked with her to the gate. She had been silent since leaving the bathhouse. Now she punched in the security code without a word.

"Talk to me, darlin'."

"I'm all right." She stared at the sixty-foot decorative screen behind the iron fence. Its hand-glazed tiles depicted colorful dragons chasing oversized pearls and snarling at each other. "I just thought I'd said good-bye to this place for the last time."

Thanks to him and her father, she had plenty of reasons to want to. As the gate swung open, he said, "Kameko, if you'd rather wait outside—"

"No." She dragged her attention away from the wall and squared her shoulders. "I know the house better than you, and we have to find those swords."

Seeing the way she had her jaw set made him want to carry her away and never let anything hurt her again. He'd come close to poisoning Jimmy and drowning Fa, just for thinking about putting their filthy hands on her. "You're sure?"

"I'm a lot tougher than you think I am, Sean." She pushed her hair back from her brow. "I didn't panic in Chinatown, did I? Even when it looked like I was about to be sold as a gemologist/slave?"

"Point taken." He took her small hand in his. "Let's get to work."

They had to step around a stack of old mail that had piled up inside the front door from the mail slot.

"My father's groundskeeper must have quit," Meko said as she eyed the pile. "I'd better go through it before we leave."

Together they searched the house from front to back, checking all the rooms, closets, and spaces large enough to accommodate three hundred antique swords. By the time they reached her father's private room at the back of the house, they were both covered with dust.

"We've looked everywhere else. They have to be in here." Meko took a deep breath before she pushed open the heavily carved rosewood doors.

As they stepped into her father's reception room, they left the twenty-first century behind and entered seventeenth-century China. The inlaid marble floor led to a raised platform, where a narrow ramp allowed a visitor to approach an immense dais, decorated with urns for burning incense, bronze figures, and a vertical tablet of inscribed stone. In the center, the Chinese characters for "purity" and "righteousness" hung over an elaborately decorated throne.

The room was, to the last detail, an exact replica of Emperor Qianlong's throne room.

Sean recalled how shocked she had been the last time he'd brought her here. "Did you ever find out if these are the originals?"

"I made some inquiries. The originals are evidently still in China." She trailed her fingers over the inscription on the stone tablet. "It still gives me the creeps, though. What was he thinking, building all this?"

"He wanted a place where he could feel like a king." Sean sat down on the throne for a moment. "Uncomfortable bloody chair. I'd rather have a recliner myself." He waggled his eyebrows at her. "Fetch me a chalice and a turkey leg, wench, and be quick about it."

Meko's pale lips finally curved. "You can fetch them yourself, your majesty. I've got swords to find."

She helped Sean search through the large cabinets lining the walls, then under the platform itself. There was nothing but more dust, and an odd powdery substance that left white marks on her jeans.

"What is this?" she asked, showing him the white powder on her hands.

He gazed around the room, then looked up and identified the source. "Plaster dust. Probably from chiseling out these crosses."

Meko frowned as she studied the decorative reliefs along the moldings and across the ceiling. "Sean, those aren't crosses. They look more like clashing swords."

Sean grabbed one of the heavy reception chairs,

dragged it over to the wall, and climbed on it to have a closer look. The X-shaped carvings had odd symbols etched along each bar. "Hand me your cell phone, Kameko."

"I'm going to go look through that mail," she said after she gave it to him. "Yell if you need me."

Once she'd slipped out of the room, Sean dialed an old number and let it ring five times before hanging up and dialing it again.

Raven answered after the first ring. "Hello, Irish. Want to tell me why you're calling me from a fugitive felon's cell phone?"

"Nice to hear your voice, too, sweetheart." Sean sat down in the chair. "Is the general about?"

"He's briefing someone who has more stars than him. Why weren't you at my wedding, and you still haven't answered question number one."

Up until two months ago, he'd wanted to see Raven's husband's career and life destroyed, but he wouldn't remind her of what an ass he'd been. "I'm helping the lady, and I wasn't presentable. I need your help, girl."

"You're never presentable, but I'll forgive you." The teasing note left her voice. "What can I do?"

He read a series of symbols to her from the carvings. "Punch those into your laptop and see if they correspond with anything in Jian-Shan's inventory."

There was a pause. "That's a match. Give me another." After he recited another series of symbols, Raven's voice sharpened. "And another. Sean, those swords are both from the missing collection. You have to turn them in."

"I don't have the blades, darlin'. I'm working off

a reproduction. Kameko's father definitely had them before he left for China." He let his eyes drift around the room. "Now we only have to figure out where he put them. He sent her a photograph, and a note." He quoted Takeshi's message, which he'd memorized back at the hotel.

"Sounds like a coded message—and you need an update on the situation. Kameko's brothers are here in the U.S. Either they or Shandian snatched the kid. And by coincidence, Shandian's head honchos have started disappearing all over the place. Ju-long last week, and now three of his captains."

"I'm thinking the brothers."

"Me too, but you've got another problem. Picture the largest explosion you've ever seen."

"Okay."

"Now, double it," she said. "That's how Kalen's going to react when he finds out you're involved."

He plowed a hand through his hair. "Then don't tell him, and I'll keep you updated."

"I stopped lying to him when I took the vows, you know. Then again, I owe you for covering my ass when I did." Raven sighed. "This had better be worth it, Irish."

"Last time, sweetheart, I promise." He chuckled at the disgusted sound she made. "Keep the faith and see what you can do with that message Takeshi sent her. I'll be in touch."

After three more hours with no results, Brooke finally summoned a replacement surveillance team and drove back to command with Kinsella.

"Coffee."

She didn't smirk when Kinsella handed her the cup—at least, not on the outside. He *had* volunteered to walk to the bagel shop while she went to work on the computer. She could be gracious about it.

"Thanks." She took a sip and nodded toward the charge listings on her terminal screen. "I pulled the last three years of Kameko Sayura's phone records. This woman barely talks to anyone. All I've got here is her store, a couple of suppliers, the kid, and one long-distance call to a hotel in Tokyo three months ago."

"That was to the ex-husband—he went over for her father's funeral. She didn't." Kinsella took out a notebook. "We checked the store lines. Nothing there but the ordinary business traffic. What are you looking for?"

"A connection to the brothers, a best friend, a boyfriend—some way I can track her down. So far, looks like she has a pretty dull life." *Just like me.* Brooke eyed the bulging envelope in his hands. "What's that?"

"L.A.P.D. tossed her house before putting out the APB. There are her home files—bills, loan papers, car and house title, the usual stuff." Kinsella opened it and dumped the contents on Brooke's desk.

"Gee, thanks." She stood up, then winced as her ribs throbbed. Without thinking, she reached to adjust the torso support brace she still had to wear, and her jacket fell open.

"Jesus Christ." Kinsella came around the desk and pulled her jacket away from her side. "What the fucking hell is this?"

"A brace." Brooke's face burned as she tried to close her jacket, but his big hands were already spread on either side of her abdomen. Which made her think of other ways he could touch her. "Do you mind?"

"Yeah, I do," he said as he carefully probed. Then he dropped his hands, and his voice went low and menacing. "How many were broken?"

She buttoned her jacket. "Six, but they're almost healed. Some tong thugs worked me over on my last op." And that was all she was going to tell him.

A muscle pulsed along his jaw. "You should be on fucking medical leave."

"And your mother should have washed out your mouth with soap a few more times, Agent Kinsella." She turned toward the desk and began sorting through the paperwork. "There's nothing here I can use. Why don't . . . you . . ." she trailed off as she pulled out a small business contract. "Oh, for God's sake, how could I have missed this?"

"What is it?"

"Like everyone else on the planet, she's got a cell phone." She sat down at the computer and accessed the records for the digital service provider listed on the contract. A long page of charges appeared. "Local, long distance, yeah, this is what she uses for most of her calls."

Kinsella picked up the phone and dialed a number. "Grace? Liam Kinsella. I need you to start a trace-and-locate on this number." He recited the number from the contract, then waited a minute. "Thanks." He hung up the phone and leaned over to look at the screen. "She's still using the phone. Signal is coming from San Francisco."

"We need to get to her before she leaves the city." She checked her watch. "It's a six-hour drive."

"The Bureau keeps a plane on standby at LAX," Kinsella told her. "We can be there in an hour. Let's go."

She had thought Sean was speaking with yet another of his informants, but as Meko came back in the room with an armful of mail, she heard the "sweetheart." Granted, Sean used the endearment freely—he'd called that hatchet-faced old woman with the oyster cart "sweetheart"—but it was the affectionate tone with which he said it that made her heart twist.

He said he's not married, but that doesn't mean he's not involved with someone. When he looked up and smiled at her, she decided it was time to find out. "Who was that?"

"An old friend." He came over and took the mail from her. "Anything interesting?"

He was changing the subject on her—again. "Some letters we should look through. What sort of old friend?"

"We've worked together a few times in the past. She's going to see if she can crack that message your father sent you." He gave her a speculative look. "Did you know your brothers are here, in Los Angeles?"

"Jiro and Ichiro?" That sent a shock wave through her, instantly dispelling her jealousy. "My brothers haven't left Japan for years. What are they doing here?"

Sean told her about the Shandian tong leaders disappearing, and how the authorities believed her brothers were responsible.

"Jiro is just like my father, and they were very close. He might be here to take control of the syndicate." She thought of the thin, gentle boy who had spent so much time with her during their childhood. "But not Ichiro. He could never hurt anyone."

"Tell me about them."

She went over to stand before the throne. It was easy to remember her father, imagine him sitting there, passing judgment like a monarch.

"Ichiro was born with a deformity in his leg, which disgusted my father. He couldn't stand to see my brother limp, and when the doctors made it clear he would never be normal, my father sent him away to school. I was only a useless female, invisible to him." She clenched her fists. "It was Jiro whom my father really loved. Jiro was fast and strong, and he knew how to make other boys do whatever he wanted." She glanced back at Sean. "My father admired that above everything."

"Why would your brothers come here together?"

"As eldest, Ichiro inherited the bulk of my father's estate. Jiro is probably using him to get access to my father's accounts, so he can regain control of the syndicate." She turned her back on the throne and returned to him, taking a handful of the mail. "Ichiro would never refuse him anything. He is a very gentle person, and avoids conflict."

Like her, he started flipping through the envelopes. "How much did your father leave to you?"

"Nothing." At his incredulous look, she lifted her shoulders. "My father didn't believe women should handle money themselves. That's a husband's privilege. After I divorced Nick, he disowned me."

Sean's eyes narrowed. "But he knew your ex-husband was a gambler."

"It didn't matter. Even a gambling addict like Nick ranked higher with my father than his useless daughter." If it hadn't been so sad, she might have laughed. "My father wasn't like American dads, Sean. He never came to my school award ceremonies, he never celebrated my birthday, he rarely even acknowledged my presence." She felt the bitterness gnawing at her again. All she had ever wanted was the one thing he denied her—his love. "The only time he had any use for me was when I got married. He thought Nick and I should have children right away. He was looking forward to having many grandsons."

"It's why you became so independent," he guessed. "To show him you weren't just another of his commodities."

"Yes. And when I demonstrated how well I could do on my own, without Nick or him, my father disowned me."

"But he wrote to you before he died. Everyone seems to think he told you where the swords are."

"That's the part I don't understand—my father would never have told me that kind of thing. Not in a million years." She picked one envelope out and set the rest aside. "This is from an attorney." She opened the letter, which detailed the final closing costs that had been paid on Takeshi's behalf. "It looks like my father bought some property, right before he left for China. No address, though."

"Does it show who the realtor was?" When she nodded, Sean took out the cell phone. "Give me the name."

He called Information, then the number for the realtor. "Mr. Steinbergen? Sean Delaney, Internal Revenue Service. I'm performing an estate audit for Takeshi Sayura, a former client of yours. Yes, a real shame. I understand you sold property to him just before his death—would you be so kind as to give me the address?" He listened for another moment, then thanked the realtor and ended the call. "He bought a vacation home up north, near Yosemite. Right near the trails going into the park. The realtor called it a hiker's dream cabin."

Meko frowned. "My father never took vacations, and he hated to walk out to the *car*."

"*Kisama!*" A thin, white-haired man came into the room, brandishing a wooden garden rake like a club. "*Bukkoroshite yoru zo!*"

Meko hardly recognized the old, stooped man from the brief glance she'd gotten during her one trip with Tara to Nine Dragon. She stepped between him and Sean and bowed. "*Daijoubu, Xun-san.*"

"*Ojousan?*" The wooden rake fell to the marble floor with a clatter. "*Gomen nasai—I—I* did not know it was you."

"*Do itashimashite.*" She bowed, then made the proper introductions. "This is my friend, Sean Delaney. Sean, this is Xun, my father's caretaker."

"*Kon'nichiwa*." Sean returned Xun's bow.

"It is my honor to meet you, Delaney-san." The old man inspected Kameko. "You real American now, eh, *ojousan*? Master not recognize you."

She wondered if anyone had even bothered to tell him. "I don't think he would, Xun, but my father is dead." She touched the sleeve of his black robe.

The gardener took her hands in his. "They send man here, tell me. I burn joss and pray for his spirit." He sighed. "Now maybe he find kingdom in heaven."

"I hope so, too." Surprisingly, that was the truth. Her father had caused her a great deal of pain, but she had never wished him to suffer in return. Maybe that was the main reason why he had never liked her—because she refused to retaliate.

"Come." He picked up his rake. "You not see garden in long time—I show you."

As they followed the old man out through the back of the house, Sean nodded at the blazing white star on the back of his robe. "You keep staring at that."

"It was my father's favorite robe." She rubbed her arms with her hands. "It kind of gives me the creeps to see him wearing it."

"Maybe it's his way of remembering him." Sean considered the old man for a moment. "If Xun was here when the swords were delivered, he might know where they went from here."

"I'll ask him." She was taken aback when they stepped outside onto the serpentine mosaic stone path leading to Xun's pride and joy. "Lord, I'd forgotten how beautiful it is."

The path was shaded by plum and peach trees that her father had imported from China, but the oleander and pomegranate were new.

"This *Suzhou-way* garden," Xun told Sean. "Not change since Ming dynasty in China. Some tend garden one hundred year before let other people see."

"I'm glad we don't have to wait." Sean admired a row of banana plants that had sprouted tiny new, green bunches of fruit.

The walled garden stretched out for more than an acre, the grounds showing signs of scrupulous maintenance.

"My *shan shui* take *qi* from water, stone, flower, man," Xun explained as he gestured to the four corners of the garden. "Always change. Never same any day."

Unlike her father, who preferred to display his dominance over others, the old gardener had managed to convey the symbolic importance of harmony through the duality of nature—the ever-changing and the unchanging.

Sean bent to sniff a fragrant froth of jasmine framing a large, oddly-shaped standing stone. "What do the rocks mean?"

"They represent the skeleton of the world, and how something as soft as water can wear down the hardest rock," Meko told him. "These Taihu stones are the most prized of all Chinese garden sculptures, though, so that's probably why my father imported them from Lake Tai." She saw a new addition to the garden statuary, and frowned. Two green stone dragons were fighting over a silvery gazing sphere—not something she would have thought appealed to her father. "Xun, where did that come from?"

The gardener eyed the statue and sniffed. "Your brothers send from Japan for Master's birthday. He say his favorite."

Fragile orchid vines blooming with large, waxy flowers clung to a sturdy bamboo *qiào* bridge over a tiny reflecting pool.

"You still keep your fish," Meko said as she looked over the railing at the enormous brightly colored koi.

"Fish keep me," the old man muttered as he produced a handful of pellets and scattered them on the surface of the water.

"Xun-san, I need your help. My father had a large shipment of swords delivered here. I have to find them. Do you know where they are?"

His brow wrinkled. "I remember. They come late one night, bring in many boxes. Master say his treasure. They gone next day."

She exchanged a glance with Sean. "Did he take them with him to China?"

"No fit in suitcase." The gardener chuckled at his own joke, then sobered and added in Japanese, "You should leave this *hakujin* and go to your brothers, little one. They will help you find your father's treasure." He crossed the bridge and disappeared into the bamboo.

"Xun, wait." Sean followed him, then emerged a moment later. "He's gone."

Meko sighed. "He's still got an excellent disappearing act."

She went back in to finish going through the mail, but Sean took her arm and turned her around. "Come on, we have to go."

"What's wrong?"

He nodded toward the front of the house. "We've got company."

She glanced back at the reception room. "But my cell phone—I need to get it."

He shook his head and urged her toward the garden. "That's probably what they used to track us down. Come on."

Chapter 11

Kinsella finished his sweep of the grounds and met Brooke outside Emperor Qianlong's room. "Nice garden out back, but no one's home. You find anything?"

"A bunch of mail and some expensive Chinese antiques." She showed him the cell phone. "And this."

"Shit."

"My sentiments, exactly." She walked back toward the front of the house. "They went through this place looking for something—all the closet doors were left open, and you can still see their handprints in the dust on the furniture."

"They?" Kinsella's brows knitted. "I thought it was just the woman."

"The handprints come in two sizes—small and large. She's either got a very big girlfriend, or a man with her." Brooke rolled her shoulders, trying to ease the tension out of them. "If they found the swords, they're on their way back to Los Angeles to make a deal for the kid. But if they didn't, where would they go?"

"Let me see the phone." Kinsella examined it, then pressed a button and held it to his ear. After a few seconds, he said, "Hello, who's this? Mr. Steinbergen, Special Agent Kinsella with the FBI. We're trying to trace a call that came into your office this morning—did anyone phone you regarding a Takeshi Sayura?" He listened for a moment. "I see. No, sir, no problem with releasing that information. May I have the man's name, and the address?" He took out his notepad and wrote a few lines.

Brooke came over to read what he'd written, saw the name "Sean Delaney" and smothered a groan. *Not him again.*

Kinsella ended the call. "Realtor named Steinbergen. He said an IRS auditor named Sean Delaney called him to get the address of a cabin in Yosemite that Takeshi Sayura bought a few months ago." He studied her face. "You know this Delaney guy?"

"I think he's one of her old boyfriends." She didn't like lying to him, but admitting that an ex-CID officer was involved in a kidnapping and extortion case would only throw gasoline on the fire. "If they're heading up north, we'd better get moving."

"I'm not playing Batman and Robin so we can chase all over the state after them." Kinsella checked his watch and took out his own cell phone. "Time I brought the task force in on this."

"What task force?" At his ironic look, Brooke clenched her teeth. "In case you've forgotten, this is *my* operation. If I need more rent-a-goons, I'll requisition them myself."

"We've got an unknown involved now with this Delaney character, the prime suspect is all over the place, and you've got to pull your agent and the kid out in L.A. soon. Even if you req' a whole platoon of your spy grunts, you've got to brief them. My men are already on the job." He held up a hand when she would have responded. "You're spread too thin and you know it." His mouth curled. "But I'll make sure you get credit for the takedown."

"Don't start a pissing contest with me, Kinsella."

Unbelievably, he laughed. "You're not exactly equipped for one, Captain."

"Shut up." Furious for rising to the bait, she turned her back on him. Then Kinsella's heavy body plowed into her, driving the breath from her lungs and knocking her to the floor.

Her ribs screamed as she rolled out from under him before his full weight pinned her, but she ignored the pain and drove her arm into his face, feeling a surge of primitive pleasure as her elbow connected with his jaw and snapped his head back.

"Bastard." She tried to lever herself up on her knees, but he caught her jacket and yanked her back down beside him. "Let go—"

Automatic gunfire smashed through the windows overhead and sent a deadly shower of shattered glass over both of them.

"Stay the fuck down." Kinsella jerked her against him and covered both their faces with one arm while he unholstered his weapon with his free hand. "Are you carrying?"

The shots ceased.

"Yeah." Brooke reached into her jacket for her service revolver. "How many?"

"I saw two." He started to rise, then ducked down and covered them both again when a second spread of shots finished destroying the windows. "Machine guns, ski masks, on motorcycles."

"Street tong, probably teenagers." She shook the fragments of glass from her face and pointed toward the front door. "Cover me."

As soon as she was ready to move, Kinsella rose and returned fire. Brooke used the time to run, crouched over, to the door and press herself against the wall beside it. A third volley of machine-gun fire drove Kinsella back down to the floor, where he inched over to the window and stood up just out of sight.

"Go, Brooke," he said as he turned and started shooting through the window.

Brooke shoved open the door but stayed behind the wall, out of the line of fire. No more machine-gun fire erupted, but she heard two motorcycle engines being gunned. Quickly she darted across the door's threshold to the other wall, and saw the motorcycles heading down the drive toward the street. "They're taking off."

She ran out, shooting at the tires of the motorcycles, but they were already outside the walls and on the street. By the time she and Kinsella got to the gate, they were gone.

"I think we just lost that pissing contest, Captain," he muttered.

"Yeah." She brushed some shards from her sleeve. "But the question is, who won?"

Conor had tried a dozen times to find a way past the guards, but they spelled each other, and they were paranoid enough to keep checking on him and the girl at least once an hour.

Which had forced him to get creative.

"No way, I won't fit in there," Tara whispered as she stared at the doors to the dumbwaiter.

"I've roaches in my apartment bigger than you," Conor murmured back. He'd managed to lever up the door with a broom handle, and while the shaft was narrow, the lift still worked. "We'll wait until they bring down the food—that's when they'll go to eat upstairs—then we can split this egg roll stand."

"How will you get out?"

"I'm going to walk up and tell them I need some air. I'll bundle up some rags next to the pipe and cover them with my jacket; they'll think that's you." He pointed to the ceiling. "When you get out on the first floor, go down the hall to your left. There's a fire exit at the end, and I'll be waiting on the other side for you."

"Okay." She shivered and nestled closer to him. "Vincent, I know I said I could handle this and all, but I'm . . . I'm really scared."

"Me too, honey." Conor ran his hand over her short, fine hair. "Hang in with me, okay? A little bit longer, then we'll be home free. And I'm taking you out for the biggest hot fudge sundae you've ever had in your life. My treat." The stairwell door opened. "Grab some pipe, here come Abbott and Costello."

Tara immediately hugged the pipe, while Conor arranged the chains to make it appear as though she was still bound to it.

The tall, cadaverous guard scowled at Tara and shoved the box of food at Conor. "She trouble?"

"Not anymore." He produced a faint smirk as he thought of how much he was going to enjoy personally tossing the Stickman behind bars. By way of the prison infirmary. "Any word on when we can do her?"

"No." The Stickman went over and pulled Tara's head back by her hair. "You be good now, eh?"

Tara bit her bottom lip, tears of pain springing into her eyes, then she nodded quickly.

"No more fight?" He snickered and released her, then climbed the stair. Halfway up, he turned and said to Conor, "Watch her. She crazy."

Tara nearly bolted from the pipe as soon as the stairwell door closed. "He cuts me, kidnaps me, and beats me and *I'm* crazy? *God*, I hate that guy."

"He'll have plenty of time to comb his hair in the penitentiary." Conor unwrapped the chain and helped her to her feet. "Ready to give this joyride a whirl?"

Tara never had the chance to reply. The staccato sounds of heavy gunfire echoed overhead, and several bullets punched through the stairwell door.

"Move." Conor hustled her over to the dumbwaiter, pushed up the sliding access panel, and boosted her through the opening onto the lift cabinet. "I'll stop it at the first floor. When it stops, climb out and find an exit, any exit, and get out of here."

She panicked and reached out to him. "I can't leave you."

"I'll be right behind you, honey." He caught her hand and pressed it to his mouth, then pushed her back and slid the door down.

The lights flickered, then dimmed. He punched the lift control, but nothing happened.

"Piece of shit," he muttered under his breath, pushing it over and over, praying a breaker hadn't blown.

Someone started bouncing into the stairwell door, trying to force it open. Bullets whined off metal, and the deadbolt blew apart. He reached under his shirt, ripped the wire off his chest, and threw it behind the pipe before moving quickly away from the dumbwaiter.

A group of masked men armed with machine guns barreled in and climbed down, one of them shouting at him in Japanese.

Let them think she escaped hours ago. They'll do me and leave. Conor didn't want to die, but they had him hemmed in and outgunned. He slipped a hand into his jacket and curled his fingers around his pocketknife. *I can still take a couple with me.* "How are you, boys? Having a party tonight?"

One of them laughed and stepped forward to pat him on the shoulder. Conor drew out his blade and pressed it against the man's heart.

"Put that away," the man whispered, then slid up his mask.

Conor rammed the tip in a little harder. "What the fuck are you doing here?"

"Saving your ass," Nick muttered back. Then in loud Japanese he called out, "This is my American friend, Vinnie. He's been taking care of the girl for us."

"I don't see any girl," one of the other men snarled.

Nick scanned the room, and his smile faltered. "Where is she?"

"I'm here." Tara climbed out of the dumbwaiter shaft. "Don't shoot him. I'm right here."

Two of the men grabbed her and hauled her over in front of Conor. He tried to catch her gaze, but she was intent on Nick. And then it hit him—she didn't understand Japanese. She thought he was in danger.

Tara had climbed out of the dumbwaiter to *protect* him.

Somehow he had to stop her from blowing his cover. "Kid, keep your mouth shut."

She ignored him. "You can't kill Vincent," she told Nick, her voice flat. "He's a government agent and he's wearing a wire. His people will be here any second."

One of the men stepped forward and jerked up Conor's shirt, revealing his bare chest.

"I don't see any wire, kid. A government agent? Is *that* what he told you?" Nick rolled his eyes at the rest of the men. "Vinnie, you got to stop making up all these stories. I can't keep them straight."

Conor forced a laugh. "Yeah, well, it kept her quiet and cooperative until you got here."

Tara shook her head. "You're lying. You were

helping me escape." All the color drained from her face when Nick handed him a gun. "Vincent?"

"Sorry, kid. Just doing my job." He leveled the pistol at Tara. "Nick, tie her hands. She's got a mean right."

"You creep!" Before Nick could grab her, she dodged his hands and scrambled around the other men. Conor swore and went after her, catching her by the waist before she got halfway to the top of the stair.

"Somebody hand me that rope," he snarled as he carried her down. Tara fought wildly, kicking and shrieking until he clamped a hand over her mouth and jerked her up to his eye level. "Shut up, or I'll knock you out."

She sank her teeth into his hand, screaming again as he jerked it away.

"Feisty little thing," Nick said as he came up and stuffed a handkerchief into Tara's open mouth. He helped hold her squirming body while Conor quickly bound her wrists behind her back, then flung her over his shoulder.

She kept struggling as he carried her from the basement to the van waiting in front of the building. As they slid the side door open, she drove her foot into his belly, and Conor nearly dropped her. He pulled her down in front of him and cradled her face.

"Remember what I promised you, Tara," he said, hoping that would be enough to reassure her. Then he tossed her inside the van and climbed in after her.

"According to the map, the turn should be just up ahead, on the left," Kameko said.

Sean eyed the sturdy wall of majestic sequoias

lining each side of the road, and slowed down when he spotted a lone mailbox near the shoulder. Beside it, a dirt road led off the highway and disappeared into the redwood forest. "Have you ever been in the Sierras?"

Meko shook her head. "I kept meaning to take a drive up here when I was younger, but something always came up." She caught the door handle as the Jeep bounced on the road's uneven surface. "The swords have to be here. I can't imagine my father *wanting* to live in the middle of the woodlands."

The tree line parted to reveal a small meadow with a substantial A-frame cabin built on one side. Sean drove up and parked in front of the home, which had comfortably silvered wood siding, a natural stone chimney, and a glassed-in loft on the second floor.

"Pretty place." Sean climbed out of the Jeep and got the sacks of groceries they had picked up after leaving San Francisco. He eyed the satellite dish on the roof. "Not what I'd call roughing it, exactly."

In the distance behind the cabin, Meko saw two huge waterfalls, one of which was still frozen from the winter months. "I think I'm in love." Then, at his quick glance, she ducked her head. "I mean, with the mountains and the scenery."

Sean went to the front door, knocked, and waited for a moment. Then he set down the bags and felt along the frame. "No spare key." He removed a thin strip of metal from his pocket. "Don't watch, darlin', and you won't be an accessory."

He picked the lock quickly and walked inside. The interior was cold, but a pile of cut logs sat next to the open fireplace. Sturdy golden oak furnishings and a sophisticated interior design with hunter green, chocolate, and snowy white accents offered a warm enough welcome. He saw a private deck outside the back picture windows, complete with grill and patio furniture for entertaining.

Meko had already gone exploring and discovered the kitchen. "Sean, come in here. You're not going to believe this."

He joined her in front of an open cabinet. Nonperishable food filled every shelf. Modern appliances sat waiting to be used, along with a wood-burning stove and a portable generator for winter months when the electricity would become unreliable.

"Microwave, dishwasher, a packed freezer." She picked up a package of dry noodles in an Oriental-labeled package. "And these are all my father's favorite foods." She glanced up at him. "What do you think?"

Sean rubbed the back of his neck. "Either he got bitten by the hiking bug or he planned to use this place as a retreat."

"A hideout, you mean." She slammed the cabinet door shut. "Why would my father need to hide out in the mountains? What was he planning to do?" Whatever it was couldn't be done in the city, or he would have never left his beloved Nine Dragon. The very existence of this cabin troubled her deeply, but the possible reasons her father bought it frightened her even more.

"We'll find out." Sean put a hand on her shoulder. "You have to stop worrying so much."

She nodded. "I know. I'm sorry. It's just, every

time I think I understand what's going on, something changes and I'm lost all over again."

"I know the feeling." He drew her into his arms. "I've been trying to get a handle on you for days."

"I'm easy," she said, then winced. "I mean, I'm not difficult to understand."

"Then I must be thick in the head." He filtered his fingers through her hair. "Or I'm lost in you."

Why his touch made her want to purr like a cat, she didn't know. Maybe because she'd never been comforted and aroused at the same time. "I don't know what you mean."

"Let me show you." He tilted her face up to his.

His voice struck a chord deep inside her, but it was the touch of his mouth on hers that liquefied her bones. The way he kissed her ignited a slow, heavy burn under her skin, flooding her with heat until she forgot all the reasons to keep a safe distance and pressed herself against him.

"There, right there," he murmured against her lips, easing one of his long thighs between hers. "You can feel it now."

She could—the throbbing emptiness between her legs, the swollen ache in her breasts. Was it like this for him? She slid her hand down between them, gliding it over the thick ridge beneath his zipper. Just touching him like this made her go wet. She wanted to tear her clothes apart so he could caress her breasts and feel how ready she was for him. She wanted to cradle him with her thighs and take the hard thrust of his stiff penis into her body, over and over again. One time hadn't been enough, would never be enough. She could spend a week in bed with him, right here, right now—

Tara doesn't have a week.

She must have said the words, because Sean lifted his head and reluctantly released her. "Let me light the fire and turn up the hot-water heater. Then we'll start looking for the blades."

She went still, appalled at how she'd lost control and how quickly he'd regained it. Then she saw his hand tremble as he dragged it through his hair, and the scalding heat in the look he gave her.

He wants me as much as I want him. That's enough, for now.

Moving away from him, she took a deep breath. "Yes. Good idea."

The army cryptographer handed Brooke a report. "We scrambled recovery as soon as we heard the first shots over the receiver, Captain. By the time our first team got here, they were gone."

"I should have pulled them out yesterday," Brooke said as she bent down to pick up the ruined wire Conor had hidden behind the basement pipe.

"Perry wouldn't have ditched it unless he thought his cover was compromised," the officer said. "We didn't find any blood, so there's still a chance."

Not for Conor. "Thank you, Lieutenant." She went over to the cops working the scene to get an update.

"Couple of kids across the street said they saw a white guy carry a young girl out over his shoulder," a patrolman told Brooke. "Climbed into a van with about eight Asian males, took off. We're working on getting a license, but this time of night, in this kind of neighborhood . . ." He shook his head.

"I called L.A. Medical," Kinsella said as he joined them. "Neither of the guards made it." He took the wire from Brooke. "What are your man's orders for a total blow?"

"He goes last option and gets the kid out. Nothing else." She wasn't going to hang around so he could grind her face in it, so she left the basement and spoke to the detective in charge of the scene. Then she went and sat at the console in the van. She should have been typing up her prelim report, but all she could do was stare at the computer screen and wonder how she could have prevented this disaster.

"Captain." Kinsella climbed in through the back and slammed the doors. "We need to talk."

"Later. I have reports to file with Washington." She began typing blindly.

"Fuck the reports." He spun her chair around. "What's the last option? What's Perry going to do?"

"His duty."

His eyes narrowed, then his expression changed. "Come on, Brooke. Tell me."

"When he sees a window, he'll get the kid out. He does it by using himself as a distraction. He's going to deliberately blow his cover." She dragged in air. "Con Perry is one of the best agents I know, and he shouldn't have to die because I screwed up."

He looked up at the ceiling liner for a moment. "You knew this might happen. So did he."

"I was his backup. If I hadn't been in San Francisco, I'd have been here for him." She was not going to cry. Not when she was safe and Conor was out there somewhere, preparing to commit suicide to protect Tara Jones. "I can't follow up on the Yosemite connection now. I've got to try to find them."

"I'll send a couple of my men up north." When she would have replied, he held up a hand. "You're overextended as it is, and they can take Kameko and this Delaney character into custody as well as you can."

Suddenly it was just easier to agree. "All right, fine."

"Since the guards were Shandian tong, I'm betting they were hit by the Sayura. I've got names of some local informants who might help us nail down who." He pulled out his notepad, then glared at her. "You are done sulking, aren't you?"

"I don't sulk." She got up, went to the driver's seat, and started the engine. She missed the grin of satisfaction on Kinsella's face as he moved up to join her.

The lieutenant who had briefed her jogged up to the driver's side window. "Before you take off, Captain, a message came in for you from Washington." He handed her a fax, then saluted and walked back to the tenement.

Brooke read the brief communiqué and crumpled it in her fist.

"What is it?"

"Change of plans," she said, reversing out onto the street. "We're meeting with General Grady downtown in one hour."

Chapter 12

They started at opposite ends of the house, with Sean working on the ground floor and Meko searching the loft. She was surprised again by how large the cabin was. Four guest rooms and two baths had been prepared, in addition to the master suite on the second floor. There were televisions and entertainment units in every room, and a mini bar at the back of the master suite. All the comforts someone would need to entertain at home.

"But this wasn't his home." Meko turned around and saw nothing of her father's touch in any of the furnishings. It was as if he had bought it intact from a previous occupant—which made her wonder exactly who were the previous owners.

She found no evidence of the swords, and thought once more about her father's trip to China. Xun had said the swords had disappeared from Nine Dragon overnight. If Takeshi had taken them with him overseas, she and Sean might never find them. Even if they did, they would almost certainly never get them back in time to save Tara.

If we ask for more time, will they say no? Will they kill her?

Her thoughts drove her back downstairs, where she saw Sean kneeling in front of a short, wide storage chest near the fireplace. "Did you find them?"

"The swords? No. Jim, Jack, and José, yes," he said, standing to reveal a full array of liquor bottles. "Your father was planning on company."

"Maybe he meant to drink it himself."

Sean shook his head. "A hard-drinking man is pretty faithful to one type of poison, darlin'." He bent to take out a bottle of Irish whiskey. "This is more what you stock for a big party."

He wanted a drink. She could hear it in his voice, see it in the loving way he held the bottle. It made her stomach clench. She didn't want him to drink, because if Sean got drunk, she was on her own—and she needed him now more than ever. At the same time, seeing the way he looked at the liquor made her furious.

She could never compete with what that bottle gave him—no woman could.

"I found some boxes in one of the guest bedrooms," he was telling her. "Looks to me like all of your father's financial records."

"We can take them with us." She glanced outside. If they left now, she could get him away from the whiskey—but then, he could stop at any liquor store and simply buy his own bottle. Still, she could try. "Can we drive back to San Francisco tonight?"

He set the bottle down on top of the storage chest. "No, we should stay here tonight. I'll need you to help me go through the receipts and all, see if there's anything you recognize as out of the ordinary. Then we can get some sleep, start fresh tomorrow."

"Get drunk, you mean," she muttered under her breath.

He frowned. "What did you say?"

"Never mind." She went to the door. "I need some fresh air. I think I'll go for a walk."

"I'll go with you."

"No, that's okay." She paused before going out, but didn't look back at him. "I need a few minutes alone. Please, Sean."

Meko followed the path from the front door to the stack of cordwood at the side of the cabin. She looked around for an old-fashioned ax stuck in a tree stump, then noticed a gas-powered chain saw hung on the wall above the woodpile. *So much for getting Sean to take off his shirt and chop some wood for me.*

The path continued on into the black oak trees framing the back of the cabin, and she decided to follow it. Anything to get her away from her father's mysterious hideout and Sean Delaney.

The smell of pine and cedar filled her nose as she wandered into the woods. Three-petaled white mariposa lilies and bolder, yellow mule ears speckled the carpet of dried pine needles and oak leaves, while squirrels and birds went about their noisy end-of-the-day business overhead. Despite the animal chatter, the air seemed very still, as if the forest were holding its breath.

I'd better turn around and head back before some bear jumps out and attacks me. Yet as she turned, the sound of moving water caught her ear, and she hesitated. *Well, maybe just another minute.*

Following the sound proved simple—the further she went along the path, the louder it got—and she soon discovered the source, soaring three thousand feet straight up.

"Whoa." She knelt down beside the pool at the base of the mountain, so she could look up at the high, thin waterfall falling from its flat-topped peak. Most of the water was diverted by outcroppings overhead, but a small amount had been siphoned off by a clever series of ducts to supply water to the man-made pool, which had been constructed and landscaped to look as natural as possible. She trailed her fingers in the water, expecting it to be cold, and snatched them back. "How can it be so warm?"

A careful inspection of the area around the pool revealed a solar-powered heating unit and an automatic cleaning and filtering system.

Meko paced around the edge of the pool, tempted by the sparkling depths. She didn't have a towel, she was in the middle of nowhere, and she had never skinny-dipped in her life.

A woman is always modest in her dress, her father had told her during her teen years, when she'd wanted to wear hip-hugger jeans and smock tops, like all American girls. *She does not display her body for the world to look upon. She does not stare into a man's eyes. She does not raise her voice. She is always ready to serve her elders and her family.*

She'd listened to that. She'd *believed* that. And

until this moment she'd unconsciously been trying to be the woman that her father had thought ideal.

That has to stop. Right now.

"I can dry off with my jacket," she muttered as she tugged it off.

Stripping naked in the middle of the forest felt terrifying—and totally liberating. Her father would have beaten her for it. For feeling the sunlight and the mountain air on her bare skin. For the pleasure of swimming in a warm pool in the middle of all this beauty. But Sean wouldn't. Sean would see her like this, and—

Don't even go there.

She stepped to the edge of the pool and dipped her toes in. Whoever had owned the cabin before her father must have had this installed; Takeshi had been like a cat about water. She lowered herself in, astonished to find the pool deep enough for her to be submerged to her shoulders.

This isn't so bad. The warmth sank into her, and she closed her eyes and sighed. *If Sean comes out here, I'll get him to come in with me.*

Then she saw Sean watching her as he moved out from behind a tree.

Brooke got through the briefing without a wobble, although it was hard to meet Kalen Grady's shrewd gaze as she took responsibility for losing Conor and the girl to the syndicate. She was also aware of Raven's eyes shifting between her and Kinsella, who had remained unusually quiet throughout the meeting.

When she finished bringing the general up to

date, she sat-back down and rubbed her damp palms against her skirt. She didn't cower, though. If she was facing discharge or a court-martial for her actions, then she'd go out as she had come in—with dignity.

"Sir," Kinsella said, breaking the interim silence, "Captain Oliver neglected to mention that I insisted that she accompany me to San Francisco. If anyone is to blame for dropping the ball here, it's me."

Brooke opened her mouth, then saw Kinsella give her a shut-up look and closed it, hard enough to make her teeth click.

"I don't think anyone's to blame." Raven gave Kinsella one of her slow, megawatt smiles. "And are you sure you work for the FBI, Liam?"

"Sarah." The general gave his wife his own warning glance before he addressed Kinsella. "Forget accountability for the screwup. What we need to do now is concentrate on recovering Tara safely and getting to Kameko Sayura before she hands the swords over to anyone."

"What about Lieutenant Perry?" Brooke had to ask.

"Con's been in worse situations than this and walked out alive," Raven put in. "If there's a way he can land on his feet, he'll find it."

"General, my task force is assembled and prepared to move in on the syndicate and Shandian," Kinsella said. "We can pull all the ringleaders in for questioning, get most of their goons on weapons charges, and shut down their operations. That will cripple both organizations for at least forty-eight hours."

"I think it's too dangerous to make an open move against either side," Brooke countered. "They get word of a crackdown and they'll clean house. Tara and Conor will be the first to go."

Liam leaned forward, his gaze intent on Brooke's. "All we need is one of them to flip, and we can get them back."

"Or get them killed." She made a cutting gesture. "It's better to find Kameko Sayura and use her to recover them."

The general began to respond, then Raven turned her head and murmured something to her husband. His expression didn't change, but something flickered in his eyes.

"Both of you have valid arguments," Kalen said at last. "We will bring in the FBI task force, but not for another twenty-four hours. Agent Kinsella, see if your people can locate Kameko Sayura without making a splash. Brooke, pull in Kameko's ex-husband, make him earn his pay."

"Yes, sir."

As Brooke left Kalen and Kinsella in her office, Raven caught up with her. "Hey, got a minute?"

She nodded, and followed Raven into the interrogation room. "What's up?"

"I could use some help on a message. I think it's some kind of encryption." She handed Brooke a handwritten note. "Sort of a side project of mine. Think you can do anything with it?"

"I'll run it through the computer." Brooke slipped it in her pocket, then met Raven's canny gaze. "I didn't have to go to San Francisco. Kinsella lied."

"I thought so." The general's wife only grinned.

"Don't worry about it. I'm going to go make Kalen take me somewhere expensive for lunch now. Want anything?"

"No, thank you." Brooke hesitated, then glanced back at the office. "What did you say to him in there?"

"I told him to give you twenty-four hours, or I'd stop eating soda crackers." Raven waved toward the office. "You do need to make peace with the G-man, Brooke. I really think he's on your side. And he's so . . ." she shook her hand as if she had burned it.

"Yeah, I guess he is." She thought of how often she'd wanted to deck Kinsella over the last week. "I'll try to strike a truce."

After Raven went to retrieve her husband, Brooke made her way to the first-floor supply room. She needed a few minutes to walk off her nerves, regain her composure. Then she could get back to the job. And to making peace with the G-man.

Unfortunately, Kinsella stepped in and slammed the door shut behind him. "That was interesting. Do you try to throw away your career at every briefing?"

Resentment made her spine straighten. "I told the truth." She paced from one end of the room to the other. "And I didn't ask you to cover for me."

"Hey, I just took my fair share."

"You *lied* to my *boss*." She stopped and waved at the door. "Would you leave? I can't do this with you right now. I need to cool off."

"Tough." He leaned back against the door. "We're settling this."

"There's nothing to settle." Had Raven sent him in here? Brooke wouldn't put it past her. "We're both on the job. You may even get to use your precious task force. So what are you worried about?"

"I'm not the one who looks ready to punch out the cinder blocks, blondie. All I was trying to do was help."

Hearing him use the hated nickname—the same one Raven had called her back when Brooke had her arrested, then had nearly gotten herself and the general killed—made her snap.

"I don't hide behind a man, Agent Kinsella. I take responsibility for my actions. And I wouldn't ask you for help if I was down bleeding in the street." She wanted to slap the knowing smile off his face, but settled for watching it disappear. "Like I'd *ever* need some sexist jerk like you to pat me on the head and tell me everything's going to be all right."

The skin above his broad cheekbones reddened. "That's enough, Captain."

He was *still* trying to tell her what to do. "I'll decide when it's enough. I *stomped* over plenty of guys exactly like you at the Point." She measured him from nose to toes and back again. "That's what really bothers you, isn't it? You don't want to cover my ass. You just want to grab it."

Kinsella moved so fast she was up against the door and under his hands before she could react. "Enough, Brooke." He jammed his mouth against hers for an instant, then broke it off to catch her fist before it struck his face.

Nervy fear made her heart skip a beat. "See?"

Her chest heaved as she tried to push him off. "This isn't about the job."

"Yeah. You're right. It's not." He forced her arm down and kissed her again, and kept her pinned while he took his time with her.

Superior strength and the advantage of leverage kept Brooke from getting out from under his mouth, but she could bide her time. The next time he raised his head, she would use hers to break his nose. Maul her like some bimbo? Well, she'd show him. She hadn't spent ten years studying martial arts to let some ape overpower her. He was in for a world of pain. Just as soon as he stopped kissing her.

Only he wasn't stopping.

Kinsella went at her with no finesse whatsoever, kissing her like a starving man gorged, using his lips and tongue and teeth in ways Brooke wouldn't have thought possible—or altogether legal.

Anything that feels this good should carry the maximum penalty.

The room spun away as something deep and dark surged to life inside her, and then she was kissing him back, meeting that angry mouth with her own fury, pouring her need into him as much as she was being demolished by his.

A dim sound pounded into her head, and Brooke realized someone was knocking on the door. She wrenched her mouth to one side. Kinsella growled something and tried to kiss her again, but then he heard it, and went still.

"What is it?" she called out, watching the shock register in his eyes. They were both panting as if they'd just run a ten-mile with bivouac packs on.

"Captain," one of the agents said, "you've got a call waiting on line four."

"I'll be right there." She waited until the agent's footsteps retreated, drawing on every ounce of energy she had to push back the shrieking need to put her hands and mouth on him. *You're a commissioned officer in the United States Army. Pull yourself together.* "Are you finished? Or did you want to give me the full frontal?"

"I want you to stop pushing me away," he said, his voice low and furious. "You feel it." He brought her hand up and pressed it under his against his heart, which pounded under her palm like a speeding engine. Then he turned it and pushed it against her own racing heartbeat, and kept his hand over hers. "Fuck, I can't believe this. If I'd known you felt the same before, I would have—" He broke off and shook his head, as if overwhelmed by the thought.

"You're a man, I'm a woman." She shrugged. "No big deal, Kinsella. It happens."

"Don't do that. Not with me." He got in close. "I don't know what the hell this is, but I want more. And so do you. When this is over—"

"I'm scheduled back at the Pentagon, and you can go somewhere and get laid. Take your hands off me." When he did, she sidestepped him and tried to open the door. He shoved it closed with a fist. "I have work to do."

"Me too." He kissed her, hard enough to make her swollen lips sting. "I'm not through with you yet, Captain." He jerked the door open. "Be sure and stick that on your schedule."

Kinsella stalked out.

* * *

"Item number two-six-nine-oh-seven," the officer in charge of the evidence storage said as he placed the long, narrow plastic crate on the worktable. "Tag reads 'sword, Japanese, antique.'" He lifted the hinged lid. "This what you folks wanted?"

Val leaned over and held her breath as she examined the blade. "Yes."

"It was used in a suspected homicide, so it can't be removed from the premises. You can photograph and measure it, but try not to disturb the dried blood on the surface. Put these on before you handle it." The officer handed her two pairs of latex gloves. "If you need anything else, press seven on the wall intercom."

After the officer departed, Valence spread out a thick, soft cloth on the table, while Jian-Shan pulled on a pair of the gloves and lifted the sword from its crate.

"I think this is the sword my father acquired right before I left China," he told Valence. "He called it the star blade."

Val removed the two swords from the case she had brought, and set them on the cloth. "I'll have to unwrap the tang to see, but it appears to be a Naga-toki."

She photographed the sword first, then sat down and carefully unwrapped the fragile leather bindings that formed the hilt. Beneath it, ancient symbols had been carved into the raw, notched end of the blade. She moved the star blade closer to the unwrapped tangs of the other two swords.

The symbols on all three blades were identical.

Val gripped the edge of the table. "She made this one too."

Jian-Shan stood behind her and rested his hands on her tense shoulders. "You sound disappointed."

"I'm afraid, *cher*. All I've ever wanted was to prove that Lady Kameko took over the forge and made these blades for her husband when he went blind." She leaned back against him. "But now when I look at them, I see your father fighting you, and killing your mother. Raven and Kalen almost died for them, too. And now Kameko is out there somewhere, trying to find the rest so she can save that young girl."

"I share your distress, *xia*." He bent down to wrap his arms around her. "Yet the swords themselves were forged with love and honor. Only the men who have coveted them created the misery and evil that follow them."

"You're right, of course." Taking a deep breath, she moved the dragon and phoenix blades to form two sides of a triangle, then finished it by matching the edge marks on the star blade to the other tangs. Some of the markings became whole Mandarin characters, others did not.

She was almost relieved. "This doesn't fit. It's not the key sword." Carefully she replaced the bindings and put the bloodstained blade back into its crate. "Just another dead end."

Her husband frowned. "Dead end? What does that mean, precisely?"

"It's a slang phrase for a street that ends suddenly and doesn't go anywhere. You have to go out the way you came in." She watched his face. "What is it?"

"Raven tells me there is an old man who still lives on the Sayura estate," Jian-Shan said. "I believe I will go and see him tonight."

"I'll go with you."

"Not this time, *xia*." He studied the sword in the plastic crate. "I want to search the grounds first."

"You mean that Lily doesn't need *both* of her parents being arrested for trespassing." Val replaced the lid, then stripped off her gloves. "Do you think he knows what Takeshi did with the third blade?"

"He may have seen or heard something that will help us." He put the other two swords into their case. "Or he may be another dead end."

She knew her husband, and sensed he was holding something back. "What is it, Jian? What's bothering you?"

"I'm not sure. It's simply a feeling." He took her hand in his. "Perhaps I will find the reason for it at Nine Dragon."

He should have stayed in the cabin.

Sean watched Meko swim to the center of the small pool, her narrow back like gleaming alabaster against the dark blue water. He hadn't intended to follow her—he'd meant to have the drink he'd more than earned—but as soon as she left, the whiskey only reminded him of what he had to look forward to after this was over.

He'd had enough drunken, lonely nights to last him forever.

Sean hadn't even realized he was still holding the

whiskey bottle as he trailed her, then stood guard over her. Not until he moved in and it bumped into a tree with a gentle clink. He looked down at the amber liquid that promised warmth, forgetfulness, and the only decent sleep he ever got. Then he looked at the woman in the pool.

He wanted Meko, not the oblivion in the bottle. He also knew he couldn't have both. He tossed the bottle into the brush.

"Are you going to stand there forever?"

He looked up to see her at the edge of the pool, watching him now. There was an odd smile on her face, as if she'd known he would be there. "I don't know."

"Come and join me. The water's beautiful."

Sean was no saint; he couldn't get naked with Meko and not make love to her again. It would only add more complications when it came time to leave her. And she deserved better than him, delicate, proper little thing that she was. He prayed his willpower was better than it had been, and walked down to the edge of the pool. "I'll go back to the house and get you a towel."

"I don't want a towel." Smiling up at him, the delicate, proper little thing clamped both hands around his ankles and pulled him in, fully clothed. When he surfaced, she slid into his arms, laughing with delight. "I want you."

"You're ruining my good intentions." He tried to hold her at arm's length, but she was as slippery as a mermaid, and twice as beautiful. As she wrapped her legs around his, he stifled a groan. "Kameko, sweetheart, you'll only end up regretting this. Like you did in Sonoma."

"I loved what you did to me in Sonoma." She nuzzled his cheek. "I've tried to fight it too, *nagare*, but it doesn't work. Every time you look at me or you touch me, I remember how it felt. I remember what you and I did to each other. I want to be with you again." Her voice dropped to a whisper. "I want to be with you, always."

"Think about that, *a chuisle mo chroí*." He made her look at him. "You know I've got a real problem with the whiskey, and I've never stayed with any woman for very long." He bent to brush his lips over her damp brow. "It's better that you find another man to love you."

Her lips curved. "And you're going to walk away from me now, so I can save myself for that other man?"

It might kill him, but he'd do it for her. "Yeah, I am."

She pulled his head down to hers. "Not a chance."

Meko knew from the moment Sean threw away the untouched whiskey bottle that they would make love. She'd never felt such pleasure, knowing that he had made her his choice. It had given her enough courage to offer herself to him, and even to pull him into the water.

He wasn't lying about his drinking problem, and it was a cause for serious concern. But she knew he was avoiding the truth about his relationships with women. He had loved T'ang Kuei-fei, enough to try and avenge her death. Maybe he drank so much because he was still in love with her.

It doesn't matter, she thought as she kissed him. *I'll take what I can get.*

"*A chuisle mo chroí,*" he breathed against her mouth. "The last time neither of us was thinking straight. I don't want to take advantage of you again."

"Why not? I certainly plan to take advantage of you," she teased as she pressed little kisses against his jaw.

He closed his arms around her. "I think the last of my good intentions just rolled over and died."

"Good." She started unbuttoning his shirt. "They were being a nuisance."

The last rays of sunlight filtered down through the pines, making irregular patches of light and shadow move over them. This time Meko saw the old battle scars she had only felt in Sonoma, small reminders of the dangerous life he had led. Tears stung her eyes as she pressed her lips to the jagged line a knife had left just above his left nipple.

"Who did this to you?" she asked him, her throat so tight that it hurt to speak.

He touched his chest. "A Russian soldier who wanted his tank back."

She pulled off his shirt and slipped her hand around to the twisted scar running along the small of his back. "And this?"

"An Iraqi soldier who didn't like his SCUD launcher being blown to bits." His mouth hitched. "They were all a long time ago, darlin'. Lucky the Irish are hard to kill."

"Oh, Sean." She closed her eyes and rested her forehead against his shoulder. "I can't bear to think of what they've done to you."

"Everything still works fine." He lifted her face to his. "Let me demonstrate."

His mouth moved over her skin, erasing the tears that had spilled from her lashes, then came to brush her lips with soothing, gentle pressure. Warm water swirled against her body as his hands stroked down her back, gathering her in and caressing her at the same time.

The same hot, tight urgency she felt every time he kissed her shot through her limbs, and she reached between them to unbuckle his belt and remove the last barriers between their bodies. The wet leather and denim frustrated her, until Sean backed away and hoisted himself out of the pool.

"Next time you want to dunk me," he said as he worked off his sodden jeans, "ask me to strip for you first."

Her face burned as she watched him undress, but she couldn't look away. She liked seeing the tense lines of his muscles, the way his abdomen rippled as he straightened. She watched the erect shaft of his penis as it strained up from the curly dark hair and heavy weight of his testicles, and an answering ache clenched between her thighs.

She moved to the side, reaching up for him. "Come down here." When he would have slipped in, she nudged him back so that he sat on the edge of the pool. "Like that."

He looked down at her, bemused. "What did you have in mind, darlin'?"

She smiled, positioning herself between his thighs as she took him in her hands.

"You don't have to do this." He traced her lips with a fingertip. "Though I confess, I've had a few fantasies about your mouth and my—" A groan rumbled out of his chest as she licked the round, swollen tip like a cat.

"So have I," she murmured before she took him into her mouth.

She'd heard her brothers talking once about women, and Jiro had claimed that only whores used their mouths on men. Nick had never encouraged her to do anything even remotely adventurous in bed, and as a result Meko had no idea if what she was doing was right. She could only follow her instincts and Sean's reactions as she kissed and licked and sucked his penis. His size made her doubt she could take him completely into her mouth, but she was determined to try, even if it meant a little discomfort.

"You don't have to do this," he said, his voice tight.

She glanced up. "Don't you like it?" Then she took him in her mouth again.

"My head is about to explode, darlin'. And that's not all." His hands sifted through her hair as he drew back out. "But I'll pull out before I come."

"Will you?" She ran her lips down each side of his shaft before delicately licking the ridge beneath the head. "Why?"

Sean made a strangled sound as Meko rested her hands on the tops of his thighs, then slowly pushed her mouth down. She looked up to see his expression, and the new angle allowed her to take more of him. She gradually worked her way down until the tip of her nose touched his belly. The sense of power and delight was so intense that she rubbed herself once against his shin and climaxed right there.

She felt his hands curled tight against her scalp as she moved her head up and down to produce a luxurious, unhurried caress, and then he was thrusting himself deep into her mouth, his penis swelling and hardening even more. The thigh muscles under her hands strained as Sean went rigid, then shuddered.

For you, my love, she thought. It was such a powerful, primal act that tears spilled down her face. *For both of us.*

Reluctantly she took her mouth from him and rested her hot, damp cheek against his thigh. His hand moved over her wet hair in an unsteady caress, before he reached down and lifted her up into his arms.

Suddenly she felt shy. "I wasn't very good, was I?"

"Dreams can't begin to compare with what you just did to me." Sean slid into the pool as he kissed her, licking her swollen lips before pushing his tongue into her mouth to taste himself there. Gently he eased her down until she was floating on her back, her head resting against the side of the pool. He moved around until he was between her thighs. "Now let's see if I can catch up."

Sean supported her with his arms as he used his mouth and fingers on her, but there was nothing tentative about it. He drove her to her first peak within seconds, then kept her there with the merciless skill of his tongue until she screamed from the unbearable pleasure.

"Sean, oh, God," she gasped out the words as she tried to draw him up. "I can't take anymore."

"Easy, love." He turned his head to kiss the inside of her thigh, and allowed her to spiral down into a sweet abyss. "I'm neglecting some other lovely places here, aren't I?" He eased two fingers into her, testing her and stroking her.

"Yes," she whispered, feeling the need begin to build again. "That's where I need you."

He pressed his mouth against her one more time, then stood up and lifted her into his arms. As he lowered her into the warm water, his shaft grazed her, making her hips move urgently against him.

"There," he reached down and fit himself to her, pressing in, filling her by degrees. At the same time, he spread her folds, seating her so that every stroke of his penis rubbed against the hard knot of her clit. "Does that feel better?"

She closed her eyes and let her head fall back. "You're going to kill me."

He put his mouth to her throat. "I'm going to try."

Water rippled around their bodies as he held her bottom with his big hands and thrust slowly into her. She could feel the tension building inside him even as he left a leisurely trail of kisses across her wet breasts. Yet he made love to her as if they had all the time in the world, and this night would last forever.

It might have to, a sad little voice inside her warned.

No. She wouldn't go back to her sterile life and pretend none of this had ever happened. She wouldn't let him go back to his empty nights of whiskey and regret.

Meko wrapped her arms around his neck and her legs around his waist, and pushed herself down on him until he was deep inside her, then held him there. *"Kimi o ai shiteru."*

He went still. He understood what it meant.

"Yes, Sean." When he started to shake his head, she cradled his face between her palms. "I love you."

"Kameko." He groaned her name over and over as he pumped into her, hard and fast. The last of the sunlight shimmered over them as Meko kissed him, and Sean poured himself into her.

Chapter 13

Bypassing the security mechanism at Nine Dragon's front gate would have been simple for Jian-Shan, but he preferred not to be seen on the street. And his wife's last words to him were still echoing in his head.

Don't get caught, cher. I don't think the general wants to explain to the police why a samurai is working undercover for the army.

He scouted the perimeter of the property, then went in over the back wall, using a nylon rope looped over the high branch of an oleander tree. His all-black clothing allowed him to blend in with the shadows, but he was careful to keep his footsteps and movements soundless.

Night-blooming jasmine poured its heavy perfume onto the air, but he detected something artificial beneath it—scented oil. He found the source when he moved up to the large stones placed around the pool and the labyrinth within Takeshi's gardens. At first glance some of them appeared to be on fire, until he spotted the small oil lamps tucked into their crevices.

Why does he light the lamps when there is no one to see them?

He swiftly searched the gardens, checking the various places where the White Tiger swords could possibly be concealed, then used a powerful and highly illegal subsurface radar scanner to be sure they had not been buried beneath the soil. The thought of searching the house tempted him, but his gaze was drawn to the gardener's shack at the far right of the property.

A street that ends suddenly and doesn't go anywhere, Valence had said. *You have to go out the way you came in.* At the time, he couldn't explain to her why that had disturbed him so much. He still couldn't.

Jian-Shan pocketed the scanner and made his way to the shack. The tidy little structure had roughcast walls with bamboo pillar accents, and after a glance through the screened window he slipped inside. Here, too, an oil lamp had been left burning on a small table beside a futon on the floor. The interior walls had been mended in a few places with a type of clay mixed with straw that Jian-Shan had never seen outside Asia. He scratched at the surface of one wall, and found more gray clay beneath. However, a few quick passes with his scanner revealed nothing metallic beneath the surface or under the dirt floor.

The rest of the shack was remarkably bare—a few simple garden tools hung from pegs beside the door, and a sack of organic fertilizer sat tucked in one corner. There was no air-conditioning, and the thin walls afforded only minimal protection from the elements.

Sayura lived in that multimillion-dollar mansion while his servant dwelled in this refugee shack. He looked through the window at the main house. *The old one must be delighted to be able to sleep inside now.*

Yet even that logical conclusion bothered him.

He left the shack and started toward the main house, but the sound of shuffling steps made him draw back behind the twisted trunk of a budding plum tree. From the hesitant, uneven footfalls he judged it to be the arthritic gardener Raven had described. That was confirmed when a hunched-over figure wearing a black robe approached the reflecting pool.

"*Anate ne,*" the old man said, searching in the long square sleeve of his robe before tossing a handful of pellets into the water.

Jian-Shan suspected the pool was full of the gardener's pet fish. Many Asians enjoyed keeping them, especially as they did no damage to their precious gardens.

"There is a little more work to be done, and then she will come home." The gardener knelt down and pulled the hood of his robe back, exposing his white hair and deeply lined face. He reached out toward the surface, his crippled hand trembling. "When she does, my friends, everything will be as it was before. I promise."

The same sense of something being terribly wrong fell over Jian-Shan, and he decided not to approach the old man or attempt a further search. He needed to meditate on the matter, pinpoint exactly what was setting off all his internal alarms.

Following his instincts, he waited until the old man returned to the main house, then slipped out of the garden.

The night came close to lasting forever.

Meko woke in a tangle of sheets, her body still throbbing from the hours she'd spent making love with Sean. She didn't open her eyes right away as she savored the pleasant aches and pains of satisfaction.

We were like a couple of kids.

She rolled over, determined that his face would be the first thing she saw, but found only an empty, cold space. Disappointed, she pulled the sheet to her breasts and sat up.

"Sean?"

A vague memory of him getting out of bed in the early hours came back to her. *Maybe he's been up for a few hours. The man never sleeps anyway.*

She got up and slipped into the robe he had found for her last night, then padded downstairs. A glance at the clock revealed it was almost noon. She didn't smell any coffee, but maybe he had had some trouble with the complicated-looking appliances. If that was the case, she would make it for him, along with the biggest brunch he could handle.

She smiled as she walked into the kitchen. "Good morning."

There was no one to answer her. The coffeemaker sat unused, and the sink was empty of dishes.

Something sank inside her as she turned around, listening to the stillness. "Sean? Where are you?"

Meko jumped as she heard the sound of a car pulling up to the front of the house. Why would he have left? Where had he gone?

She hurried to the front door and stepped outside, ready to scold him for deserting her again.

The Jeep was gone. In its place was an unfamiliar silver sedan, with a black-haired man wearing dark glasses sitting behind the wheel.

Meko clutched the lapels of her robe together and backed up as the man got out of the car.

"Kameko." He started walking toward her.

"Who are you?"

"I know it's been a long time, but"—the man took off his glasses—"don't you recognize your own blood?"

"Jiro?"

He gave her his usual cocky grin. "Live and in person, little sister. All the way from Tokyo."

She looked behind his car and around the cabin, but there was no sign of the Jeep. "What are you doing here?"

"It's too cold for you to be standing out here, dressed like that." Her brother gestured toward the house. "Let's go inside and I'll explain."

She didn't want to let him in, but with Sean gone, it wasn't as if she had a choice. "Yes, of course."

Once inside, she wandered over to one of the sofas and sat down. And immediately got up again. Relaxing was impossible, and the smile on her brother's face made her want to run into the woods and hide. At last she busied herself by placing some small logs on the banked fire.

"This is some place," Jiro said, walking around the front room. "Father must have paid a lot for it."

"How did you find me?" she heard herself ask.

"Ichiro found the paperwork from the realtor at Nine Dragon." Her brother took out a cigarette and lit it. "Since the phone lines were dead, I told him I'd drive up and see if this is where you were hiding."

After she stoked the fire with some additional kindling, she sat back on her heels, then glanced over her shoulder at him. "Why did you and Ichiro come here? To the States, I mean?"

"Ichiro wanted to put some of Father's property up for sale. I came to help him." His smile faded. "Kameko, I have some bad news. The police in Los Angeles contacted us yesterday. They found that girl's body, abandoned near some highway."

All the color went out of the world, and she stumbled to her feet. "They found Tara? Tara's dead?"

"Yes." He came to her and helped steady her. "I've come to take you back."

Conor spent a moment getting himself and his gear ready before he went after Nick.

"I need a minute," he said as he stepped into the restaurant manager's office.

Nick, who was on the phone arguing with someone in Japanese, nodded to the two guards. As soon as they left, Conor reached over, took the phone, and hung it up.

"Hey!" Nick scowled at him. "That was important business."

"So is kidnapping and double homicide." Conor locked the door, then took out his gun. "You want to explain to me why you snatched me and the kid, and handed us over to the Sayura?"

"The word came down to move in and take the girl." Nick was chewing on his nail again, so hard he looked like he was sucking his thumb. "I had to go along with it, but I didn't kill anyone."

"No, you didn't. You just watched." Conor jerked him up out of the chair and slammed him back against a metal filing cabinet. "I'm taking Tara out of here."

"I can't let you—not yet." Nick shook his head frantically. "The boss is on his way over. They think Kameko has the swords and is coming to make the exchange. If she's not here, I'm a dead man."

"I'll light a candle for you." Conor applied an efficient punch to Nick's head, then let him slump to the floor. "Next time I'm in church."

He left Nick locked in the office and went back to the room where they were keeping Tara. She'd started running a fever back in the basement, and by the time they'd arrived here she'd become semi-delirious. He'd untied her and left her to sleep. Once they were clear, he would get her to the nearest hospital. As he went in, he saw a crate propped under an open window, and his jacket lying on the floor.

"Damn, no!" He went to the window and stuck his head out. Tara, her hands still tied behind her back, was already halfway down the alley, running at a quick trot. He swung himself through the window and went after her.

She tried to run as soon as she heard his footsteps, but looking back made her stumble and fall. "No! Leave me alone!"

"Listen to me," he said as he pulled her up and began to untie her hands. "Everything I told you was true. I'm not one of the bad guys. We're getting out of here." He nodded toward the street. "All we need is some wheels."

"You're not one of them?" Her voice rasped out the words. "Then how come that guy knew you? How come he gave you a machine gun?"

He pulled the rope off her wrists. "I work undercover, remember? They're supposed to think I'm one of them." He grabbed her arms before she could swing at him, then heard someone shouting from the restaurant. "Tara, stay behind me." He took out his gun, then swore as she took off toward the end of the alley. "Damn it, kid, wait!"

Shots rang out behind Conor as he chased her. He nearly caught her sleeve when they rounded the corner and emerged onto a busy street. Tara didn't hesitate but ran directly out into traffic, screaming for help as she waved her arms.

"Help me! Please!"

Cars dodged around her but no one stopped, and she was nearly run over by one before Conor could get to her and haul her back to the curb.

"Don't be an idiot!" he shouted at her when she lunged for the street again. "You'll get yourself killed!"

"Bite me!" she yelled back, then kicked him and

wrenched free of his grip. A pedestrian approached, and she ran up to the middle-aged man. "Please, help me!" She pointed at Conor. "That man right there, he kidnapped me!"

"Of course I'll help you, my dear." The man, who was leaning heavily on a cane, lifted his hand. A moment later a black car pulled to the curb.

"No, Tara!" Conor recognized the man from the surveillance photos he'd seen in Washington. "Don't get in that car!"

Ichiro Sayura pulled Tara in front of him like a shield and raised his arm. She looked down at his hand and screamed.

Three shots hit Conor in the chest, propelling him backward until he slammed into a brick wall and fell. As he went down, he saw Sayura force the girl into the black car. Pain made him black out for a few minutes, then he heard a familiar voice call his name.

"Tara?" He blinked, then struggled to get his feet under him.

"Thank you for following procedure, Lieutenant," Brooke pulled him to his feet and, when he would have gone around her, held him against the wall. "But you're not going anywhere."

"Shit, this hurts," Conor gasped out the words, and grimaced as she pulled open his shirt. The Kevlar vest he had strapped on before going after Nick had stopped all three bullets.

"Liam, give me a hand." As the big man with her grabbed Conor's arm, Brooke ripped off the securing straps and removed the armored vest.

Conor glanced down to see deep purple bruises

already blooming over his chest. When he tried to take a deep breath, his lungs filled with fire.

"Ichiro shot me and took Tara." He stopped and peered at the man who was keeping him from sliding back to the ground. "Who are you?"

"Kinsella, from the Bureau." He scanned the street. "Do you know where Sayura's taking the girl?"

"He's going to meet his sister," Conor said. "Nick said he thinks Kameko has the swords now."

Brooke turned toward the diner. "Then we'd better go have a word with our boy Nick."

He'd thought one night would never be enough, but two nights with Kameko had only made it worse. A man could survive a glimpse of paradise, but walking away from it a second time only guaranteed the direction he would take.

The sign above the liquor store/bar marked the road to hell with the welcome words "Open 24 hours."

He pulled into the parking lot and eyed the paperwork on the seat beside him. It had taken him a few hours to piece together from the financial records exactly what the gardener had done with the swords. Then he found Takeshi Sayura's detailed plans of what he intended to do with the Star King, written out like a shopping list.

> *Gain control of the satellite laser system.*
> *Assassinate all leaders who will not join the alliance.*
> *Evacuate members of the alliance from the cities.*

*Destroy key areas within the metropolitan areas if
government does not meet demands.*

The plans, had they been carried out, were
enough to make him sick. He wouldn't subject
Meko to the knowledge that her father had been
fully prepared to murder millions to get what he
wanted.

No, leaving her behind was for the best.

He locked the paperwork in the glove box before
he went into the bar. There was no one inside, except for a short, chubby woman bartender washing
glasses from the night before.

Sean sat down on the stool nearest the sink and
put a twenty on the bar. "Whiskey, Irish, if you have
it. And a phone I can use to make a collect call."

"Bushmills, the breakfast of champions." The
woman's silver-streaked ponytail bounced as she
produced a bottle and poured a healthy shot.
She set that and a cordless phone on the bar in front
of him. "You look a little tired, pal. Been on the road
long?"

"All my life."

"I know how that is. I started in Alabama and
ended up here." She took off her glasses and polished them with the hem of her shirt, then had a better look at him. Like any good bartender, she saw
that he didn't want to chat. "If you need anything
else, just holler."

"Thank you, ma'am." Sean waited until she went
back to the sink, then took the phone and dialed
Raven's number.

She answered the second ring with, "Kalen won't

have to put your Irish ass in front of a firing squad. I'll personally shoot you."

"Save your bullets. I'm likely to do myself. I know where the swords are."

"The swords are not the priority anymore," Raven said, and rapidly filled him in on the deteriorating situation. "We need Kameko, Sean. She's the only way we're going to get the girl back alive."

He thought of Kuei-fei. "No. She's been through enough. Use a decoy. I'll be in touch." Before Raven could say another word, he switched off the phone and reached for the whiskey.

He'd earned a drink—moreover, he didn't think he could keep his sanity without one. He could taste the smooth malt on his tongue already. Whiskey had never complicated his life, had never broken his heart. It had been his friend when no one else could be. Loved him, when no one else cared to.

Except Kameko.

As he stared down into the amber liquid, he admitted that much. She'd told him that she loved him last night, and she wasn't a woman to use the words lightly. Like him, she knew how love could grab a heart and squeeze until it shattered. Only she hadn't run from it like he had. She'd accepted it, welcomed it.

The same way she'd taken him.

"I've got some apple turnovers in the freezer," the bartender said as she came up and eyed his glass. "Only take a minute in the microwave to heat up a couple."

Sean stared at her. "Apple turnovers?"

"Thought I'd offer you something to eat, just in

case"—she nodded at his whiskey—"you've changed your mind."

"The jury's still deliberating." Sean picked up the glass, and wondered why fate had such a grand time playing the same game with him, over and over. "Have you ever been in love?"

"Oh, yeah." She started wiping up the counter. "I married the great love of my life."

"What happened?"

"He had a midlife crisis and decided a younger woman would cure it." She showed him her bare left hand. "Got three gorgeous kids out of him, though." A dimple appeared in her cheek as she nodded toward the mirror behind the bar. "That's my crew right there."

He studied the photo of her children—two healthy-looking boys and a petite blond girl. "Would you do it again? Marry again?"

She shook her head. "One husband was plenty for me."

"What about love?"

"Love's different." She cocked her head. "You can run, and you can hide, but in the end love always finds you. Whether you like it or not." She picked up the phone and excused herself, then went into the back room.

Love always finds you.

He'd loved Kuei-fei, but she would have never loved him. Whatever feeling she had left after enduring her tragic life had been reserved for and focused on her son. Kameko was completely different. She had come to him in fear, then learned to trust him, enough to put her life in his hands. She had accepted what little he'd given her with joy, and showed him nothing but love in return.

And he had repaid her by leaving her.

Sean hadn't left to protect her from the truth. He'd run from her love. He'd abandoned her because he was afraid of what it would mean, to accept such a gift. To return it. To share her troubles, and to trust her to share his.

There wasn't enough whiskey in the world to absolve him of that.

"Good-bye, old friend." He picked up the glass of whiskey, reached over the bar, and poured it into the sink. "I've got to go see a lady about some swords."

Jian-Shan listened to his daughter's happy chattering before he wished her good night and handed the phone to Val. Then he studied the photographs she had taken of the star blade again.

"Shikoro says Han has set up a new sandbox for her in the garden," Val told him after she hung up the phone. He'd been very quiet since returning from Nine Dragon, so much so that it was beginning to worry her. "It's like a big purple plastic caterpillar."

He made an affirmative sound and gave her arm an absent caress.

"I told Han to paint the house the same color," she continued smoothly. "And I thought I might redo our bedroom in hot pink and aqua. With orange lace accents."

"Whatever you like."

She rolled over onto her stomach and propped

her chin on her hand to watch him. "Then I plan to invite my ten new lovers to move in with us, so we'll definitely need more beds."

"They won't fit in the master bedroom," he said mildly. "You'd better plan a new addition and have Han paint that as well." He looked at her. "And if any of them ever touch you, I will kill them."

"So you *are* listening." She nodded toward the photo. "Is it the blade, or the old man at Nine Dragon, *cher*?"

"Both. And neither." He set aside the photo and rubbed the scar on his neck. "I'm missing something. Something so simple that it appears as it should, but is not . . ."

His hand fell away.

She caught his hand in hers. "Is not what?"

He edged off their bed and reached for the case containing the two key swords. "I must go back to the police department. At once."

Val grabbed the keys to their rental car. "I'm going with you."

The officer in charge of evidence storage grumbled as he brought out the star blade again. "Can't be hauling this in and out every day, you know."

"This will be the last time," Val promised.

As soon as the officer departed, Jian-Shan took out the key swords and arranged them on the table, then removed the star blade from its crate and handed it to Val.

Without another word, he knelt on the floor. "Hold the blade in your left hand and place the tip at my throat," he told her.

Val automatically recoiled. "Jian!"

"Please." He tugged open his collar, revealing the old scar on his neck. "I believe this is the sword my father used to make this. I saw something that day. Something I'd forgotten."

Val reluctantly lifted the sword and held it so that the tip hovered a few inches from her husband's throat. "This is going to make me sick."

He stared at the blade. "Turn your wrist slightly to the right. Yes. That's it." He got to his feet and took the sword from her, then held the blade at a down angle to the overhead light. "On this side, you see the etched marks near the back of the blade."

"Yes, and they don't match."

He turned the sword over. "And these?"

Val peered at the barely discernible marks on the opposite side of the blade—which she had never checked. "Oh, my God."

"My father was left-handed. Every sword he held was inverted." Jian-Shan reversed the blade in the triangle pattern with the other two key swords.

"The characters match." Val sat down in front of the triangle and began following the line of symbols with her fingertip. "It says, 'Control the treasure of power and death over the earth.' Then there are some numbers—a set of ten, and then a set of five." Her pale face turned up to his. "I don't understand it."

Jian-Shan took out his mobile phone. "Read the first set of numbers to me." As she did, he dialed them in and switched it to the hands-free speaker.

"Bank of Canton," a pleasant female voice answered. "May I help you?"

"Where are you located?"

"On Washington Street between Kearny Street and Grant Avenue, sir, in the center of Chinatown."

"May I speak to the person in charge of your safe-deposit boxes, please?" Jian-Shan waited until the call was transferred to another, male bank employee. "I am interested in renting a safe-deposit box. Would you tell me what access services you provide for box holders?"

"Certainly, sir. We have the traditional keyed boxes, and PIN boxes. Which do you prefer?"

He looked at Val. "The PIN boxes don't require keys?"

"No, sir," the man replied. "All you need is a five-digit personal identification number to access the box."

Meko got dressed in a numb haze, her fingers fumbling absently with every button and snap. She heard her brother moving around downstairs, but even his presence barely registered. The only thoughts she had were an endless loop of horror and shame.

Tara was dead.

Jiro had come to take her home.

Sean had left her.

Tara was dead.

Her brother had told her they had to return to Los Angeles, so she could turn herself in to the police. Tara's death would actually clear her name, he said, as long as she could substantiate her whereabouts—but she had to go, there was no debate about it. As long as she remained a fugitive, the police would consider her the prime suspect.

"Kameko." Jiro entered the master bedroom carrying a tray. "I brought you tea."

"Thank you." She tucked her blouse into the waistband of her jeans, and bent to tie her sneakers. "Is Ichiro in Los Angeles now?"

"Yes. He is eager to see you." Jiro studied her with a frown. "Where did you get those clothes?"

She glanced down. "Sean bought them for me."

"You've been with a Caucasian man?" As she nodded, her brother's dark brows rose. "I never thought you would turn into a *gaisen*."

His casual use of *gaisen*, which referred to those physically attracted to non-Japanese people, made her cringe. Then she thought of her father, and lifted her head. "I wasn't just sleeping with a Caucasian, brother. I'm in love with him."

"As he stranded you here, it is safe to assume he does not return your affections." He let that sink in, then added, "Perhaps next time you decide to take a lover, you will remember how you were treated by this *hakujin*."

Meko followed Jiro downstairs, and took one last look around the cabin. Sean had left nothing behind. She had no memento, no lover's token to take out and caress during the long, lonely nights to come. Then she remembered the old lady and her oyster cart in Chinatown, and slipped her hand into her purse. The tiny pearl still lay safely tucked within the back inside pocket. She took it out and closed her fist over it as she remembered how touched she'd been when he'd given it to her.

"Kameko." Jiro sounded impatient. "We must go *now*."

The bright sunlight and her wet eyes rendered her momentarily blind as she stepped outside, but the familiar sound of the battered Jeep made her knuckle her eyes.

"Who is that?" her brother demanded.

A strange calm settled over her. "It's Sean."

"That old man?" Jiro made a disgusted sound. "He could be your father."

"Shut up, Jiro." She watched Sean jump out of the Jeep and head toward them. He didn't look happy. "I didn't think you were coming back," she said as he reached them.

"Neither did I." He turned to her brother. "Who are you?"

"Jiro Sayura, Kameko's brother. I've come to bring her back home." He went on to repeat what he had told her about Tara, and finished with, "Naturally my sister is very upset, but it is imperative that we clear up this matter with the police. Excuse us now."

"No."

Jiro put his hand into his jacket. "What did you say?"

"I said no." Sean punched him in the face, sending him sprawling on the ground. "You're not taking her anywhere."

"Sean!" Horrified, Meko dropped down beside her brother, who was out cold. Then she saw the gun in his hand. "Oh, my God."

"Take it." Sean pushed the gun at her, then picked Jiro up with a grunt. "Stay here." He carried her brother into the house, and returned a few minutes later. "I've tied him up. We'll send the police round to collect him later. Come on, we have to hurry."

"I can't go with you. I have to go back to L.A.— tell the police where I've been—"

"Kameko, Tara isn't dead. I spoke to Raven, and she confirmed it. Your brothers are the ones who are holding her hostage." Sean caught her as the shock made her knees buckle. "I'm sorry. I'll explain on the way, but you have to come with me now." He guided her to the Jeep.

"Where are you taking me?"

"To get the swords," he said. "They've been right under our noses the whole time."

Chapter 14

Kinsella left Brooke and Conor with the paramedics responding to the scene, and went into the diner to question Nick Hosyu. He came out a few seconds later.

Meko's ex-husband, along with the kidnappers, had vanished.

"The police have an APB out on him, for what good that will do." Kinsella watched the medics loading Conor's gurney into the back of the rescue unit. "You want to go with him to the hospital?"

"No." Brooke turned on her heel and headed for the van. "We need to talk to the Sayura brothers again."

They came up empty at the Hilton as well.

"My desk manager says they're still checked in, but she hasn't seen either of them for a couple of days," the house detective said as he let them into the empty suite. "Just lock it up when you're done in here, if you would."

The suite was empty, except for some half-packed suitcases. Kinsella motioned to Brooke when the door to the suite opened and an older Japanese man carrying an armful of garments in dry-cleaning bags entered.

"Hold it," Brooke said, knocking the garment bags away and pointing her gun at his head. "Up against the wall, now. *Now!*" She shoved him forward, and as his hands smacked against the wall, she kicked his legs apart. "Got any goodies for me?" She patted him down quickly, then tossed the man's wallet to Kinsella. "Who are you and what are you doing in here?"

"I am Master Sayura's valet," the man said, sounding terrified. "Have I done something wrong?"

"Yeah, you work for killers." She pulled him around to face her. "Where are they?"

Sweat beaded above the man's trembling mouth. "I don't understand. I don't know any killers."

She grabbed the front of his shirt and jerked him closer. "Sure you do. That cigarette-sucking bastard you work for and his gimp brother. Where are they?"

"Captain." Kinsella's voice held a distinct warning, and Brooke reluctantly released him. To the man, he said, "Mr. Tomuki, we need to know where Ichiro and Jiro Sayura are."

The valet's expression became guarded. "I do not know, sir. The master does not tell me his plans."

"But you were packing their suitcases," Brooke circled around him. "They must have told you something."

Tomuki shook his head and made a vague gesture toward the bedroom. "I was told to pack, nothing more. I am only a servant."

"You're interfering with a federal investigation, sir," Kinsella told him.

"And that makes you an accessory to kidnapping, racketeering, and multiple homicide," Brooke said, moving in between the two men. "Take a walk, Liam. Mr. Tomuki and I are going to have a private little chat."

The valet paled.

"No job is worth spending the rest of your life in prison, Mr. Tomuki," Kinsella said. "Or having a private chat with the captain here."

The older man's shoulders sagged. "Master Ichiro left last night. He mentioned he was collecting something and moving on to the house in San Francisco. I was to wait for his brother to arrive and inform him of the same."

Brooke caught Kinsella's gaze. "Collecting what?"

"He did not say, but I gathered it was of great importance."

They left the valet with the house detective, to be held for questioning by the police, and returned to the van. Brooke contacted General Grady with an update, then slid behind the wheel. "I have orders to head up to San Francisco."

"I'm going with you."

"Fine." She drove out of the hotel parking lot and headed for the expressway.

Kinsella made one call to his field office, then remained silent for some time. He was so quiet that when he did speak, he startled her. "He'll be all right."

"Who?"

"Perry."

Brooke kept her eyes on the road. "Thank you for your opinion, Dr. Kinsella."

"Look, Captain, this won't work. I'll call Grady and explain things, then take you back. It's time we transitioned command anyway." He opened his briefcase and took out a report. "I'll copy you on all the briefs, and one of my men will call you with updates."

What he was saying made no sense. "What are you talking about?"

"I'll take over command of the operation, and you can monitor Perry." He glanced sideways. "You can't work like this, you'll snap. You almost did with Tomuki."

Brooke hit the brake and pulled off the highway, heading for a deserted rest area.

"What are you doing?"

"I have to powder my nose," she said through her teeth as she pulled in and rammed the van into park before she flung open her door. "Excuse me for a minute."

For a smart man, Kinsella was remarkably stupid. Instead of giving her five minutes to get her temper under control, he climbed out of the van and came after her. "Brooke. Wait up."

Five minutes. Couldn't she have five goddamn minutes to herself? "Go play with your briefs, Kinsella. Maybe some small but important detail will pop up."

He didn't. He got in front of her and blocked her path. "I'm not letting you play GI Jane with your Roscoe so you can comp for Perry getting shot. You'll just end up dead."

She shoved him out of the way, but Kinsella only used the momentum to pivot and wrap an arm around her. Rage shot into new, icy channels inside her. "Assaulting a military officer engaged in official duties is a federal rap, Kinsella. Being Bureau, you should know that."

"I understand how you feel. Most days I get the feeling you'd cheerfully fire a few rounds into my skull." He hauled her back until her shoulder blades hit the trunk of a scrub pine, then got in her face. "Personal shit is one thing, but I'm not letting you blow my case."

The ice began to solidify, until she could barely speak. "It's not your case, Liam," she said, very softly. "Back off."

Something in his eyes changed. "No." He dug his fingers into her hair, ripping out her clip, dragging it out to fill his hands. His big frame pressed her against the tree and knocked the last of the air from her lungs. "You want to take it out on someone? Try me."

Performing a shoulder throw from her position was difficult, but not impossible. Brooke stepped out until her foot was planted just in front of Kinsella's, then twisted one hundred and eighty degrees, shoving her hip in and bending her knees. An elbow to his right armpit and a lift with her knees, and she'd have him on his back in three seconds.

"Nice *seinage*," he said as he countered her move

and clamped her against him in an unbreakable hold. "You didn't mention you're a black belt in judo." He looked down at her chest. "But then, neither did I."

"What are you going do now? Kiss me?" Brooke sneered. "Go ahead, stick your tongue in my mouth. See what happens."

"I thought I'd start somewhere else first." Kinsella shoved one big hand down the front of her blouse, working it under her bra until he had her breast in a firm grip. Then he began to knead it slowly. "Tell me something, Captain. Is it the violence that turns you on, or is it me? I'd really like to know."

Blood roaring in her ears, she swung a side chop at his neck, but he blocked the blow. The deliberate rhythm of his fingers against her breast was making her burn from the inside out. Enraged even more by her body's response, she reached for his testicles, only to encounter his hand again.

"No, it's not your turn yet." He forced her hand back, threading his fingers through hers and using them to pull up the hem of her skirt. The touch of their joined hands against her bare thighs made her stiffen, but he was already tugging her panties down with his thumb and pressing the back of her hand against the trim patch of hair over her mound. "Come on, baby. Tell me it's me who does this to you. That makes you so hot."

She twisted against him, trying to dislodge their hands. The constant stroking of his other hand made her hips roll. "It's not you, it'll never be you."

"Liar." He used her own fingers against her, sliding them back and forth over her folds. "Feel how wet you are now?" He dipped his head and nipped the side of her throat. "You're primed and ready. For me."

It took everything she had to still her shivering body and ignore her screaming nerve endings. "I don't want this, Kinsella. I don't want you."

"Okay." Incredibly, he pulled his hands out from her bra and her panties, and stepped away. "Don't look at me like that, blondie. You're the one who said no."

"You son of a bitch."

"Oh, yeah. Signed, sealed, and certified." He cocked his head to one side. "So what are you going to do now, Brooke? Slap me?"

She pulled her blouse together and stalked back to the van, only to stop at the back doors. She was so angry she couldn't see straight, much less drive. She wiped her eyes with her sleeve, then braced herself against the doors, fighting to get back the control that had never deserted her before.

"Hey." He was right behind her. "Turn around."

Slowly, like an old woman, she faced him, and found herself in his arms. She saw his eyes, and heard herself make a low, needy sound.

"Jesus, I'm sorry." He lowered his mouth to hers, and the world exploded.

Brooke didn't think, didn't move. She was too busy drinking in the sensations, opening her mouth under his, letting him have what he wanted. Taking what was hers. He tasted hot and dark and his tongue was just as relentless as she remembered, only now there was nothing to hold her back. She reached back and grabbed the handle of the van door.

She got the door open. Somehow.

Then she was on the floor of the van, under Kinsella, who had his mouth on her breast now, sucking the nipple through her blouse as he pushed her skirt to her waist and tore her panties off with a single jerk.

He returned to her lips, giving her short, biting kisses as he unzipped his trousers to release his erection. "I can't hold off," he said, panting into her mouth. "I've got to be inside you."

"Do it." As soon as she felt the smooth dome touch the inside of her thigh, she lifted her hips, insane with need. "God, Liam, now!"

He drove into her, the heavy length of his penis filling her in one brutal stroke. She screamed as she climaxed over him, squeezing him and holding him inside her as she writhed, and then he began pumping, pushing her past the first peak to the next, pinning her wrists down when she clawed at him and grunting as he wedged himself deeper with every stroke.

"That's it, baby," he urged her in a hoarse voice as she arched her back and shuddered again. He ripped her blouse apart, taking her breast and rolling and pinching the nipple in time with the strokes of his hips. "You come on my cock for me again, just like that. I want to feel it, Brooke, give it to me."

She got one hand free and grabbed his hair, pulling his face down to hers so she could taste him again. She sucked on his tongue as she planted her heels and bucked under him, driving her hips up to take him as deep as possible. It felt as if jolts of electricity sizzled through her belly, connecting with the hot, slick pleasure from the mindless friction of his flesh in hers.

They wouldn't last much longer. She could feel it in the way he hunched over her, hammering her into the floor of the van with each stroke. She wrenched her mouth away and flipped him, keeping his penis clenched inside her until she was on top and driving herself down on him, dragging her hands down his chest until she reached the place where their bodies merged.

"Liam," she said, caressing the base of his penis with her fingertips before she began stroking herself. "Fill me up." Then she braced herself, her feet on either side of his hips, and lifted her weight completely off him. Then she began working herself over him with a smooth, rapid pumping motion.

"Ah, Christ." Kinsella grabbed her hips and pushed her down, holding her there as he jerked and jetted into her.

Brooke watched his face until she followed, and sagged to collapse against him in a tangle of sweaty limbs and wrinkled clothes.

After a long time, he asked, "How many years for assaulting a military officer again?"

"Five to ten." She reached blindly, stroked his short hair. "I don't think my testimony will hold up in court, though."

"Hell, my ears are still ringing. God, you're something else." He studied her face as if he'd never seen her before. "What's your middle name?"

"Allison." The way his lips curled made her glower. "What's so funny about that? It was my grandmother's name."

"Your initials—B. A. Oliver." He kissed her nose. "Captain Bad Attitude."

She was considering where to punch him when what he'd said struck her a different way, and she rolled off him.

"What?"

"It couldn't be that simple." Swiftly she pulled her skirt down and reached in the side pocket for the note Raven had given her. After she read it again, she swore.

He touched her arm. "Brooke, what?"

She looked up. "Liam, I know what the encryption says."

Kalen threaded his way through the heavy Chinatown traffic. "Tell me about this bank, Sarah."

"It was once the only Chinese telephone exchange in the United States," Raven said as she consulted her laptop. "And San Francisco's first newspaper, the *California Star*, was published here. Otherwise, it's completely legit—serves the local merchants and residents, maintains normal assets, etc." She pulled up the bank's Web site. "Pretty decent rates on CDs, too."

He pulled up to the front entrance of the Bank of Canton and parked at the curb. The pagoda-style red-and-green building stood between two larger brick buildings like a jewel set into stone.

"You're going to get a ticket," Raven said as she got out of the car.

"I'll let you tear it up for me later," he promised her as they went inside.

Val was sitting in the reception area, and got up as soon as she saw them. "Jian's in the vault with the bank manager. They're opening the box."

The bank was nearly deserted. As Val quickly relayed what they had discovered from the swords, Jian-Shan emerged from the vault. He returned the bank manager's bow, then joined them.

"The safe-deposit box is empty," he said, and handed Kalen two photocopied ledger sheets. "According to bank records, it's been accessed only twice—once when it was rented in 1999, and three months ago. The signatures don't match."

Kalen skimmed both copies. The name Li Chen—one of T'ang Po's aliases—appeared on both. "Two visits by two different men."

"According to the date, my father couldn't have made the second visit. He was already dead." Jian-Shan glanced at Raven. "What about the Dai's son?"

She shook her head. "He was in Washington that week."

"Which means we have a third player." Kalen folded the copies and tucked them into his jacket. "But who, and what was in the safe-deposit box?"

"What was the exact date of the second visit?" Val asked, and grew thoughtful after Jian-Shan told her. "Something happened around that time— something we've talked about before, when we were discussing the investigation."

"Gangi and Portia were killed the next day," Raven said. She frowned. "I came to the U.S. three days later."

Kalen rolled through his mental files. "No, it wasn't the Dai. It was Sayura. He left the United States the day after someone emptied the box."

Jian-Shan muttered something in Chinese, then went still as all the emotion went out of his face.

Val put out her arm. "Jian?"

"That is what was wrong," he murmured. "What he said to the fish."

"Takeshi talked to some fish?" Raven's brows rose.

"No. His gardener did. We must go there at once." As Jian-Shan headed for the door, he glanced at Kalen. "How many men do you have in this area?"

"We have a situation team of twelve on twenty-four-hour standby. They can be on the move in thirty minutes." Kalen's voice sharpened. "Why?"

"Contact them, and have them meet us at Nine Dragon immediately."

"Ichiro can't be involved in this," Meko said as they drove through the open gate up to Nine Dragon. They had gone over every detail of what Raven had told him during the drive from Yosemite to San Francisco, and it still had her shaken. "If anything, he would try to protect Tara from Jiro and my father's men. As for those Shandian leaders who were killed, it had to be Jiro."

Sean took her hand and squeezed it. "Let's get the swords and find out."

"Someone's been here." Plywood covered the front windows, but she could see bullet holes in the wall around them. "Why would they shoot up the house?"

Sean studied the damage. "Machine guns—they were aiming for someone standing inside at the windows."

The door to the front of the house remained unlocked, and Sean took out his gun and pushed Meko behind him as they entered. The faint smells of incense and something sweet and floral lingered on the air.

Xun appeared, carrying a tray filled with precisely prepared food and a bottle of sake. He glanced at Meko and his mouth stretched into an odd smile. "I knew you would come back."

Meko controlled a shudder. "Take me to my brother, Xun."

He led them into the Emperor's Room, and carried the tray to the throne. "Your sister is here, Master."

"So I see." Ichiro, who was seated on the throne and wore one of their father's elaborate dragon robes, looked up from the scroll he was reading and smiled. "Come closer, Kameko. Introduce me to your companion."

"This is my friend, Sean Delaney." She walked up the ramp to the dais, but stopped when she saw that Tara was tied to the frame of the stone tablet. She was dirty and thin, and one of her arms had a long cut on it. "Tara. Are you all right?"

"My arm hurts," the girl said, "but I'm okay. I just want to go home."

"She has not been the most cooperative of guests, so I was obliged to restrain her." Ichiro rolled up the scroll and set it aside to accept a tiny cup of sake from Xun. Just as casually, he pointed a gun at Tara's head. "You seem surprised to find me in our father's place, *kappa*. You, who were always so eager to see me succeed in obtaining that which I desired."

It broke her heart to see him like this. "I thought you would become a teacher, or a scholar. Not what Father was."

He glanced at Xun. "I believe he shared your opinion of me, for a little while. Until I proved to him that I could be even more valuable than our little brother."

"Look at what you've done, Ichiro." A cold hand tightened on her heart. "You've kidnapped an innocent girl. Did you kill Father, too?"

He smiled at her, as if she'd told a joke. "Do you have any idea what our father was trying to achieve here, in the United States? An alliance with all of our enemies—to make peace between the tongs and the syndicate."

Meko knew her father was no peacemaker. "So he could control them himself."

"Someone must be in charge. T'ang Po would have been, with our father as his second-in-command, but he met an untimely end in Paris. After Po's death, Father naturally assumed control. There was one problem, however." Ichiro took a sip from his cup. "T'ang Po entrusted only one man with the secret of the swords. A man who, for mysterious reasons of his own, gave that secret to you."

"I don't understand any of this. I don't know any

secrets." Meko cautiously approached the throne. "Tara is injured and exhausted, brother. Let me take her away from here now."

"You may"—Ichiro set down his empty sake cup and cocked the pistol—"as soon as you give me what I want." He nodded toward Sean. "And please tell your friend to put away his weapon. He is making me feel very nervous."

"Sean, do as he says." Meko never looked away from her brother's face. "Ichiro, you already have the swords."

"Do I?" He looked around. "You mean you actually had a clever moment and concealed them somewhere here?"

"The gardener did, boyo." Sean picked up the gong striker, went over to the wall, and struck it against one of the clashing sword reliefs. Plaster rained down in small chunks, destroying a section of the relief and revealing the antique sword beneath it. "He scheduled the work to be done after Takeshi and he left for China. Now, give us the girl and we'll leave."

"He won't let any of you leave alive." Nick Hosyu strode into the room. "Meko, move away from him. Ichiro, I told the authorities everything. They know about the killings you ordered. It's over."

"The wisest thing my sister ever did was to divorce you." Ichiro swung the pistol forward and shot Nick in the head.

Meko screamed and dropped to cover Tara with her arms.

"There, *kappa*," she heard her brother say. "I believe I have finally cured Nick's gambling problem."

It was too much for her. "Sean!"

"I'm here, *a chuisle mo chroí*." Sean dropped the striker and advanced on the throne, his gun out.

"I don't agree with some of my father's philosophies, but"—Ichiro pointed the pistol at Meko—"no *hakujin* will pollute my family bloodlines. Put your weapon on the floor and kick it toward me, Mr. Delaney. Or I will shoot my sister next."

Sean slowly complied. "If you hurt her, you'll die. Slowly. Badly."

"Brother." Meko stepped between him and Sean. "We would leave you in peace. You have the swords, you and Jiro have control of the syndicate. What more do you want?"

"I don't want the swords. I want the Star King. Specifically, the control and firing sequence codes for the Star King." He studied her face. "Of course, I see the wisdom of it. You still don't know. We now control a laser in orbit on a Chinese military satellite."

She looked at Sean. "Is this true?" When he nodded, she said to her brother, "Why would you want to control a laser in outer space?"

"The laser's beam can be adjusted to target and eradicate anything from a single human being to the entire city of Los Angeles." He sounded as if he were discussing the weather. "With that kind of power, a man can control a great deal. Now, tell me where the codes are."

"I don't have any codes."

"He entrusted you with their location in a letter,

mailed just before we had him killed." Ichiro reached down and pulled her to her feet. "What did he write in the letter?"

Meko recited from memory the letter her father had sent her. " 'Use this historic evidence to identify. Good example rank sword, the real evidence as specified under research. Everyone is skeptical, guarded. Until a representative delivers everything, don't betray your dear relatives.' " She glanced up at her brother and let irony enter her voice. " 'All goodness only needs someone to find it.' "

For the first time Ichiro looked uncertain. "He sent someone to you?"

"No. It's meaningless. Nothing but a bunch of . . ." Her eyes moved up to the characters representing her father's name. ". . . gibberish . . ." She looked at Xun, who was hovering by the door.

Ichiro leaned forward. "I can see it in your eyes, clever girl." He pressed the gun to Tara's temple again. "Tell me, what does it mean to you?"

She thought of the green stone dragon statue. "It has to be outside, in the garden."

"Then untie your young friend, and take me to it."

Meko helped Tara to her feet and with Sean's help guided her outside. Ichiro followed, leaning on his cane as he held the gun on them.

"Oh my God, you're burning up," Meko said, pressing her hand to the girl's flushed face. "I am so sorry, Tara."

Tara shook her head. "No way could you have known." She swore as Ichiro grabbed her hair.

He hauled her back against him. "You talk too much."

For the first time in memory, Meko wanted to kill her older brother. She settled for blocking his path. "You stop hurting Tara this instant, or I won't tell you anything."

Ichiro let go of Tara's hair, but kept her pressed against him. "I forgave you for your disrespect toward our father, and for leaving your husband. I will never forgive you for betraying us with this foulmouthed brat and your *hakujin* lover. Get me the codes, little sister, or I'll do much worse to her—and I'll make you watch."

She walked up to the fighting dragon statue. Lifting the striker, she smashed the silvery glass gazing sphere.

"He hid them in our birthday gift to Father?" Ichiro sounded mildly indignant. "That was rather disloyal of him."

Meko turned to conceal the fact that there was nothing inside the statue's sphere, and saw dark-suited men closing in all around them.

Her ruse wouldn't work; they had run out of time. Now she had to save Tara.

"Sean? I love you." Satisfied that she had been able to say it one more time, she met her brother's amused gaze. "You're right, Ichiro. I have betrayed you, and I deserve to be punished. You don't need Tara. Let her go, and then you can do whatever you like to me." She caught Tara's gaze, and then looked down to her brother's deformed leg.

Tara gave her a small nod.

"You're still determined to be the noble lady. Little sister, Nick was quite right," Ichiro told her. "None of you are leaving here alive."

"I doubt that." A man dressed in black stepped out of nowhere and slashed a long blade at Ichiro's hand. The gun went flying through the air and landed in the reflecting pool.

"Jian-Shan." Sean sounded relieved. "How the devil did you end up here?"

"I heard a man speaking to fish in the wrong language. Or, as my wife would say, it's a very long story." He gestured at Ichiro with the sword. "Release the girl."

Meko whirled to see Xun running at Jian-Shan, brandishing his rake like a club. At the same time, Ichiro lifted his cane, twisted the handle, and pulled out a hidden sword.

"Watch it, boyo," Sean snapped, launching himself at the old man and knocking him to the ground.

As Jian parried a blow from Ichiro's sword, Tara ducked and knocked the crippled man off balance, lunging away and hurrying to disappear into the labyrinth.

"Kameko, get down!" Sean shouted as guns began to fire all around them.

Meko crouched behind one of the Taihu stones and flinched as a bullet ricocheted off it a few inches from her face. Ichiro's men also took cover as a new wave of armed men in black fatigues moved in, led by a red-haired man and a gorgeous brunette woman she thought she recognized.

Raven?

Since no one was paying attention to her, Meko hurried over to Sean, who had the old gardener pinned to the ground. "Be careful, he's very old, Sean."

The SWAT team of agents swiftly overpowered Ichiro's men, but just as the firing ceased, someone grabbed Meko from behind.

"He's not as old as you might think." Ichiro wrenched her away from Sean and Xun, dragging her back, his sword pressed against her back. "Release him, or I will lay open her spine."

Jian-Shan moved around them in a circle like a boxer, waiting for an opening. "Sean, do as he says."

Sean let the old gardener up, and Xun gave Jian-Shan a look of intense hatred. "How did you know?"

"The fish." Jian-Shan gestured toward the reflecting pool. "You spoke to them in Japanese. An old man by himself would speak in his native tongue— Chinese—not the language of his master."

The old gardener moved to Ichiro's side, but something was wrong. He was no longer limping or hunched over, and he looked taller—much taller. She forgot to blink as the gardener lifted perfectly functioning hands and began to peel off his face. No, not his face.

His mask.

It took her a moment to find her voice. "Father?"

Chapter 15

Sean watched as Takeshi Sayura finished removing most of the prosthetic makeup. Jian-Shan couldn't disarm Ichiro, not the way he was holding Kameko. And if Sean shot him, he still might have time to thrust the sword into her spine or neck.

"And so my prodigal daughter finally comes home." Takeshi dropped the pieces of rubber and foam to the ground and brushed off the front of his robe. "Where is Jiro?"

"We left him at the cabin. The police will have him in custody by now." She looked from her father to bits of makeup on the ground. "Why were you pretending to be Xun?"

"I believe Xun went with your father to China," Jian-Shan said softly. "Loyal servant that he was."

"He was never loyal to me." Takeshi glowered at Jian-Shan. "T'ang Po sent him to infiltrate my household years ago. One word from your father, at any time, and he would have cut my throat while I slept."

"So you killed him?" She was horrified. "Xun

was just a harmless old man who loved fish and growing things. And he worshiped you."

Her father grunted. "More like he watched me. For thirty years."

"We needed a body, little sister, or the American authorities would never have believed he was dead." Ichiro jabbed her with the point of his blade, making her jump. "And who better to serve the purpose than a traitor like Xun."

"Unfortunately, the old man didn't trust your father, and before he left, he took certain precautions," Jian-Shan said. "He removed the Star King's control codes from my father's safe-deposit box and hid them, along with the swords. Then he gave the secret of their location to the one person he knew would never give them to the syndicate."

Sean saw understanding dawn on Meko's face, and knew she had figured out where the codes were.

Takeshi went over and examined the broken sphere. "They're not here." He came over to Meko. "What did you do with them?"

"They're exactly where Xun left them. Guess." She didn't cower, not even when he slapped her hard.

"Keep your hands off her," Sean said.

"I'm all right," she told him. Then, to Takeshi, she said, "Xun was right, Father. I would burn in hell before I gave those codes to you."

"It's over, Sayura," Kalen said. "Tell your son to put down the sword."

"With me, Father!" Ichiro shouted as he locked

his arm around Kameko's throat and dragged her into the house. Takeshi followed.

Sean's blood turned to ice.

"Delaney!"

Reflexively he caught the gun Kalen tossed to him, then ran after them into the house, Jian-Shan hard on his heels. Ichiro's lurching footsteps scraped over a gasping sound.

The woman he loved was not going to die.

He burst into the Emperor's Room just as Takeshi pushed over the emperor's throne, revealing a recessed staircase. As Ichiro held Sean off with his sword, Takeshi forced his daughter down the stairs.

Sean aimed for the crippled man's upper arm. "Put down the blade."

"If you want her, you have to get past me."

Kameko stumbled in the dark and fell to her knees as her father pushed her away from him and shut something over her head. Lights came on, blinding her for a moment, then she saw the computers and equipment all around her.

For a moment, she felt as if she had stepped into another world. Beneath the grandeur of the ancient Emperor's Room, the high-tech monitors, keypads, communications stations, and databanks looked like something out of *Star Wars*. "Father, what have you done?"

"The past is dead, my daughter," Takeshi said as he jerked her back upright. "I am taking my place in the future."

He pushed her toward what appeared to be the central control terminal. The wide-screen monitor showed an electronic map of the United States, with red glowing dots above each major American city. A wavy line ran across the map, and the small blinking symbol slowly followed the line.

The room scared her, but not as much as the sealed hatch cutting them off from the Emperor's Room—and not as much as her father's eyes. "What is this place?"

"The satellite control room. I had it built according to T'ang Po's specifications." He gestured around him. "From here I have complete control of the Star King. You cannot imagine the power it will bring to my name."

"You wouldn't kill innocent people with that monstrous weapon. Not even you could be that cruel."

"There are no innocents in the world, Kameko. Only the powerful and the weak." He stared at the electronic map, and his thin lips curled with satisfaction. "With the Star King at my command, no country in the world will dare refuse me anything."

She wiped a trickle of blood from her chin. "You can't play God without those codes."

"You're going to give them to me." When she shook her head, he slapped her, hard. "No more of your foolishness, girl. You have interfered enough with my plans. Give me the codes!"

"Or you'll do what, Father? Beat me until I do?" Slowly she straightened. "Go ahead. I'm not afraid of you."

"You will obey me." As he lifted his hand to strike her again, Kameko shoved him away with both hands and ran for the stairs. When he caught her on the stairs, she kicked him, and he fell backward. There was a crunch of bone as he landed at the bottom and shrieked in pain. "Ichiro!"

Kameko found the switch that opened the hatch and emerged from the control room. As she stood, she found herself facing the razor-sharp tip of her brother's sword.

"I won't give you the codes," Sean heard Kameko say. "It doesn't matter what you do. You'll never get them from me."

"Then you can go and see Xun, *kappa.*" The crippled man's face contorted with hatred. "Tell him how well his plan worked." He lifted the sword high.

Sean didn't stop to think, but took three running steps and lunged at Meko, knocking her out of the way. Cold steel pierced his back, driving through muscle and bone.

He fell against the emperor's throne, and held on to it for a moment before collapsing. As his vision dimmed, he rolled onto his back and a series of gunshots deafened him. Then Meko was kneeling over him, her pretty eyes wet, her sinful mouth shaping his name. Over her right shoulder, the wavering image of another woman appeared.

Kuei-fei.

We make the best of what fate gives us, Irish. Be happy, for me.

"Sean."

Meko's voice dispelled the ghost of his former love, and he focused on her pale, frightened face.

She was holding his gun. Behind her, Ichiro lay crumpled and still on the floor.

"Be happy, *a chuisle mo chroí.*" Darkness crowded around him, making him impatient. "I love you."

Then Sean Delaney stopped breathing.

Meko watch his chest rise and fall, then still. The strong heartbeat under her palm ceased. She should have collapsed on top of him and wept, torn out her hair, gone insane with grief. Instead, a white-hot surge of fury shot through her, and she threw the gun away from her. With tight hands, she gripped the back of his neck, pushing it up, and pinched his nostrils closed. Then she covered his mouth with hers and forced her own breath into his lungs.

You're not going to die on me, nagare.

She lifted her head, clasped her hands into the correct position as she'd learned from her Red Cross class, and started compressions. "Does anyone know CPR?" she shouted.

"I do." The red-haired man knelt on Sean's opposite side, and took over doing the compressions. Meko counted until it was time to breathe for Sean again, and checked his neck for a pulse.

After ten compressions, there was nothing. After twenty, she felt a faint fluttering. "Wait." As Sean's chest moved, she looked into the angry green eyes across from her. "It's okay, he's breathing again."

They stayed right beside Sean until paramedics arrived on the scene a few minutes later. As they were loading him onto a gurney, Raven brought Tara over.

"Is he going to be all right?" Tara asked as Meko caught her in a careful hug.

"He will." She had to believe that, or she would go insane. She looked over Tara's head, and smiled her gratitude at Raven. "We all will."

Meko rode in the front of the rescue unit that took Sean and Tara to the hospital. Tara was taken to assessment, while Sean was quickly transferred to severe trauma and then on to surgery, where the doctors began the long fight to save his life.

A nurse took Meko to a waiting room, where she watched the clock in silence until the door opened and Jian-Shan entered, accompanied by a striking-looking woman.

The woman, whose exotic face went perfectly with her blazing red-blond hair, spoke in a familiar voice. "Ms. Sayura, I'm Valence St. Charles." She touched her lethal-looking husband's arm. "I believe you and Jian-Shan have already met."

"Yes." Meko went to shake her hand but found herself in a gentle embrace. She allowed herself to lean against the other woman for a moment before stepping back. "Forgive me. I'm waiting to hear some news about Sean."

"Is he still in surgery?"

"Yes." She turned to Jian-Shan, and recalled how calm he had been, facing her brother's rage. "I don't know what to say about my family."

"Our fathers were much the same. We cannot choose them." He touched her shoulder. "But they do not own us, ever."

That made her feel better, and she nodded.

Val smiled. "Would you mind if we wait here with you? We'd like to tell you how this all started."

Meko was still listening to the story of how Val and Jian-Shan had met in Paris when the red-haired man who had helped her perform CPR on Sean arrived with Raven.

"Hey, sweetie." Raven took her hands and kissed her on both cheeks in Parisian fashion. "I've just been down to see Tara, and she's doing fine. How are you holding up?"

"I'll be fine." She glanced back at the door. "We haven't heard anything about Sean yet. Dale Taggart, the heart surgeon, is the husband of a client of mine." She looked down at her hands. "I know he's the best in the state."

"Then he'll fix him. Besides, Irish has been stabbed and shot so many times he should moonlight as a pincushion. I doubt one more time will do any damage." Raven scowled at her companion. "Oh, and this important guy is my husband, CID general Kalen Grady, whom I will beat up later on Sean's behalf."

"It's a pleasure to meet you." The general shook Meko's hand. "Please ignore my wife. She's expecting our first child, and the hormone changes are pretty brutal."

The story shifted as the five of them sat down and Raven related how Kalen had brought her over to the U.S. to find an assassin and the White Tiger swords.

"Which brings us to you," Raven said as she finished her harrowing portion of the tale, "and Sean. And the Star King."

Meko took up the thread of the story and explained what had happened since Tara's abduction, leaving out only the more intimate details.

"I know that my father murdered Xun in China in order to switch places with him," Meko said. "What I don't understand is why. Xun worked for my father for thirty years. Why would he wait all this time to kill him? Especially when he was the only one who knew where the Star King codes were?"

Before anyone could respond, a well-dressed couple came in, accompanied by a tall brown-haired man with his arm in a sling.

Meko slowly rose to her feet. "Mrs. Jones, Mr. Jones. How is Tara?"

"They've admitted her for observation, and she's already kicking up a fuss," Rebecca Jones said. "She says she doesn't want to be stuck on the pediatric ward with all the little kids." She snorted. "I swear, that child is sixteen going on forty."

"She'll live," the man with the sling said. "I'm Conor Perry, Miss Sayura. I was with Tara most of the time, and she's a very tough kid."

Rebecca Jones enveloped Meko in a perfumed hug. "John and I just wanted to stop by and thank you for saving our daughter. We shouldn't have blamed you for this mess, and I hope in time you'll forgive us."

"Of course."

The Joneses left, but everyone else remained with Meko to keep the vigil. Raven disappeared briefly, only to return with a cart filled with sandwiches, coffee, and soft drinks.

Meko glanced up and for the first time noticed that there were dozens of people waiting in the corridor—some in black fatigues, others in suits and coats. "Who are all those people?"

"Everyone who has worked with Sean Delaney who was in the immediate area," Kalen told her.

"Yeah, we're like cops that way," Raven said, handing a tray of sandwiches to two of the agents who had also been at Nine Dragon earlier. "One of us goes down, the others stand watch."

Her husband inspected the cart. "Hungry?"

"You would not believe the kitchen in this place," Raven said as she sat down and attacked a large croissant stuffed with chicken and lettuce. "I think I'll stay and have the baby here."

The general's eyes narrowed. "And someone just *gave* all that to you?"

"No, but they won't find any fingerprints at the scene." She smiled at his scowl. "If you're mean to me, I won't share."

Meko couldn't eat anything, but she gratefully accepted a cold soda and sipped it. The hand on the clock seemed to slow and drag as it ticked off the minutes. The others kept up the conversation, but as the hours passed she became more quiet, until all she could do was stare at the clock and pray.

They all got to their feet when a doctor, still dressed in a surgical gown, walked in.

"Is there a Kameko Sayura here?" he asked, looking grim.

She braced herself. "Yes, that's me."

"Mr. Delaney came through the operation quite well, but we're having a bit of a problem in recovery." The surgeon pulled off the cloth mask that was still hanging around his neck. "He's refusing to co-operate with my nurses. He says he won't, until he can speak with you."

Raven chuckled. "Yep, that sounds like Sean."

Meko went with the surgeon to the recovery room, where she had to don a gown, mask, and gloves before entering Sean's room. He lay very pale and still on the bed, but as soon as she stepped inside the curtain, he opened his eyes.

"Darlin'?" His voice sounded dry and thin.

"Yes, Sean." She went to his side and took his hand carefully in hers. "You have to stop giving these people a hard time. They're only trying to help."

"Hate hospitals," he murmured, and brought her hand up to his lips. "Had to see you. You're too far away, come down here."

She bent over him and smiled when he tugged her mask down. "I'm right here."

His eyes moved to the door. "Tara okay?"

"Yes. They admitted her for observation, but she'll be going home in the morning."

"Good." He dragged in a deep breath, struggling to get out the words. "Don't go."

"I won't leave you." She kissed his brow. "I'll be right here until you feel better."

"Never go." He closed his eyes, then forced them open. His fingers squeezed hers. "Marry me."

Kameko stayed with Sean, leaving him only long enough to shower, change her clothes, or catch a quick meal. Quickly realizing they'd have a much

more cooperative patient if she was in close proximity, the nursing staff set up a cot in an adjoining
room for her. A week later, Sean's condition was up-
graded enough for him to be moved from intensive
care to a regular ward, and Kameko could finally
breathe again.

"Well, Irish, you've lived up to your reputation
again," Raven announced as she came in to inspect
Sean and the new room. "I don't think anything
short of a nuclear attack would kill you." She
hugged Kameko. "But if you don't marry this
woman, I might have a go at you."

"She's mine." Sean met Meko's gaze, and smiled.
"The second I get out of here."

Raven chuckled. "I guess if I want to borrow your
lady, I'd better do it now." She checked her watch.
"We've got a debriefing with the powers that be in
an hour, and we'd like her to be there."

"Yes, there is something I have to do." Kameko
went over and kissed Sean. "I'll be back soon."

He trailed his fingertips over her cheek. "Are you
sure you want to do this?" She nodded. "All right,
then, *a chuisle mo chroí.* Good luck."

Raven kept up a constant stream of chatter as her
limo whisked them from the hospital to the FBI's
San Francisco office, but Kameko remained quiet
and thoughtful. So much had happened since she'd
met Sean, but almost losing him had been the worst.
She knew it was time to set things right, and she
was the only one who could really do that.

"Basically this is an information exchange and
wrap-up among the various agencies involved,"
Raven told her as they were escorted to the meeting

of CID, FBI, and other government officials. "Lots of high-powered men with no hair in dark suits. You'll love them."

Kalen met them at the door, and showed Meko to a chair beside Val St. Charles and her husband. Raven introduced her to Liam Kinsella and Brooke Oliver, and added, "I know you have some questions about your father and brother. Liam would be the one to ask."

Meko knew they'd be spending the rest of their lives in prison. "I would like to know why my father faked his own death."

"Probably because my task force was on the verge of indicting him on multiple counts of racketeering, fraud, and conspiracy to commit murder," Kinsella said. "We had just wrapped up a two-year investigation on him when he fled the country."

Brooke Oliver reacted more strongly to this than anyone. "You knew he wasn't dead?"

The agent made a seesaw gesture with his hand. "We suspected he might try to assume a new identity—it's a common practice among Asian crime bosses. And when our source came back into the country and didn't try to make contact with us, I got suspicious."

"Xun?" Meko's jaw sagged. "You mean our gardener was informing on my father?"

Kinsella nodded. "Since our source lived in the household, and Sayura had extensive contacts within various local and national law enforcement agencies, we had to keep a tight lid on everything."

Kalen leaned forward, looking serious. "We still need to locate those control codes, Kameko."

"I cracked the encryption, for what it's worth," Brooke said, taking out a slip of paper and handing it to the general. "It was so simple I didn't see it at first. He used initials."

Meko nodded. "Xun was a simple man. The message begins with the word 'use.' If you take the first letter of each word between that and 'to find it,' they spell out the location. *The tiger's treasure is guarded by dragons*."

"Your father called T'ang Po the tiger. And control codes for the Star King are obviously the treasure." Raven took the slip from her husband and studied it. "But which dragons? We thoroughly searched the house and the grounds."

"There's a small blue dragon on the edge of the tile wall at the front of the property," Meko told them. "I believe you'll find the codes hidden behind the blue dragon's pearl."

A senior FBI official called on Liam Kinsella to relate the details of the investigation.

"The control room at the Sayura estate has been dismantled, and the equipment turned over to the army for further analysis. Our ambassador has made a special report to the United Nations, and the resulting sanctions have forced the Chinese government to remove the laser satellite from orbit. U.N. inspectors will make sure they don't send up a replacement in the future."

He went on to list a series of arrests in major cities across the country. "Indictments from this and other, related investigations will send most of the tong leaders to prison. We haven't put an end to

Chinese organized crime here in the U.S., but we've taken out the major players."

Raven lifted a hand. "Where are the White Tiger swords?"

"They were removed from the Nine Dragon property and are being held in evidence by FBI officials until the Sayura trial. There is some legal paperwork to be filed, as they were used in the commission of several felonies." He exchanged a look with the general. "But under the circumstances, I believe the entire collection will eventually be returned to you, Ms. Sayura."

She nodded. "May I say something?"

He gestured toward her, and Meko got to her feet. "Those swords don't belong to me or my family, and I would like to give them back to their rightful owner." She looked at Val's husband. "Jian-Shan, I also want to make amends for what our fathers have done. If you're willing, I'll donate the Nine Dragon estate, to be made into a museum for the swords." She smiled at Val. "I know it's far from New Orleans, but after everything that's happened, it feels right."

"I think it's a wonderful thing to do," Val said.

Jian-Shan rose and bowed to Meko. "I am honored." Then he took her hands in his. "We will add to the history of the swords—a new chapter, one of hope and honor."

"Yes." She thought of Sean. "And we'll write it with love."

Epilogue

Several weeks later, Kalen and Jian-Shan stood with Sean before a wall mirror. Kalen wore his dress uniform, while the other two men were in tuxedos.

Still pale from his stint in the hospital, Sean scowled at his image. "I look like a bloody damn penguin in this thing."

"Every groom does," Kalen told him. "It's how the women get their revenge for childbirth."

"You don't have to wear one."

"I'm a general," he said, and grinned at Sean. "I don't have to do a lot of things."

In another room on the other side of the church, Tara, Valence, and Raven were fussing over Meko from all sides.

"Hold on, the veil isn't hanging straight," Tara said, tugging it into place from behind. "God, Meko, this dress is just so fat."

"A bride is not fat. She's ethereal," Val insisted.

"I was a fat bride. And I'm getting fatter by the minute," Raven said as she adjusted a fold of the snowy train. "Though I have to say, I agree. You can't go wrong with Vera Wang."

"Lily?" Valence got a panicked look on her face as she looked around them. "Lily, where are you?"

Meko smothered a laugh and pointed down.

Valence lifted the hem of Meko's gown and hauled her daughter out from under it. "What are you doing down there, you little monkey?"

"High-dig." Lily giggled. "Time fro fowers, Mama?"

"Almost." Valence handed her stepdaughter a small basket of rosebuds and loose petals. "You behave now, *cher*. How do you feel, Kameko?"

"Like a big *fat* walking meringue," Meko admitted, then inspected her three friends. "Anyone want to swap dresses?"

"That would lead to bigamy charges against me and Val," Raven said. "And I think Tara is holding out for Brad Pitt."

"He'll get tired of Jennifer one day," the teenager predicted. Her expression sobered as she looked down at Meko's hands. "I have to tell you something—Sean asked me to make your ring. I hope you don't mind, but I really wanted to do it." She ducked her head. "I owe you so much."

That explained why Tara had been acting so secretive lately, and the thought of having her protégée's first piece of professional work delighted her. "I think Sean has excellent taste in jewelers."

The teenager grinned, then cocked her head as the opening chords of the Wedding March drifted down from the sanctuary. "They're playing your song, boss."

"Lily?" Valence sighed as her daughter popped out from behind Meko's gown. "Come on, sweetie, time to fro the fowers."

The four women hurried out of the dressing room and down to the entrance to the church. Kalen was waiting for them, and held out his arm for Meko as Valence led Lily inside, followed by Raven and Tara. At the altar, Meko saw Sean waiting with Jian-Shan.

"Ready?" Kalen asked her.

She kept her eyes on Sean. "Oh, yes."

As she walked down the aisle with the general, Meko watched Sean's mouth curve into a beautiful, warm smile. They had come so close to losing each other so many times that now it seemed like an utter miracle that they had arrived at this, the first day of the rest of their lives together.

She passed the pew where Neala Ryder and Laney Tremayne sat with their husbands and sons, and caught Neala's wink and her sister's warm smile. Although she had only just met Sean's nieces and their families when they flew in for the wedding, she was already in love with them.

"She's a cute little thing," Neala said to her sister. "Doesn't look like she'll take any crap from him, either." She certainly had taken Sean's crap herself when he'd gotten her mixed up in Senator Colfax's murder. Happily, she had ended up hiding out in Montana, where she had met her husband, Will.

"I can't believe Uncle Sean is getting married," Laney murmured with a dreamy look in her eyes. She was pregnant again, and held her sleeping toddler son propped against her softly curving stomach. She smiled as she felt her husband's hand caress the back of her neck. If not for her uncle, she would have never met her husband during the CID operation at the Dream Mountain Mine in Colorado. "Aren't you glad you didn't shoot him at the mine, Joe?"

Neala's husband, Will, held on to their wideawake, squirming infant son and eyed her uncle. "I'm still wondering if I should have shot him up in the mountains," he muttered to his brother-in-law.

Brooke Oliver and Liam Kinsella watched from their positions on the bride's side of the church. "What's that stuck in the back of her veil?" Kinsella asked Brooke.

Brooke peered. "Looks like a couple of banged-up roses." She caught the look in Kinsella's eye. "We have to make an appearance at the reception, you know."

"For how long?" He stared at her mouth. "Fifteen minutes?"

She refused to smile. "Ten ought to do it."

Raven also spotted the last-minute decoration Lily had added to Meko's veil. "Uh, Val? I think your kid has aspirations in the fashion industry."

"I noticed." Valence pressed her lips together to keep from laughing. "Which is why we're giving her to you and Kalen as soon as she hits thirteen."

"With this ring, I thee wed," Sean murmured, slipping a filigree band over Meko's slim finger.

She caught her breath when she saw the small paragon pearl, flanked by a circle of rubies and diamonds. It was the loveliest thing she'd ever seen. "Sean, it's beautiful."

"Like the hand that made it," he told her. "And the hand that wears it. I love you, *a chuisle mo chroí*."

As she gave him his ring, Meko looked into Sean's eyes. She saw love, and faith, and trust there. She expected no less, and couldn't ask for anything more. "And I love you, *nagare*."

The smiling priest pronounced them man and wife, but he didn't have to repeat the rest of the traditional words.

Mrs. Sean Delaney was already being thoroughly kissed by her new husband.

"A soul-deep love story and
wild adventure." —Catherine Coulter

Jessica Hall
The Steel Caress

Raven had no intention of ever returning to her life
as an undercover government agent.   The stunning
beauty didn't doubt that years ago she'd been
betrayed by the agency she worked for—and by her
devastatingly handsome boss, General Kalen Grady.

Now, Raven has launched a new career—and a new
life. But just when she's certain the past is behind
her, Kalen turns up on her door—step with one final
and crucial assignment.

0-451-20852-8

Available wherever books are sold, or
to Order Call: 1-800-788-6262